CH00843242

Stephen Dearsley's Summer of Love

Colin Bell

Ward Wood Publishing
www.wardwoodpublishing.co.uk

Published by Ward Wood Publishing
6 The Drive
Golders Green
London NW11 9SR
www.wardwoodpublishing.co.uk

The right of Colin Bell to be identified as the author of this work has been asserted by him in accordance with the Copyright, Designs and Patent Act, 1988. © Colin Bell 2013.

ISBN 978-1-908742-07-0

British Library Cataloguing in Publication Data. A CIP record for this book can be obtained from the British Library.

All rights reserved. No part of this publication may be reproduced, stored in a retrieval system, or transmitted in any form or by any means, electronic, mechanical, photocopying, recording or otherwise without the prior written permission of the publishers. This book may not be lent, hired out, resold or otherwise disposed of by way of trade in any form of binding or cover other than that in which it is published, without the prior consent of the publishers.

Designed and typeset in Garamond
by Ward Wood Publishing.

Cover Design by Mike Fortune Wood
from original artwork by © Luis Santos
Titled: Barefoot on rock
supplied by Dreamstime.com

Printed and bound in Great Britain by
Imprint Digital, Seychelles Farm,
Upton Pyne, Exeter EX5 5HY.

All the characters in this book are fictitious and any resemblance to actual persons (living or dead) or to institutions is purely coincidental.

To Andie
with love (all you
need)

23/10/2014

Stephen Dearsley's
Summer of Love

Bliss was it in that dawn to be alive,
But to be young was very heaven!

William Wordsworth
The Prelude, Bk. XI, l. 108

For Linda Bell

One

In the summer of 1967, three naked young men took a shower in a fountain in the centre of Brighton. It was hot, and good-humoured mischief was in the air. The bus that circled the dolphin-ornamented fountain gave its passengers an uncensored view of the fun. Hilarity competed with outrage – all eyes focused in unison on the same, usually hidden body parts. Almost oblivious to the drama but not quite, one young man was intent on other matters; he was still rolling his ticket into a perfect cylinder as he got up from his seat at the front of the top deck. He was on his way to the Library.

Stephen Dearsley, no older than the fountain invaders, had a better excuse for public nudity than the frolicking, loose-limbed bodies that were dancing in the water. Grey nylon socks stuck to the swelling feet that he refused to let escape from his tightly-laced black shoes. Cavalry-twill trousers, old-fashioned by a generation, a woollen maroon shirt and a thick brown corduroy jacket; this was his usual look and he wouldn't change it just because of the weather. His outfit contrasted vividly with the disposable summer chic all around him and, in the case of those young naked lads, clothes, chic or un-chic, had been discarded altogether. The tightly knotted brown tie was his final and most aggressively unseasonable fashion statement.

Stephen disliked the whole idea of summer clothing. He disapproved of seasonal sartorial changes just as much as he hated the idea of fashion itself. Clothes were clothes, that's all, a human uniform distinguishing us from other mammals. Uncomfortably hot, he hurried on his way, shy, confused and disorientated. The dark green and yellow wall tiles and faded grey marble floor of the Library's entrance hall felt better to him than any cooling shower. He felt safe with both sun and noise locked out as he climbed the ironclad staircase to the Reference Library, his sweat turning refreshingly cold on his back.

The nineteenth-century building that now housed the Public Library, Art Gallery and Reference Library was Stephen's daily destination. Originally serving some frivolous function concerning the Prince of Wales' horses, it had now settled into dignified municipal respectability. No mop could bring a shine to its faded splendour but that made it all the more attractive to Stephen, who delighted in the quiet understated values of decay. This was his natural habitat. Maybe that was not altogether true. There was just one minor problem here – people.

Of the three departments, the Public Library was just much too busy and the Art Gallery was even worse now that it had become fashionable with exhibitions designed for art students and the much too fashion-conscious elite of Brighton's bright new intelligentsia. Both departments, on occasion, and to Stephen's irritation, attracted people in from the street. Not silent unassuming loners like Stephen, who respected this mausoleum, but people just like the ones he had escaped from out there in the sunshine: lively, laughing, happy folk looking for fun. No – for Stephen, the search for the perfect environment had driven him up the staircase to the Reference Library.

Antique books, encyclopaedias, gazetteers and brown box-files full of yellowing newspapers were crammed onto shelves reaching up to the ceiling. Porcelain-shaded lamps hung from unpolished chains, their off-white bowls dimmed by the dark shadows of fossilized insects. Beneath them, filling the room, were long oak tables, book-laden and solid, attended by wooden chairs with well-worn maroon leather upholstery. Stephen was, by far, the youngest of the regular visitors to this, his sanctuary. Dusty amateur academics, probably retired schoolmasters, came here to research books that they had never had time to write during their working lives. They planned to record the minutiae of a way of life that was already dying around them by reading the complete works of forgotten Edwardian poets and searching through back-numbers of local publications long out-of-print. Elderly people came here for somewhere to sit, to read the newspapers without having to buy them and for an excuse to leave their musty bed-sitting rooms. It was a favourite place for respectable vagrants. The Reference Library preserved fading ideals, battered pride and precariously held self-esteem. No one spoke here, so illusions flourished in the silence. Stephen had an unformulated affection for these familiar people.

He was twenty-four, of medium height, medium build, pale with black-rimmed glasses and well-clipped, thick and strikingly dark hair. Unbeknown to himself, he possessed natural good looks, what his elderly relations would call bone structure and, superficially at least, he was more than a little like Buddy Holly even if he had never heard of that dead American singer. The product of a rather incompetent private school, he had flunked his exams so badly that his university ambitions had been thwarted and he had lost the little confidence that he had possessed as a child. He suffered from malaise, or so one of his teachers told him, and he would never come to anything unless he took himself in hand.

A long list of educational failures had depressed him but he still retained the ambition that had haunted him since he was very young. He wanted to be a writer, but not of poetry or fiction; he had no faith in his own imagination. No, he wanted to be a biographer, a chronicler of other people's lives, a dispassionate observer. He was a quietly spoken, often silent, student of history. He took a job as a waiter after school but he had no social skills and soon he was out of work, invisible to all but his parents who decided to throw money at the problem. So he moved to Brighton from his childhood village in Kent and, for three years now, he had been coming to the Reference Library where he continued his education in isolated dedication, surviving on a small allowance from his bewildered and disappointed parents. Stephen had found, or so he had decided, his perfect environment, his temple of fustian delights.

Sitting in his usual position at one end of a long table, with the summer light barely filtering through the large dusty window at his side, unusually for him, his concentration wavered. Remembering the fun in the fountain, fleetingly and disconcertingly, he felt alone as he thumbed through a book about the Metaphysical poets, his current self-imposed project. He had seen those young men, naked and free, and had been left with a mild sense of disappointment that he could never have done anything so recklessly exciting. These thoughts distracted him from the Metaphysical poets. He admired their clever play with words, but love poems weren't really his sort of thing and literary studies discussing sensuality were even worse. He tried to imagine the professor who had written this book and whose photograph was reproduced on the inside cover. The egg-shaped head of a late middle-aged intellectual frowned through the cellophane book wrapping.

John Donne – who wasn't unduly coy about sex – was the professor's favourite. The poet wrote that love without its sexual consummation meant that 'a great prince in prison lies'. That was enough about an old academic's sexual fantasies, Stephen thought, suddenly unable to carry on reading dispassionately. There the professor was, dancing in the fountain, before Stephen could jettison the image. It would not do to imagine professors any more. Let imprisoned princes lie, he thought; yes, they should lie well buried and forgotten under the academic tweeds of men who were old enough to know better.

The silence was broken by a wheezing cough from an old man sitting nearby. He met Stephen's stare with a frown. The library was unusually full today and, as he watched his familiar but never-spoken-to companions, he began, for the first time, to think of them as living bodies. Human flesh was haunting him today, and now the professor's hidden prince and the old man's cough alerted him to other noises and smells everywhere around him – the sucking of false teeth, stomach rumblings, the shuffling of feet and the smell of moth balls, paraffin and pipe tobacco.

A whiff of sweet perfume accompanied the assistant librarian as she walked apologetically down the line of tables with a pile of books. She was in her early thirties, or maybe late twenties, he assumed. Her pale, makeup-free face was a full moon dominated by black-framed spectacles, rather like his own pair. As she worked next to him, he noticed that her thick dark hair, pulled back into a ponytail, had a light coating of scurf. She was small-boned and skinny limbed so that anyone looking at her was drawn to her magnificent and well-supported breasts. Stephen caught her eye accidentally and she blushed and turned away. A secret princess was imprisoned there, he thought, as the blood rushed to his face.

The next chapter, 'The Metaphysical Poets and the Church', interested him even less than the one about sex. He pushed his fingers through his hair and scratched his scalp. Stretching his legs under the table, he was trying to repress his boredom just as the door opened and a young man and woman, the same age as himself, centuries younger than everyone else, shuffled into the room, arms entwined. They were already one body – as the Elizabethan church would say – identical long hair, sun-browned skin, flowing cheesecloth shirts and faded jeans. They looked irrepressibly happy. Giggling at the silence and the hostile looks, they floated to Stephen's table at the back of the room still clasped to each other. The assistant librarian tried to ignore them while she stacked books fussily onto shelves.

'Have you got any Dürer?' the man asked.

'Right next to you in the art section,' she replied curtly.

'Cool!' said the girl, starting to pull out large art books in a limp, unfocused way and stacking them on the table. 'Fantastic!' 'Amazing!' 'Unreal!' Admiring adjectives hurtled around the room with enthusiastic sibilance. When the couple reached Dürer's 'Head of the Dead Christ', a projected male whisper filled the room. 'There it is! It's fantastic. Look. He's tripping, man. Brilliant!'

The assistant librarian hissed through her teeth and approached them, but her eyes settled on Christ's head with its brutal crown of thorns, its vacant eyes and ecstatically opened mouth. Stephen looked too. Until then, he had only seen the suffering. 'Look, you'll have to leave if you keep making such a lot of noise,' the librarian said harshly, her eyes still focused on the Dead Christ. 'People are trying to read.'

'Okay, man. Keep cool, okay? We're going. All right,' said the young man.

'Yes,' said the girl. 'We love your books, that's all.'

So they left, slightly sunken now from their bouncy selves, but wrapped up in each other once more and already oblivious to the others. As they slipped from the room, raised eyebrows and sighs accompanied them on their way. Stephen stuffed his papers into his briefcase and hurried out, catching up with them on the stairs but not knowing why he was there.

'Hello,' he said.

'Hi,' they replied. There was a pause while they all smiled. They stood there for a lingering moment, not quite embarrassed but silenced. 'See ya around,' said the man.

'Yes,' said Stephen. 'That would be good.'

Then they had gone leaving him stumbling out into the sunshine. He felt foolish but also inspired by such an uncharacteristic surrender to his subconscious. He was still not sure, though, why he had followed the couple out of the building. He would go home, of course, he could think of nothing else to do now that he had left the library, but something had changed in him and, today, he would do things differently. Instead of going straight to the bus stop, he walked across the green and back towards that fountain. People, his generation, were lying in the sun and a radio was playing a song about love.

Nothing new there, he thought, but as he walked on he inhaled the change. It wasn't just all that exposed flesh or the evocative smell of French cigarettes or whatever people were smoking, and it wasn't even the electric guitar cutting through the airwaves; it was a small gentle sound that got to him and brought more of his hidden emotion to the surface. Somewhere, in the distance, he heard the tiny tinkling of bells. Again, for the second time that day, he did something without thinking about it – he unfastened his collar and slipped off his thin brown knitted tie.

Two

'Don't look for me any more – any of you who knew me well. No more crotch-focused stares or furtive glances. No more flesh on flesh or leaping hearts. Leave me here drifting between two worlds looking for someone new... my judge, perhaps or, maybe, a second opinion. I am waiting for you, drawn to you, holding on for you, my unsuspecting friend.'

Austin Randolph, Tung Ping Chau, June 1967

Stephen rented a room in a nineteenth-century terraced house in Hove, Brighton's respectable, some would say dull, Victorian neighbour. The two towns meet seamlessly along the same broad promenade but there has never been any doubt about which is which. Brighton was a small fishing village until, in what seemed like moments, in the late eighteenth century, it was transformed into a playground for the future King George the Fourth and his hangers-on. Ever since those heady, so-called Regency days, it had been a place for fun and sex. Hove, with its gull-fouled statue of the great Queen and Empress, had always been Victoria's child – sensible and solid with its mysteries well concealed under its ample skirts. In that summer of 1967, the sun sparkled on the sea and the crumbling white stucco terraces of Regency Brighton but, away from the shore, down streets of dirty yellow brick, Hove was dusty and stifling – somehow diminished by its twin. Naturally, Stephen preferred Hove.

The house was ten minutes' walk away from the beach so, apart from adventurous and raucous herring gulls and the luminosity that the sea's reflection lent to the sky on a sunny day, No. 47 Gresham Villas could have been in outer London. Two or three overgrown dusty shrubs filled a small, unkept front garden and hid most of the litter that sea breezes dispatched efficiently and regularly in through the gateless entrance.

Once the home of a Victorian doctor, solicitor or some such worthy, the house, three floors and an attic, like most of its neighbours, had become a complex of bedsits with an inadequate bathroom and a grubby separate lavatory shared by too many tenants. An art student had converted the entrance hall into an

15

oriental fantasy of primary colours with a mural of loosely clad and very non-spiritual-looking Asian monks sharing erotic positions with even less clad but highly flexible and long-suffering young women. The exotic ambience was increased by the heady scent of incense and the frequent sound of sitar music that emanated from the ground floor rooms. Stephen liked to think the atmosphere was Baroque but he knew he was deluding himself. He tried to ignore the other tenants, preferring to live in seclusion in his attic room three floors above. Up there, with his eye for historical detail, he took his surroundings to an opposite extreme. The room was monochrome with old, if far from antique, furniture and the walls were, of course, the correct shade of magnolia.

Lighting a cigarette, one of his greatest pleasures, he ignored a brilliantly sunny Saturday morning sitting back in his threadbare but immensely comfortable brown wing-backed chair. He had found this unloved piece of 1940s soft furnishing dumped in the garden of a mansion which, like so many of Hove's largest houses, was about to be demolished and replaced by a block of flats. The effort of dragging it to his lair had been amply rewarded by the many hours spent within its comforting wings with nicotine and Marcel Proust's languid, voluminous novel *À la Recherche du Temps Perdu* – Remembrance of Things Past – his perfect weekend relaxation.

He never went to the library on Saturdays and it was closed on Sundays. Immersed in this multi-volume novel, and hoping that he would never reach its end, Stephen had long gone home to the nineteenth century when his door opened. This had never happened before. He never invited people in and none of the other residents ever came up to the top of the house. Nevertheless, the door had opened and Stephen jumped to his feet shocked, surprised and slightly angry at the intrusion. It was the girl who lived downstairs.

'A man came round with this. He was a postman or something, I think. It's got your name on it, I think, here.' She dangled a letter in front of him as he stood there in his striped pyjamas and black socks. 'You'd better take it,' she said, in that trendily modern vague tone that so annoyed him.

'Thank you,' he said. 'Yes it is for me.' He was neither friendly nor hostile but he held back, embarrassed and awkward, making no

16

effort to start a conversation even though it was obvious that she wasn't about to leave. She stood staring at him with large, very memorable and inquisitive green eyes. She was small, thin and light-boned, with long and very straight black hair that came down to her waist. She was barefoot and wore an ankle-length, faded blue muslin dress with a string of purple beads and a small bell on a chain dangling over her shallow chest. Stephen thought that she looked liked the heroine from a Victorian novella. She would not have liked that. She was very brown but almost immediately her complexion changed to white and then to a livid green as they stood frozen in non-communication. She grabbed the arm of the chair and for a moment she looked as if she was going to faint. She righted herself and smiled.

'Look, I'd better sit down, You don't mind?' she said, immediately lying on his bed.

'Can I do anything to help?' he asked, quietly panicking in his own reserved way.

'No, thanks. I'm fine now.' Her colour returned and she sat up still staring at him like a child fascinated by a new experience. 'You're not as strange as you look, you know.' She leapt up lightly like a ballerina and left the room as suddenly as she had entered it.

'Thank you,' he said, feeling a touch of unexpected warmth, but the door had already closed.

He felt like a fossil or as if embalming fluid had congealed in his veins, freezing him and preventing him from going after her to start their meeting again. It was not to be, she was gone, the moment had passed. The letter, however, was still in his hand. He recognised the shaky but elegant handwriting. It was from one of his few acquaintances, actually the only person in this town that he could think of as a friend, a ninety-five-year-old French literary historian, Georges Villard. They had met when Stephen attended one of Villard's lectures – 'The French novel after Victor Hugo'. It had been held in a small room at the town hall on a wet Wednesday evening and, unsurprisingly, it had been sparsely attended with Stephen as the only member of the audience to ask a question. He had been reluctant to speak but even he was embarrassed for the old academic who had spoken with such passion.

Consequently, the two had struck up a friendship of sorts and, since then, for nearly a year now, Stephen had visited the old man who had recently had to move into a nursing home on the other side of Hove. Villard was frail but mentally alert and continued to work on his latest literary project for a few hours every day. He was putting the final touches to what he knew would be his final book on his literary hero, Victor Hugo. He occupied that dignified but unrewarded position of being old, respected and out-of-print. Stephen was deeply impressed that Villard had not only known his favourite novelist, Marcel Proust, but, as a young man, had modelled nude for Degas who had introduced him, still naked, to an unphased Claude Monet. Proust, Stephen assumed, would have loved the finished painting. Villard was happy, to a certain extent, to talk about the past, but he never said much about his meetings with Proust; he preferred his young friend to tell him about the modern world – unfortunately that was hardly Stephen's speciality. It was a relationship that sustained two lonely people – the old man nurturing Stephen's writing ambitions, the young man being Villard's only visitor. They did not usually write to each other, so the envelope with Villard's noticeably feeble handwriting was an ominous sign. The short note asked him to visit.

Since the beginning of the year, Villard's health had deteriorated and he was now bedridden in the small and cosy Hove nursing home, which was in high contrast to the dynamic spirit of the man confined there. Chintz curtains and flowery wallpaper reflected the nursing home's well-intentioned cheeriness but Villard's possessions clashed with the English suburban décor. Piles of books obscured the orange-brown veneer of the mock Regency dressing table, and signed photographs of long-forgotten literary celebrities in ornate frames looked bizarre on a white Formica table. The bed was a strange mixture too; the pink roses of the eiderdown struggled to emerge from the cascading piles of paper covered in the old writer's pencil-written notes.

A large plaster bust of Villard on the narrow windowsill was already a more life-like image of this minor legend of La Belle Époque than the living face of the man who, when Stephen walked into the room, looked as if he could have been carved from stone. Still strikingly handsome, his aquiline features recognisably those of the sculpture, Georges Villard lay in a bed surrounded by the memorabilia of nearly a hundred years. He was still a handsome man: a fine long nose, deep blue eyes sparkling with ironic humour, and a mouth that had retained its wry curve which could condemn, terrify or charm with the most nonchalantly subtle muscle movements. His shoulder-length white hair had been recently combed by his nurse and, unintentionally, she had given him the look of an old rock 'n roller. He would have liked that if he had known about such things. His skin was anaemic, the texture of tissue paper, and it declared that these were the well-preserved features of a dying man. His body, except for his long expressive fingers, was pitifully wrecked. Once a muscular six-footer, he was now skeletal and frail, almost invisible beneath the covers. The aroma of antiseptic filled the room but could not conceal the smell of disease. Stephen recoiled. He had not seen death before. Until this moment, it had always been just a date in a book, a historic event, not a process at work on the human body.

Villard greeted Stephen warmly with a voice that always took him by surprise. It was a deep, rich bass with only a hint of French accent, projected with the clarity of a classical actor. To Stephen, it was the voice of the nineteenth century.

'How is the world?' it proclaimed ironically.

'Confusing,' Stephen answered truthfully with a shy smile.

'Sickly, like me, I expect,' the old man laughed. 'It will outlive me anyway, even though it has been dying for so much longer. Well, let's not mind about that now. Come round here out of the light. I want you to read this letter.'

Stephen was reading it already. It had been sent from Hong Kong and was written in an even frailer hand than Villard's.

'Dear M. Villard,

We do not know each other but we have a mutual friend in Professor Julian Maynard. He said that you dabble in biographical matters and that you might consider undertaking an account of my life – wretched though it is.

Maynard knows a lot about me so forgive the brief nature of this note. My health is poor and, unlike you, writing has never been my talent. If you are interested, consult Maynard. He will tell you that I have lived an eventful life and that is no exaggeration even if I wish it had been otherwise. There is, in Maynard's opinion, a lot of material that should be published one day and that you would be the ideal person to do this work.

Let me know your answer as soon as you can.
Yours sincerely,
Austin Randolph.'

'Who is Professor Maynard?' Stephen asked.

'Dead. He was an historian and a fool. He believed in reincarnation.'

'So he didn't tell you anything about Austin Randolph?'

'Not yet,' Villard grinned. 'But I have written to this pushy Mr Randolph, telling him that I have more pressing business and that I would not be able to undertake his book.

'So that's the end of it?'

'Not quite. I have recommended you. Here is my letter. I did not send it in case you are not interested or too lacking in confidence to take it on. You can use it as an introduction. If you're not interested, don't call yourself a writer, my young friend.'

He smiled mischievously and pressed a button on the wall, sinking into the pillows with a wry grin. The nurse came in immediately.

'This young man has a lot to do and this old one has done enough. Show him out and then come back and jab me with that hellish syringe. I have that pain again.'

He took Stephen's hand in both of his and squeezed it feebly, bringing unexpected tears to the young man's eyes. It was a moment of benediction.

Three

It was a warm October day in 1914, the first autumn of the Great War, the last war, everyone hoped. Sitting on the balcony of his elegant suite at the Metropole Hotel, Brighton, Maurice Irving gazed out to sea. Comfortable on his wicker chair, wrapped in a tartan blanket, his eyes focused somewhere beyond the horizon. He might have been thinking about the war, his early departure from it, the horror, the death of friends, the passing of the old order, or even the tentative future, but he was not. He was really just sitting, put there by his wife with the help of his nurse, who hoped that the sea air would do him good. What passed through his mind, if anything, was a mystery. The war had left its mark.

Margaret Irving missed her husband's wit, his sense of adventure and his protective arm. She had not expected a wounded manikin to return from the front, especially after just one battle, and she wasn't equipped to deal with it. A nurse was all that was needed. She had her own requirements, her own needs. Maurice had been beautiful, she thought. It was not his wealth that had drawn her to his side; a strong physical attraction had brought them together but almost immediately the war had destroyed the erotic charge. She could not go near him now – not in that way. She had always been beautiful and her beauty, if that were possible, had blossomed with enforced chastity. Her physical yearning gave her an allure that unsettled every male that she met and not a few women too. Then, in that sinful seaside town, she fell from grace. For her the relief was great, and for Henry Randolph the prize was beyond his dreams.

In those trench-foot-stinking dugouts, Henry had dreamed of many things. Soft feminine skin with the odour of peaches, Belgian whores, country girls, beds with sheets, and English beer. He was a workingman, young, handsome and athletic with healthy animal instincts. He had admired his employer's young wife, of course, joked about old Irving's luck; but he had never thought of bedding her, not for real, not on his first home leave and not in such a way: the bed with its laundered sheets, the opened windows letting in the midday sun and the restless sound of the sea. He had underestimated the energy of the woman, the ferocity and the shamelessness of doing it there with her husband sitting out on the balcony, wrapped in tartan.

Four

The girl from downstairs was called Dys. It was typical, thought Stephen, of her contrariness. She would always disagree with his observations, disobey the rules, dislike his taste; the name was appropriate, a contradictory prefix, Dys. Since her visit, he had felt her presence constantly. When he came back from the library filled with enthusiasm, she could destroy his euphoria with a simple comment. Remarks like 'Hello' or 'What are you reading?' sounded like sly attacks. When she joked, he could never think of a clever reply. She reduced him to monosyllables with those penetrating green eyes and ironically pouting lips. Every day, she killed a little more of his privacy just by being there on the stairs, in the hall, in the street. Now that Georges Villard had sunk under the power of his painkillers, she had become his only acquaintance and he, in turn, had become her latest toy. Irritating as she was, he felt a certain pride in her attention, even a touch of vanity. Was his hair too short? Maybe it would look better if he stopped brushing it back? He would make some concessions; she was, after all, interested.

It was now several weeks since he had written to Austin Randolph at the annoyingly clue-free Hong Kong box number. It was an improbable project, partly, no doubt, an example of Villard's Gallic humour and possibly, in Randolph's case, the ramblings of a fantasist; but he had written the letter, opened himself up to hope and, just occasionally, looking at himself in the mirror, he saw the writer that he had always wanted to become. Vanity kept appearing there too. The glasses were fine, just the sort that a biographer should wear, he would let his hair fall forward over his forehead and his tie could be a little looser, a little less correct. As yet, however, there had been no reply. Every morning he came down to look for the post to find nothing but Dys looking at him, rubbing in his failure but exciting him and distracting him just the same.

One morning, she was sitting on the stairs with a tawny young man, cascades of blond curly hair falling over his skinny shirtless torso; they were whispering and giggling quietly together – a tangle of hair, the aroma of musk, a secret code. Her friend moved his

23

large bony feet as Stephen squeezed past but Dys blocked his way with her legs. He glanced at the purple varnish on her toenails, then before he could escape she grabbed him, pushing her hand up his trouser leg and massaging his calf insistently and firmly. He recoiled, froze, and wanted more but his reflexes took him to the bottom of the stairs.

'You're trembling! You're not frightened of me are you?' she mumbled in a dreamy voice.

There were no letters for him by the front door. His disappointment distracted his pounding heart but he had to take a deep breath before tackling the return trip past his tormentors. He pushed through their languorous cordon, ignoring Dys's protests and her friend's mocking shrug, and hurried back to his room.

'Don't be so boring,' she called. 'I was only being friendly!'

He was angry but excited; she had touched more than his flesh – she had thrilled him. Her intimacy was meant to humiliate him, he knew that; she was showing off in front of her friend, her new boyfriend he assumed, one of those slender sun-baked aliens, those unbuttoned hedonists that were becoming the image of the age. Now she was bringing them into the house, unhousetrained strays trapping him even further behind his bedroom door. Maybe he should move. He could have lived on his own if only he hadn't felt that touch, her thumb pressing against his calf muscle. That had changed things. He sat in his chair, flustered, even breathless, turned on, his heart still pounding. This was no time for Proust; all he could think of was that hand on his leg.

He flicked through the pages of yesterday's evening paper mechanically, almost desperately, trying to put her out of his head. He had to turn back a couple of pages when his brain caught up with the print. There was a short paragraph that registered on his busy subconscious. 'Writer Dies.' It was Georges Villard. There was no lengthy obituary; the piece was wedged between the main story, plans for a new supermarket, and an advertisement for greenhouses and garden sheds. 'Erect it yourself and save pounds!' Stephen was still thinking of Dys as he read on. Villard had died a week ago and the funeral was today – in an hour – at eleven o' clock.

He was thinking of Dys as he got his posh clothes from the wardrobe: his 'interview' suit, a white shirt and the black tie that he had bought for his grandmother's funeral. Changing in front of the mirror, he appraised his legs, trying to be objective. There was nothing to laugh at, no reason for him to be embarrassed – in fact, altogether, he was in good shape. Regular morning exercises, from a book by an American marine, had kept his muscles conditioned and his flesh tight. She had no reason to mock but, even so, she never stopped laughing at him or so it seemed. No matter what he wore, she would see through it; she was exposing him, stripping him and dissecting him. Thinking of her made knotting his tie a clumsy affair… the third attempt would have to do. He was ready, prepared to run that gauntlet to the bottom of the stairs.

He could hear them laughing, inane tittering, puncturing his confidence before he had even started. Obviously drug-induced that giggling, he thought; but no, that was a cheap gibe, it was more than that. She had got to him and she could not be so easily dismissed. He could not hide behind rhetoric, blame her or her boyfriend – he knew what he wanted and that he would fail. He wanted that touch again, he wanted more than that of course but he would not show it, he was good at disguise, he had had a lot of practice.

They were still on the stairs as he came down, his body respectfully covered in black.

'Going to a funeral?' she asked, with that same unsettling hint of irony.

'Yes,' he answered artfully, carefully adding a reciprocal hint of tragedy. He too could play the game, he decided.

Five

'Bloody stupid place to build a cemetery – there's always a hold up here,' said the taxi driver. Stephen just smiled; he would not engage with the man's ill temper, he was too emotional for a lecture on navigation. Pedestrians, free from the immobile traffic, were rushing about their business; everywhere faces were intense in concentration: working or shopping, bargains and deals, it was all so serious, too serious. When he died, he thought, he would have a horse-drawn hearse and make sure that it came this way during rush hour to remind people of the real reason for the hurry. There was so little time, and for someone as indecisive as Stephen, it felt as if it might already be too late. He was being called to action but his fingers were still in his ears, avoiding the call, refusing to jump, frightened of what he might find on the other side. The car behind them had its windows open with the radio playing the Marseillaise.

'So they remembered the old Frenchman after all,' he thought – of course, he knew he was wrong but, within his own reality, it seemed apt. It was the opening of a song that had been playing everywhere that summer. He had heard it in shops, on the radio and from opened windows in the street. He never listened to the words but now they hit him with unexpected force: the song told him that there was nothing he could know that wasn't already known – chilling that – and that there was nothing he could see that wasn't already shown. Ah yes, just as the old man had said, Stephen needed to look for what he wanted to do with his life. Then the lyrics continued with more of the prophecy: there was nowhere, the song said, nowhere he could be, that wasn't where he was meant to be. The record, although he had never heard of The Beatles, struck him electrically, as if it was being sung directly to him as a warning. Then, even more challenging to his belief, the words said that all this was easy and, in an époque-defining line, 'All you need is Love'.

For that moment at least, he thought that The Beatles were right. Maybe it was easy. Everything was easy, everything except love.

The taxi driver was having nothing to do with love that morning as a group of chanting but very Caucasian-looking Buddhists with shaven heads and saffron robes wound through the traffic jam offering flowers to the drivers.

'Bleedin' idiots!' he shouted.

When they reached the taxi, Stephen opened the window and took a slightly crumpled dog-daisy.

'Love means Peace,' said the smiling young monk, in a gentle Home Counties accent.

'Thank you,' said Stephen, putting the flower in his buttonhole. As he fixed it, he noticed that his hands were shaking.

'A spell in the army would do them a power of good,' volunteered the driver, but Stephen ignored him.

When he finally arrived at the cemetery, the ceremony was over and the small group of mourners was dispersing with that matter-of-fact air that accompanies the funerals of the very old. When they had gone, he went to the open grave and, unobtrusively, dropped the flower onto the coffin lying far below him in the clay. Inappropriate as it might have been, his body tingled with an exhilarating sense of hope.

'Goodbye, old friend,' he muttered. 'Peace and love, OK.' He grinned at his own foolishness and made no effort to stop a modest shedding of tears.

Six

'You are my eyes, my friend. Piece it all together, the whole sorry tale or, if you want, tear it apart. Do as you will. Go back to those days when we were new sprung and eager. Listen and look, my young scribe. Do your worst with me — that is your job.'

Austin Randolph, Tung Ping Chau, June 1967

The sunlight was pale that evening but it was still humidly hot in Stephen's dusty room, polluted still further by his cigarette smoke as he stood at the window looking at the sloping roofs and church spires through the encroaching sea mist. Seagulls screeched their lament above the distant sound of traffic. The view had lost its charm. It spoke of decay and that had lost its charm for him too. Downstairs, the sitar player was practising an oriental raga. Without wanting to, Stephen was led away by the music. The world could take care of its own death-pangs while he found another reality sitting cross-legged on the floor. Sitar music, smoke and dusty heat, a silk dressing-gown replacing his recently discarded funeral clothes, everything was telling him that he could and should move on. He should let himself out of his self-inflicted prison or, as the new jargon had it, he should loosen up. He internalised the sea mist and the filtered sunlight; the music engulfed him and he was away in a melancholy but freer place until he burnt his fingers on the forgotten cigarette.

Then he noticed Dys sitting in his chair. 'Hello,' she said quietly and almost meekly. Her feet were pulled up to her body, her chin rested on her knees, and wilting daisy chains decorated her ankles, drawing his eyes to those purple toenails and then to her face. She was smiling gently at him and he smiled back before realising that his dressing gown no longer covered his nakedness.

'I was going to have a bath,' he said, hiding his crotch.

'You looked very calm.'

'Yes, I was. Quite,' he said, getting up from the floor. It was alright, he thought; he didn't mind her seeing him like that.

'Oh, don't get up. It was good seeing you there. You've been so sad today.'

28

She wriggled her toes, snuggling them under her dress, and he resumed his now awkwardly cross-legged position on the floor.

'It was nothing,' he said. 'Just an old man who died.'

'But you loved him. I came to apologise. I was being stupid. I'm sorry, really sorry. Look, I've brought you this.'

It was a bracelet made from her plaited hair.

'You must wear it on your wrist – it will ward off evil spirits – all except me that is. Go on, let me put it on you.'

Almost invisibly she had moved to sit next to him; she crossed her legs to become his mirror image and took his arm, enclosing it, her hands almost burning him with her touch. As she knotted the bracelet around his wrist her breath warmed his arm and, while she concentrated on her task, he felt an unexpressed but radiant laugh surging through him, coming from somewhere far beyond him. He had never heard it before; it was from another creature deep inside himself. It made him blush and his eyes watered imperceptibly.

'There you are,' she said, in a tenderly distant tone that he had not heard before. 'You've got a little bit of me. Now come down to the pub and buy me a drink.'

'Just give me time to dress,' he said, fumbling for his clothes.

'I'll wait.'

He turned away and dressed hurriedly, knowing that she was watching, but happy that he didn't really care any more. Decency was achieved rapidly and, as he found his jacket, she came up behind him, putting her hands on his shoulders.

'Don't put that on,' she whispered. 'It's not that sort of place.'

The Bear was Brighton's largest pub; it was built like a baronial hall with a mock Tudor emphasis on oak beams, tapestries and refectory tables. There was a large central area and a gallery above, reached by two sets of carved wooden staircases. Nicotine coloured the walls, the lights were low and the ambience smoky and noisy. The town's student and would-be student population had claimed it as their own, coming here in their hundreds, knowing that it would be full of kindred spirits. The babble of voices rose above the rock music, which was amplified by Brighton's most discerning jukebox – it was playing a song about a girl called Emily, telling her to put on a gown that touched the ground. It could have been about Dys. She, like Emily, would float on that river forever.

Stephen liked it immediately; he was almost frightened that a song could capture his mood so exactly.

'This is great,' Dys whispered a shout into his ear. 'See Emily Play – I love it.'

'I don't know it,' he mumbled.

'It's Pink Floyd. We all went to see them in London last week. They are so beautiful, Stephen.'

'Funny name, Pink Floyd,' he said, fumbling for words.

Exotic herbal smells mingled with the familiar aroma of cigarettes, cheap perfume and dirty denim as Dys led Stephen through what was, to him, enemy territory. It was perhaps his first experience of his own generation en masse and he felt foolishly formal in his white shirt and neatly ironed trousers in a sea of psychedelic colours and ubiquitous Levi blue.

'There they are!' Dys shouted, pointing to what he took to be a group of students sitting on the stairs. 'Are you coming?'

They were just the sort of people that he dreaded. A half dozen or so young males and females of the hippie race sitting languidly in a huddle partly concealed by a cloud of their own making.

'Let me get you that drink first,' he said, needing the time to acclimatise, excited to be with her but desperate to escape before he ruined everything. He wanted to run back to safety, to hide before he was forced to enter this new world. 'What do you want?' he said, as if he was buying a round in a golf club.

'I'll have a Guinness but don't be long. I want you to meet my friends.'

The song kept encroaching, charming him but warning him that he might be entering a trap. Stephen always listened to the lyrics of songs, seeing no point in having words to songs if you didn't pay attention to them. 'See Emily Play' was warning him that there might not be another day and, if he didn't get this right, he might just lose his mind; not knowing that people would say that this did indeed happen to the young singer from, for him, the comically-named Pink Floyd. He did know, though, that he would, even only for a few moments, love to lose his mind, to leave it behind and to play – just like Emily played.

The bar ran the length of the building and was well serviced by bar staff but he still had to queue and, as he got to the front, a crowd gathered behind him blocking his view of Dys and her friends. He went hot with frustration as the smug-faced barman slowly poured the Guinness.

'Please hurry,' he said without meaning to. He was scared that it was all going to fall apart and that he was going to fail before he had even started.

'Nothing but mistakes are made in a hurry,' the barman said, with a condescending smirk.

'You're not like the others, are you?' came the slurred voice of an old man standing next to him. 'You've got more sense, haven't you, lad? I've been coming here for over twenty years,' he went on. 'In the old days, there were no juke boxes and you could hear yourself speak.'

Stephen did not need this; he was already flustered and embarrassed enough and he tried to ease himself away with his two perfectly poured pints.

'I see you're drinking the good stuff. It was even better than that in the old days. Smooth like wine it was. Like wine.'

'Really,' said Stephen, managing to break away. He pushed through the crush looking in vain for Dys. Then he heard the drunk's voice above the tumult.

'He's a good lad that one. Not like the rest of you – you load of layabouts!'

Dys and her friends had gone. Maybe he had forgotten where they'd been sitting or perhaps they'd moved. He pushed backwards and forwards looking for them, feeling more and more desperate and out of place, the beer spilling over his starched white cuffs. She had gone and he was alone, longing for her to come back, not knowing what to do, he had to just wait and hope. He found a table and tried to control himself. He was shaking with anger, embarrassment, hurt; he wasn't sure why but these feelings all seemed new, as if he had never felt this way before. Maybe once, he remembered. Once, when he was little, he had lost his footing in the school swimming pool; the water filled his lungs, blocked his nose and stung his eyes as he struggled to breathe and all around him the other schoolboys laughed and jeered. He could see the whole event all over again as he sat quietly, choking back his emotion at a small table in the corner by the door. He had never been to a pub before and he hardly ever drank alcohol, so the Guinness made its impact immediately. It unlocked some darkly

31

hidden thoughts coloured by his anger, his sadness and his hopeful excitement. He cursed himself for being such a liability in his own life. Time wore on and Dys did not return. He drank morosely – first his pint and then hers. The alcohol opened up a gamut of clashing moods, extravagantly discarding his joy and ultimately, as always, settling for depression. A hurtling feeling like a storm in his ears, which he knew was drunkenness, gave him the energy to leave, and he was about to go when the old man from the bar sat down next to him.

'I saw you here all on your own so I've bought you a drink, lad. Us loners should stick together, eh?'

Seven

It was summer in the year 1915 and it was love at first sight. There he was, snuggling at her breast, her firstborn, the saviour of her world, the fruit of her forbidden love.

Margaret Irving lay in bed, elegant with a cream gardenia in her hair, her silvery-white silk bed jacket opened to free her breasts; she was propped up by a bank of pink satin pillows, obsessed and enraptured by the sight of her son.

'You are as beautiful as your father – no, more beautiful even than him,' she whispered.

Little Austin Irving, or Austin Randolph Irving as she had insisted on naming him, already had a head of thick black hair, healthy swarthy skin, and eyes that were as blue as the sky on that sunny March morning.

'I will protect you and love you like no other,' she cooed, rocking him playfully in her arms. 'No one will ever take you away from me, no one will harm you. Mummy will never let them because you are my special reward, little Austin. You are the joy of my life.'

Eight

Stephen sat dejectedly in the Reference Library, his first hangover bringing in its wake a slow poison that worked its way ruthlessly from his brain to his bowels. The accompanying depression repeated, for him, not just his latest failure but all the disappointments that had blighted his life. His general malaise killed his concentration; sweat gathered on his brow, his stomach sent warning signs but he held out, he tried anything, everything to connect with his brain – pen clicking, tooth tapping, foot shuffling – but his limbs were elsewhere, his body was in revolt and his brain was buzzing. He could not look at any of the other library regulars but he felt their irritation; old friends they were not.

As he got up to fetch a book he made accidental contact with the assistant librarian's firm thigh: she was hot in her acrylic pink sweater, he could smell her animal scent, and he squeezed past while she remained firmly in his way. She was smiling as their bodies touched and she kept that expression as she watched him file through the rows of tables on his queasy way to the door. Only when he had gone did she continue stacking encyclopaedias methodically, alphabetically, absent-mindedly, each volume fitting into place with a dull thud. For a moment it looked as if she needed courage to survive in this place. Her mood was lost on Stephen – his stomach had issued its final ultimatum and he had to run to the lavatory.

When he returned, mouth soiled but relieved, tasting of bile and smelling far worse, he found Dys sitting in his chair. She gave him the most beguiling of her smiles and put a small package on the table.

'I've brought this for you,' she whispered. 'I won't stay. I'm going to Salisbury for a bit but I'll see you soon, OK?'

'Wait,' he said.

'Sorry, Stephen, I have to go.'

Then she was gone, her old trick – her body slipping from the room like silk on marble.

Instead of looking at her gift he followed her, pursuing her musky perfume but, impossibly and inevitably, she had disappeared. There was no sign of her in the street – just a few passers-by, the muffled sound of traffic and a suffocating intense heat that raised long dormant urban smells, stale litter and urine, human grime. 'Excuse me, sir,' came a voice. 'Could you spare the price of a cup of tea?'

'Piss off,' he hissed.

He returned to his seat; the assistant librarian smiled and looked away. Then he remembered Dys's package: it was an airmail letter with a Hong Kong postmark. He doubted his strength if this was going to be bad news – disappointment now would be too cruel. He flinched like a defeated animal waiting for its deathblow, holding off the moment with a whimper, trying to comprehend the fatal moment. His face flushed with sweat; his headache now less of a pounding thump, more a penetrating bolt, piercing his eye with electric ferocity as the bile returned to his mouth.

'Dear Mr Dearsley,

Georges Villard speaks highly of you and tells me that you know about my project. He says that you could undertake to write the biography. I am prepared to go along with his judgement. I cannot help you much as I am not in good health but I am enclosing the names of people who will give you some of the facts. I want to put the record straight and they all have good reason to remember me. A cheque will be sent to you to cover initial expenses. I trust that you will find it sufficient. I do not expect to see you until you have finished the book. Write it as if I were dead.

Yours sincerely,

Austin Randolph.'

On another piece of paper there were a few pencil jottings: 'Emilia Jeffries, Philip Irving and Stanley Finch. He used to be my valet. He is discreet, maybe over discreet, but will be of more use than the others.' The note added that Finch was working in the catering department of a London college, and ended with a scribbled *good luck* and pencilled monogram *A.R.*

The job was mysterious, improbable and, maybe, impossible, but it was what Stephen had dreamed of doing and it was also his legacy from Villard, his only true supporter. The old man had given him a chance and he had, of course, also called his bluff and

35

challenged him to actually do what he had said he wanted to do with his life. Through his nausea, he could feel a distant glow. It was growing inside him; a warm message from the grave, maybe, or just a hint that he could engage with the world, break out of this melancholy and his much too cleverly formulated façade for living. And, one day, he might be a writer and he might even dance naked in fountains: naked with Dys, always with Dys. It was up to him, it was time to stop dreaming and to act. He must accept this unlikely, forbidding challenge because it just might be his only chance. There was excitement enough in that thought. He was about to jump into his future, that murky world that he had only ever half believed in.

Naturally there was no champagne celebration in the Reference Library. No one there knew what had just occurred; he wouldn't have wanted that anyway – it was just business as usual in his hideout, but for Stephen life as a biographer had just begun. Then his stomach rebelled and he had to rush from the room as last night's Guinness returned to remind him of Dys.

Nine

Brighton Station – symbol of confident Victorian achievement – had known better days. Its roof of iron and glass would have sparkled in the sunlight when the first steam trains rolled out on their journey to London, but now over a hundred years of steam and industrial grime had blackened the roof and the rest of the edifice. Stephen loved it all the more for that. The sun, unable to penetrate the glass, flooded into the station in shafts along the railway tracks, illuminating the building like a rose window in a Gothic cathedral. As he was waiting for his train, ruffled passengers jostled and circumnavigated him; pale-faced Londoners were beginning their fortnight in the sun, while their red-faced compatriots prepared to leave with over-excited children, dilemmas over timetables and peeling skin.

The new generation of khaki-clad student travellers sat on the floor, backs propped against rucksacks, faces blank with exhaustion and indelibly tanned by their summer life on the road. The world would be discovered afresh with every new era, the democracy of travel made possible by those Victorian engineers and their armies of navvies. Stephen shared those pioneers' euphoria; he was embarking on a voyage of his own, as epic as those first steam trains passing through chiselled far-off mountains. His enthusiasm wavered, however, when he was approached by a haggard, tangle-haired stranger who had been watching him with shifty interest.

'Do you want some shit, man?' came the gravely serious question.

'What do you mean?'

'Come on, man. Don't freak me. Shit, you know, dope. Do you need some?'

Stephen surprised himself by becoming the owner of a small brown paper package, shoved roughly into his jacket pocket.

Later, on an escalator at Victoria Station, another young dealer stood next to him meaningfully.

'Some shit, man?' he asked.

'No thanks. I've already got some,' he said, trying to sound matter-of–fact even though inside he felt a leap of excitement and a new sense of belonging.

He felt a stab of regret, though, when he went through the main entrance to one of the University of London's most imposing neo-Gothic buildings. He was entering more than a building; he was reliving a childhood dream, one that had been shattered by schoolboy failure. Disappointment was soon dispersed by excitement, however. He was a visitor with a mission, so he allowed himself to enjoy the sound of his steel heel-caps as they echoed into the far recesses of cream-coloured corridors that were lined with oil paintings, not very good ones, of extravagantly robed academics. Once he had thought that he too would become one of those settled figures of intellectual prowess and now, even though he was here for an altogether more interesting reason, he imagined the gown and hood billowing behind him as he clicked his way into the inner sanctum.

A barefooted student with a colourfully embroidered waistcoat partially covering his bare stomach showed him the way to the canteen. No undergraduate gowns here and no panelled dining hall either. It was a self-service cafeteria – all steel and Formica, with shabbily dressed students sitting around drinking coffee out of polystyrene cups, stubbing out cigarettes in silver foil ashtrays; long gone were the high table, the Latin grace and the silver service.

Not for the first time that day, his expectations were thrown about; through passing disappointment to challenging reappraisal. The world pictured in his solitude had moved on. He had imagined Stanley Finch as a grandly dignified figure in the spirit of English butlers, presiding efficiently in an oak-lined hall at the heart of an ancient institution. He wondered if he had just been misdirected when he approached a middle-aged Spanish woman who was wiping down the tables with a damp cloth.

'Could you tell me where I could find Mr Finch?' he asked.

'Who?'

'Stanley Finch.'

She put her hands into the pockets of her blue nylon overall and gazed into space before laughing and clasping his arm.

'You mean Stan, dearie!' she said in her Iberian-cockney accent, at a volume much too high for Stephen's shyness. 'We don't call him mister anything,' she screeched. 'He's just Stan. He's over there, love, with the trolley. We don't have Misters and Misses here, we all muck in together.'

Across the room, an old man, looking older than his late sixties, pushed a metal trolley from table to table, scraping cold baked beans and unwanted sausages into a bucket. His straight-backed military bearing gave him a dignity hardly lessened by the regulation blue overall. His face was deeply sculpted with wrinkles that added decades to his age and spelled out his history as a melancholic. These lines, however, were insignificant compared to the jagged scar that ran unforgivingly down one side of his face.

'Mr Finch?' asked Stephen.

'Yes, sir,' he answered, stiffening to an imaginary attention.

'I believe that you used to be a butler.' Stephen regretted the tactless opening as his eyes moved to the congealed remains of fried eggs and chips in Finch's bucket.

'Yes, sir. I'm a butler by profession,' came the proud reply. 'As you can see, sir, I am in somewhat reduced circumstances at the moment. This isn't my usual line.'

'Of course, I can imagine that, Mr Finch.'

A flicker of optimism passed across Finch's face. Maybe he was thinking of the possibility of a return to his old profession.

'Are you looking for a butler, sir?' he asked solemnly.

'No,' Stephen smiled. 'I'm afraid not.'

'I assumed not, sir. As you can imagine, there isn't much demand for butlers these days. All the situations are for odd-job men. They expect you to do the gardening, clean the car and mend the fuses. All that sort of thing and, to be honest, I'm just too old for all that, so I'm doing this little job until the right one comes along. But if you aren't looking for butlers then what can I do for you?'

'You worked for a Mr Austin Randolph, I believe.'

'Look here, sir. I don't want any trouble,' Finch responded, with an instant hardening of tone and more than just a hint of panic in his voice. 'If it's all the same with you, I'd rather leave all that behind me, sir, if you don't mind.' He finished cleaning the table with a clenched jaw and an energy that wanted to wipe out more than just the coffee stains.

'Could we have a talk about it when you've finished here?' asked Stephen, noticing that the canteen supervisor was looking over at them. Finch began pushing his trolley to the next table.

'It was all a long time ago. It's of no interest to anyone anymore. So if you'll excuse me, I really need to be getting on.'

Stephen's eyes watered in frustration. He began to plead. 'I really need your help, Mr Finch. Is there anything you can tell me about him?'

'He was a gentleman like yourself, sir.' He stopped his trolley and faced his interrogator. There was a new strength in his manner and Stephen had no doubt that he was going to be firm and serious. 'He paid me to do a job, not to pass judgement on him.'

Now all eyes were on them, but Stephen persisted and followed Finch through the rows of tables.

'Well, can you at least tell me where I can find Mr Irving?'

'As I told you, sir, it's all in the past now. Can't you leave it at that? No good is done by raking it all up again.'

Stephen gave up and, with his hands trembling, he fumbled for a piece of paper and wrote down his name and address.

'Well, if you change your mind, you can always contact me here. I'm writing a book, at Mr Randolph's request, and I need any information you can give me. He told me that you would be very helpful to the project.'

'Well I can't help that, sir. Take my advice, if you will, and find something better to write about than all this stuff from long ago. It won't do you any good or anyone else for that matter. But, I'll tell you one thing. If you want to know about Mr Irving, he's probably where he always was – Frampton in Huntingdonshire. Frampton House.'

'Is everything alright, Stan?' said the Spanish woman.

'Yes thanks. The gentleman is just leaving.'

Ten

It was a seaside summer's day in 1934. The Randolphs had taken a seafront suite at the Metropole Hotel in Brighton. Unbeknown to them, they were in the very place where Austin Randolph's story had begun twenty years earlier.

Ivy Randolph, the image of modern beauty, was a study in white: peroxide blond hair ferociously permed, powdered face, silver sheen on her silk white gown. Blanched, soft-focus beauty pierced by the cruel scarlet of her lips. Ivy lay suggestively stocking-footed on a bed of creaseless satin.

'Your port, sir,' said Finch, standing rigidly to attention, his black, neatly oiled hair shining in the sunshine that burst through from the balcony. The same midday light picked out the silver tray with one finely cut glass sparkling with ruby red liquid.

A young man who had grown up fast, Austin Randolph, tall, dark, Hollywood handsome with his trimmed black moustache and flashing hazel eyes, grinned his grin of perfect teeth. Taking the glass gently by the stem, he turned it and delicately poured its contents into Ivy's blanched lap before crushing it in one flexing grip.

'Drink it, if you like,' sneered the woman, but Austin was not listening. He was standing on the balcony, holding his wounded hand as blood dripped onto the white balustrade.

Eleven

'Red liquid, sparkling crystal on a platter of shining silver. So polished and scrubbed. Decanted lovingly by masterful hands framed in starched linen. So calm and patient. So wanting that fist. Needing it. Asking for it. No shouting or screaming as it smashes. Crystal shatters. That red, red wine on madam's satin crotch. That placid look. That immobile face. Finch, you are flesh and blood like all of us. Flesh and blood, broken glass and madam's laughter. Go on, stumble away with your dignity intact.'

Austin Randolph, Tung Ping Chau, June 1967

So that was it; his first day as a biographer had been no great triumph. His notebook had only two entries: Finch's workplace and now Philip Irving's address, obviously a grand house in Huntingdonshire. He knew very little else except Finch's nervous resistance about digging up the past and Austin Randolph's bizarre wish for his own biography. Certainly, there was something to hide but Stephen's confidence had crashed at the first hurdle. He doubted his investigative abilities; he should have bullied the truth out of Finch, refusing to leave until he told him more, but instead he had just recoiled in embarrassment and escaped crestfallen out onto the London streets. This was not how it was done. The great biographies were not written like this.

Somehow he had thought of his work being conceived and executed at his garret desk, poring over dusty volumes and drawing the rest from his self-cultivated intellect and admittedly limited imagination. He wanted to be Plato, meticulously chronicling Socrates' arguments in his gentle Grecian retreat, far removed from the turbulent world of James Boswell, Dr Johnson's biographer on the partygoing, binge-drinking, pox-catching circuit of eighteenth-century high culture. He had not expected the rough and tumble of doorstep journalism and now he doubted if he could do it. Randolph's secrets might just stay hidden: a gentleman and his butler and a murky forgotten history – Stephen's performance in the canteen had, he knew only too well, been pitiful.

He took the mid-afternoon Brighton Belle – a soon-to-be axed Pullman train which belonged to a more elegant age but still ran several times a day between London and Brighton, serving breakfast, lunch, tea and dinner. The walls were panelled in dark wood; the tables covered in starched linen with heavy steel cutlery and shaded table lamps. The three o'clock train would take one hour to reach Brighton – time enough for afternoon tea served by a uniformed steward as they sped through the Sussex downlands. Alone in the carriage, his ego in dire need of pampering, he poured his tea, skilfully balancing his arm against the rhythm of the train. He liked the fading rituals of English life: tea poured first, diluted with the correct amount of hot water and then a dash of milk. With the reassuring sound of spoon on china, he was burying his failure.

The journey was made the more enjoyable by its imminent obsolescence; he had always got a frisson of excitement from ruins, savouring the ends of eras, wishing for them even, in an oddly self-destructive way. Since childhood, he had felt that every day was its own fin de siècle – each enjoyably melancholy in its unique way and demanding its own chronicle. He explored derelict Victorian mansions and, when he could gain access, disused factories from the high days of the Industrial Revolution, enjoying the desolation and savouring the thought of imminent demolition. He was always looking for the remains of a vanishing past; in a crowded street, he would ignore the fashion boutiques and advertising hoardings in favour of a Victorian post-box or an original Georgian shop front.

When he became an old man, there would be new additions to look forward to: he would visit the ruins of tower blocks or dig up the indestructible plastics and polystyrenes of the late twentieth century. He was an eyewitness to life as it passed him by. Two egg and cress sandwiches later, and, after a second cup of tea, he sat back in the well-sprung, dusty upholstery and watched the afternoon sun flickering through the canopy of trees as the train clattered on its way. Life should be always like this, he thought: never quite arriving but with your anxieties left behind, pleasantly travelling in closeted isolation. The Brighton Belle, so soon to be scrapped, was his perfect refuge.

He might have been the same age as Stephen, but the newcomer to the carriage looked very different with his brown curly hair nearly reaching his shoulders, his ripped denim jeans, dirty granddad vest and the by now inevitable sandaled feet. He sat down opposite and stuck his brown street-worn feet on the seat next to his reluctant companion.

'You don't mind?'

'No,' Stephen lied.

'Quite a train. You could have a banquet in here.'

Stephen, rather too stiffly, he thought later, poured himself another cup of tea. He did not relish another assault on his confidence and, yet again, he was hiding behind ritual.

'It's really strange, you know,' persisted his new friend. 'I mean being here with all this.' He pointed generally around the compartment. 'It's really beautiful, I know, but who needs it? I mean... there's no one on the thing except you and me. It's crazy, man. What's it for?'

'Why are you on it?' asked Stephen, sounding more aggressive than he had intended.

'I don't know. I just saw it was going to Brighton and here I am. It's amazing.'

They smiled blandly and sat in silence.

'Oh, my name's Steve,' said the unwelcome stranger.

'I'm Stephen too.'

'Why are you going to Brighton?'

'It's where I live.'

'Cool! We're all meeting down there to give out leaflets,' Steve said vaguely.

Stephen nodded and looked out of the window.

'About the war,' Steve continued. 'Vietnam. What's the feeling down here? We've got a lot of support in London.'

'For the war?' Stephen asked with irritated irony.

'No way, man! You're kidding! Will you be coming too?'

Stephen was struggling for an answer when the steward came up and told Steve to take his feet off the seat but let him off the supplementary fare. It was obvious that Steve had no money on him.

'Alright, man. Don't get hung up about it, OK?' he said, laughing.

They were drawing into the station and Steve took down his shoulder bag from the luggage rack while Stephen packed his book into his briefcase.

'See you around.'

44

'Yes. I hope you get rid of all your leaflets.'

'Here take one,' said Steve, pulling a badly printed photocopy from his bag. 'You might want to come along.'

After he had gone, Stephen stayed in his seat looking at the leaflet. It showed a photograph of a decapitated Vietcong soldier. Behind the corpse were the terrified faces of Vietnamese peasants. 'Stop the carnage' read the caption. He felt sick and ashamed as he walked out of the station into the urbane Brighton afternoon.

Twelve

A week later the Vietnam leaflet was lying on Stephen's desk, curling in the sunshine. He couldn't throw it away but he couldn't act on it either. Sitting there it was making a statement, reminding him not to forget. He would remember but he couldn't act. Not yet. He was saving it up, he thought, like the other things that were eroding his carefully balanced lifestyle, for the time when he would know what he was doing, where he was going and why. He had written to Austin Randolph to accept the job and to Philip Irving asking for a meeting but, so far, his only mail had been a postcard from Dys. The picture was a tourist snap of Salisbury Cathedral with its needle sharp spire penetrating an improbably blue sky and, on the vivid green grass, a happy family picnicking, respectably dressed in Technicolor clothes from the 1950s. The message was brief:

'Gone to Salisbury to see friends for a few weeks. See you when I get back. Love D.'

The only friends that she could have in Salisbury Cathedral would live in the belfry, he thought bitterly. He hated the idea of her having friends in Salisbury or anywhere else; she should be sitting on his chair mocking him with her searching eyes. She was mocking him, of course, with the card. She must have searched for it in antique shops, looking for just the right amount of reactionary stuffiness. He not only missed her, he thought, smiling at the picture, he needed her. She had unsettled him, disrupted his pattern and, he had to admit it, got him thinking about her most of the time.

Two letters had arrived the following morning but he pocketed them unopened; he didn't want any more bad news. Something fragile was forming inside him and he needed to let it grow unchallenged, so he grasped the moment and went outside, his body in need of some summer photosynthesis now that Brighton had abandoned itself to the growing heat wave. 1967 was going to be an iconic English summer. Ignoring the time honoured border between beach and town, swimwear was worn in the streets, office workers at lunchtime lay in the sun in any open space, stripped to a minimum, underwear promoted to sun-wear, the grass strewn with discarded pinstripes, blouses, black socks and city shoes.

Elsewhere, students and hippies – it was difficult to tell them apart – brought an ethnic exoticism to the streets: bare feet, ankle bracelets, henna-tattoos and exposed navels spoke of a different set of priorities. Somehow, stuffy old England had begun to unbutton. Street-sellers capitalised on the fashion for beads, necklaces and, especially, strings of bells. It was a time to be young and, while their elders followed the Anglo-Saxon tradition of covering up, young bodies proclaimed a new philosophy by revealing skin, lots of it. The press took notice and announced the 'Summer of Love'. Love was all you needed. It was easy, as the song said, and it was easy to love these beautiful, languid creatures with their hopeful ideology of love. It was especially easy to love while the sun shone and the air was filled with songs and the tranquil sounds of gently tinkling bells.

Sitting by the Dolphin Fountain, daring to be without his jacket, Stephen felt that, just possibly, Utopia had come of age. He had gone out, he had told himself, to get his hair cut, but then those bells and an American song about surfboarding that emanated from a clothes boutique told him to let it grow. It said more than that: it told him to let it all out, and maybe he would before it was too late, even if he only half-understood what they meant. He was intoxicated by the moment, by the joy and by the knowledge that he too was young and eligible to enlist in this sense of abandon. Instead of the haircut, he bought himself a cheesecloth shirt and a blue and red striped blazer. Even if he was still only on the outer limits, he had joined the fiesta and it felt good. Dys, he thought, would approve.

Now he was ready for those letters.

'Dear Mr Dearsley,
Glad you want to do it. Find enclosed a cheque for £200. Tell me when you need more. A.R.'

'Dear Mr Dearsley,
I was most intrigued by your letter and will do all I can to help. Come down to Frampton. Any time would suit but if you come

down this weekend, you'll find lots to amuse you. Just turn up –
I don't stand on ceremony!
    Yours sincerely,
    Philip Irving.'

His eyes watered, he couldn't help it. It might just be euphoria,
he thought, but for the first time he let himself dare to believe, not
only that he had become a biographer, but that he might escape
from his solitary confinement locked in by his own inhibitions. It
was easy. Everything was possible. The breeze caught the fountain
and he was showered with spray. He was soaked, water dripping
down his face, saturating his shirt, cooling him down but not
staunching his excitement. He didn't care; in an instant he was
dried by that all-healing sun.
    'Hey man,' laughed a young guitarist sitting on the grass
strumming amiably away. 'That was cool!'
    'Yes,' Stephen agreed. 'Cool.'

Thirteen

The same old bed but another baby. It was 1916 and Margaret Irving, in her bedroom at Frampton House, was reluctant even to look at her howling straw-haired son.

'Here, take him,' she said icily to the man standing awkwardly at the end of the bed. 'I made him for you, he's yours.'

The boy was handed curtly to his placid father. Maurice Irving concurred with a kindly nod, but his face had that distant troubled look that came from long sustained pain. He too passed the baby over, this time to the smiling face of a nurse.

'Shall we take you to see your big brother Austin? Yes, let's do that shall we?' mumbled the nurse sweetly as she took her new responsibility towards the nursery wing of little Philip Irving's family home.

'I have done my duty for you, husband,' Margaret Irving said in an unchanging tone of hostility. 'I think that settles matters between us.'

'Try to make an effort with the boy, if not for me then out of kindness for a vulnerable child. Margaret, you would feel less anger if you could only offer the baby your love.'

'I have done all that I can do. You should be grateful, you have your heir.'

Maurice Irving was trembling when he closed the door on his wife's bedroom. The twitch that had been with him since the Great War now developed into a full body shock and he fell to the floor in a fit.

At the end of the corridor, the nurse put down the crying baby and ran to his aid.

Fourteen

According to a reference book, Frampton had a Saxon church, a manor house called, unsurprisingly, Frampton House, and one of those accident-prone ponds, Frampton Pond, which had been the scene of a much recorded tragedy in 1763. Since then, it had followed the pattern of remote English villages – less and less agriculture and more and more gentrification. Stephen was expecting what the newspapers classified as a sleepy picturesque village so he was surprised to find the train, and then the small country bus, crowded with young travellers. The predictably green lanes with their undulating slopes were lined with rucksack carrying hitchhikers. It was the weekend of the Frampton Rock Festival.

Leaving the bus in the village, he followed the directions – cardboard signs with large red arrows – to Frampton House, only to find that he had joined a sporadic hippie procession that stretched round each bend, then up over a hill to Frampton House itself. A hundred improvised guitar riffs and the hurdy-gurdy sound of multiple harmonicas blended with the rural sounds of grasshoppers and birdsong, mostly the squawking of startled blackbirds. Old cars with streamers flying from the aerials, backpack-overloaded bicycles, even tandems, propelled by scrawny legs in sawn-off denim, and coaches filled with word-perfect choruses from over-excited rock fans. It was rural congestion: Philip Irving was holding open house and everyone was going Stephen's way.

The coaches turned through large wrought iron gates following clumsily hand-written signs to the coach park that was a field commandeered for the occasion. At the top of a tree-clad drive, a Georgian mansion stood radiating in the sunlight – Portland stone, Stephen noted enthusiastically. Marquees had been erected in front of the house and noisy generator vans were positioned around a large makeshift stage made from scaffolding, canvas and timber; already the parkland was crowded with small tents and a throng of people, the slightly more punctual soul mates of Stephen's travelling companions.

As he followed the drive up to the house, he parted company with the other pedestrians who were all dutifully following the arrows to their tent sites. He was alone on the drive, suddenly separate again. His newly washed hair stuck to his forehead and sweat saturated his face; he took off his glasses and wiped them with a silk handkerchief just as a large golden-haired man strode towards him. Philip Irving was telling some workmen to move a pile of scaffolding when he saw a boy in a blazer walking up to the house. He guessed that it was Stephen, bookish and unworldly in a sea of cool – he could be none other than Austin's scribe. Any anxiety that may have flickered across his face was lost to his visitor's myopia for, without his glasses, Stephen saw the world through romanticising gauze.

Irving looked very much as he would have done thirty years earlier. To Stephen's eyes, he had thick golden hair that lay in short tight curls on the handsome bull-like head of a man with the heavy frame of a rugby player. With the glasses back on, the image came into focus: the vivid blond hair was quite obviously the result of an over-dose of self-administered and cheap hair dye, fleshy jowls obscured the jaw-line and hung down to the tie-knot from a face reddened by burst veins. Philip Irving's face and form were transformed in an instant with these and several other unflattering signs of age and dissipation, culminating in a sagging stomach that filled a tightly buttoned tweed jacket. Large moist lips, lubricated by an access of Labrador-like saliva, parted to reveal nicotine-stained teeth as he shouted out Stephen's name in greeting.

'You must be Stephen,' he called jovially. 'As you can see, you've caught me at a busy time, but welcome anyway. Come inside.'

He put his hand on Stephen's shoulder and guided him with towering, straight-backed authority into the house.

The mansion, like the man, did not live up to Stephen's first impressions. The elegant Portland stone walls that had shone brightly from a distance were in reality cracked and flaking, the paintwork was of a faded municipal green and, even more surprisingly, the property itself was no longer in Philip's possession. The Irving family, Victorian industrialists made good, had bought the estate in the nineteenth century but Philip Irving, lacking his ancestors' entrepreneurial streak, had let things slip and had avoided bankruptcy and homelessness by selling both land and house to an adventurous local charity. He kept the use of his living quarters in the central section of the house – the two other wings

51

had become a rather under-used youth hostel catering for the increasingly small band of young walkers and deprived urban teenagers who were thought to benefit from Huntingdonshire's gentle rusticity, while their more fortunate contemporaries travelled to the headier climes of Marrakech or Goa. The Rock Festival, to Irving's initial horror, was the charity's new experiment in a long line of unlikely moneymaking ventures and it had attracted hundreds of rock fans and alternative lifers to the acres of tent sites prepared for the occasion – making this the largest crowd seen at Frampton since the visit of Queen Elizabeth I in the sixteenth century.

Inside, Frampton House's declining fortunes were even more obvious than they were from outside; Irving's bachelor lifestyle had reduced the former splendour of the interior to a dreariness more usual in a run-down boarding house or a municipal office. Stephen's well-tuned eye analysed the décor as they went through the entrance hall: good Victorian tiles, a bit worn but very stylish; the walls had been papered in the last ten years with a cheap and inappropriate woodchip that was already beginning to peel at the edges. The drawing room was in various states of disrepair but had a fine ornate painted ceiling depicting the ancient classical tale of Actaeon devoured by his own hounds; there was a carved wooden mantelpiece and large windows looking onto the grounds. Stephen noted the nineteenth-century glass approvingly – he loved the way it acted as a distorting mirror to the trees outside. The walls retained the oil portraits placed there a hundred years earlier, but the room itself was sparsely furnished with ill-matching sofas and easy chairs fitted with dirty loose covers of clashing shades of faded blue and red. A large oak table, probably mid-Victorian, Stephen guessed, was covered in papers; the carpet, a terrible sacrilege, once a fine William Morris with its distinctive intertwining leaves, now carried the stains of several generations of cats and dogs. It was like the staff room of a seedy private school.

'Take a pew,' said Irving. 'A drink? What about a gin?'

Stephen accepted reluctantly. Irving's gushing manner had already made him uncomfortable.

'Tonic? Indian Tonic Water. I make it myself. Lemon juice and lots of quinine – that's all you need. We made it out East during the war. I think we all got hooked on it.'

52

The drink was offered in a cracked milk glass – the gin had a murky texture and lemon pips floated on the surface with other pieces of unspecified dark detritus.

'Very good,' said Stephen, shuddering at the taste.

'Well, here's to the success of your enterprise.'

'Cheers,' said Stephen feebly.

'I have to admit it has all come like a bolt out of the blue. I thought the old bastard died years ago.'

He crossed his enormous thighs and his bravura slipped for a fleeting moment before the bonhomie returned.

Fifteen

A pale imitation of his disappointing father, thought Margaret Irving, as her sandy-haired son with his bandaged knee played with the marmalade kitten on the drawing room floor at Frampton House. Memories of his conception still disturbed her. Her flame-haired and war traumatised husband, lost to her emotionally so early in their romance, was no longer the brave young officer who had left for the front. Now he had given her this reminder of her fate: a feeble child, impossible for her to love, an irritation and an insult to her moribund passion.

It was the bandage that focused her mind. The nurse must have put it on that pale pin-like leg, soothing an unknown injury. No matter how poignant the image, she could not cross the threshold to sympathy. Her husband had continued to disappoint her even after his recovery. Post uniform, post shell shock, and in spite of his regular epileptic fits, he had mellowed into tweeds, pipes and country pursuits. Happiest with his spaniels, Maurice Irving had good reason to wish for placid, peaceful things; he had no need for passion or drama. His wife was less fortunate.

Her war hero lover, her former estate worker, her Henry Randolph, had found glory in the war and in her bed. Conceiving their child on their first shattering conjunction, Margaret Irving knew that she was pregnant even in those early gasps of ecstasy.

It was a brief affair, ended when, unexpectedly, unforgivably and uncharacteristically, Henry Randolph, weakened by battle, died succumbing to enteric fever in a hospital in Belgium, near the trenches, before they could begin a life together, before they could cool their infatuation, before she could tire of his physical attraction, and before she had to choose between wealth and love.

There was the boy, of course, Austin. From the moment of his birth, his mother noticed that same look, that spark of life and excitement that was so lacking in her womb's other desiccated fruit. Austin Randolph Irving, a servant's child but heir to his father's physical glory, was cherished secretly, and sullenly accepted by her husband as his son but excluded from any rights of inheritance. He tolerated the child, allowing it to live beyond its status as his own in the secluded, English idyll in that summer of 1915.

Margaret Irving maintained a burning love for her firstborn throughout her second reluctant pregnancy. She held onto it too, giving it over-flowingly to him while neglecting the other as the two half-brothers grew into childhood in front of her tormented eyes. She had bullied her husband into accepting little Austin – the child's security was the price she demanded for her continued presence in their marriage so, scandal ignored, Austin became Maurice's acknowledged but largely ignored son.

'Look Philip, if you don't jump, I'll leave you there,' called Austin, fourteen summers later, in their short-trousered, Wellington-booted, early teenage years. He had already jumped over the high wall that enclosed Frampton House. Nervous, tearful Philip froze in fear, high up there above him. A stone would do it, Austin decided, and, with a wicked grin, he aimed it sharply at his brother's knees. It did the trick and Philip joined him on the ground, in the lane, out of bounds, bleeding from his injured knee.

'We can do it here,' said the pale, prematurely wizened girl, no older than the boys but wearing her fourteen or so years like a prison sentence. Lizzy knew a shed quite near to her house where, naked in her thin, freckled body, she lay down in the dirt and waited curiously for Austin. Later, it would be Philip's turn.

'Don't keep her hanging around,' came his brother's proudly mocking call. 'Do it now.'

'You're trembling,' whispered the girl kindly. 'I won't hurt you. I won't tell.'

Later she bandaged that knee.

Sixteen

'We did it there. That freckled body barely budding; offered in sulky trust, uncovered for the first time, joylessly obeying her instincts. We did it in front of him, the ginger boy with the frightened eyes. Yes little brother, you can watch. This is how it's done... fearlessly, unsentimentally in the dusty dirt. Have her next, if you can. What lies behind the fear in those eyes? Is it pleasure, little brother? Bad little brother.'

Austin Randolph, Tung Ping Chau, July 1967

'I always thought he was a bastard, you know. Quite literally,' said Irving, settling into his gin. 'Someone, they said it was her husband, but whoever it was, someone screwed my mother's maid, got her in the family way and bolted. Austin grew up here at Frampton. The mother drifted away but he stayed. Did odd jobs, you know but mostly just did what all boys do. Hung around getting up to no good. We were practically the same age. We had all this space; I suppose you could say we grew up like brothers, no one really bothered about us. We were free – freer then than ever again; it was a wonderful time.

'I remember all the outdoor stuff best. You know, boyish things with catapults and bicycles; there were the horses and then, when we got a bit older, there were girls. One in particular – we shared everything, if you know what I mean! Well, anyway...' he paused, out of breath, unconvinced by his own story. 'Another gin?'

Talking had unsettled him; his boisterous manner disappeared, his voice took on a thinner tone and his face set in a frown. Staring into the past, drink became a necessity; he had already poured himself three and forced identical refills on Stephen.

'Austin was practically adopted by my parents. They gave him an education – everything you need for upper class English life – riding, shooting, dancing and drinking. He excelled in them all. After puberty things changed, things always change, don't they? I suppose we were never as close again but then that's growing up, isn't it?'

The gin lowered his morale and brought him to the verge of confession.

56

'Talking about the past is making me nostalgic, you know. I still love to remember those days; it was so different here then. And there was all that marvellous music! Do you like music?'

'Yes,' said Stephen, unconvincingly. The gin was eroding his liking for anything and, anyway, he had never been very musical. He was drowning in Irving's self-pity, feeling cornered in the summer stuffiness of the room, but ennui had only blunted the edges: this was going to be so much better than his meeting with Stanley Finch.

'I collect old gramophone records, you know. I've got all the old dance numbers. I know no one likes them nowadays but I still play them. You know, damn it, I think I'll put one on now before all that modern rubbish starts up outside.'

Loud hissing and scratching came from the antique wind-up gramophone as Irving fumbled drunkenly, trying to rest the needle gently onto the delicate Bakelite of his 78 rotations per minute recording. After a few false starts and a few expletives, the room was re-filled with the energetically nostalgic sounds of Thirties dance music that even Stephen could imagine playing there in more affluent times. Muted trumpets, massed saxophones, banjos and strings with a pure voiced crooner singing sentimentally of love and the Moon. Carried away, Philip wanted to dance; he shuffled a bit but Stephen's presence restrained him and he returned to his seat. Their eyes met and parted in embarrassment, and Stephen looked away through the distorting glass of the windows with gin-intoxicated eyes at the modern world gathering outside.

The music muted all other sounds, acting as a bizarre soundtrack to the very modern festival that was transforming the parkland out there beyond the ceiling-high sash windows. Irving might well have wanted these intrusive hordes to vanish but the emerging rock generation was not so easily wiped away. It was Irving's frail world that was under threat. Stephen knew that and a flicker of sympathy went out to his self-consciously foot-tapping host. Increasingly, he did not want to be a part of an old order, he wanted to be outside, free and part of his own generation's new world. Slumped in the chair, Irving's body visibly crumpled in disappointment; he had wanted this to be a special moment, a way of showing his young guest some of the excitement that was locked away in the past. The hissing stopped, he leapt to his feet to retrieve the needle and the old blustering manner returned.

'I've things to do for a bit, old thing,' he said. 'So whilst I'm busy, you could speak to my mother, if you want. She's very much alive, you'll find, even though she is fantastically ancient! She lives here in wilful isolation but I'm sure that she would love to talk to you about the past. It's her obsession.'

The hurriedly finished gin further disorientated Stephen as he was led into the hall and up the uncarpeted staircase. The noise from outside only emphasised the embarrassing silence within, and Irving's heavy breathing and the echoes of their footsteps carried through the empty house as if they were in a marble mausoleum. Stephen, in spite of his growing headache, smiled, albeit nervously, about the unexpected bonus of finding another witness to this confusing story. As they climbed up to the bedroom quarters though, he felt vulnerable for a moment and hoped that this wasn't an embarrassing trick sprung on him by his drunken host. Please, he thought, let the old lady really exist.

'She's gone rather cranky in her old age, I'm afraid. I think she's confused about time,' warned Irving in his most worldly voice. 'I don't spend much time with her even though I know I should. Sometimes I think she's gone back to the past altogether, poor old girl, but she'll be interested to meet you and she'll love talking about Austin.'

The pieces were fitting together in Stephen's fuddled brain and an emotional surge of excitement, still mixed with fear, propelled him onwards as Irving opened the bedroom door.

Seventeen

The tiny, frail old lady sat upright in a high-backed chair of carved ebony with scarlet velvet upholstery. Her bone-structure, which must have made her beautiful once, now gave her seventy-four years a defined dignity and a sharp bird-like intensity, but she was wearing her age badly. She dressed in black satin – accentuating her paleness and defining her in the pathos of her isolated widowhood.

'This is Stephen Dearsley, Mother. He's writing that book about cousin Austin. The one I told you about.'

'You're very welcome,' said the old lady in a lightly whispered soprano, which, like an adolescent boy with a breaking voice, descended rapidly down the octave at the ends of phrases before sliding up again for her next sentence. 'I hope we can have a nice long chat. Are you staying or going, Philip? There is no need to stay, you know, we will be fine together, this young man and I.'

'See you later then, Stephen,' Irving muttered in a knowing whisper, giving him a confidential wink. 'I'll come back for you later, old thing.'

Stephen silently objected to Irving's fraudulent show of intimacy but he let it rest and smiled politely, pleased to be free of him for a while. The mother, he thought, looked much more interesting.

'Cousin Austin!' Mrs Irving scoffed as soon as he had gone. 'He will never admit that Austin was twice the man that he will ever be. Don't listen to anything he tells you, by the way, if you want the truth in your book. He invents things to make himself feel good, or at least to make himself feel better.' She was enjoying herself already. 'So what do you want from me? You are welcome to sit and talk for as long as you want. I have nothing to do these days; I just sit here looking at my things.'

She pointed generally to the room with its dismal Edwardian furnishings, but the details were difficult to see as the heavy dark green velvet curtains were drawn and there was only one, thickly shaded, lamp to light the whole space. She indicated an ornately carved ebony chair, the twin to her own and Stephen sat down shyly.

'Are you one of Philip's young men?'

'I don't understand,' he stumbled. Once again he felt under attack.

'Come now, Mr Dearsley. Are you his lover? Is he in love with you?'

She emphasised her last question with a sneer – as if love were an obscenity for her.

'No. Not at all. We've just met. I'm here to research the book as he told you.'

'Well that's good,' she said, laughing in a tiny trill. 'Don't think that I disapprove of such things, I'm no prig, don't misunderstand me. But Philip is so disgusting. I wouldn't like to see you involved with him. He is revolting, don't you agree? I mean physically repulsive.' Again she laughed, waving her bony hand to stop him speaking, her eyes sparkling in the gloom. 'Don't answer me. I don't want to get you into trouble, my dear. Save the unpleasant truths for your book. That's what you'll do, I'm sure. Well, if you want the truth. I should give it to you, shouldn't I? There's no point in me being the dignified old lady and covering everything up is there? Anyway, I'm not ashamed of anything. People should enjoy themselves when they're young. You're a handsome young man and I'm sure that you have lots of fun.'

'Was that his relationship with Austin?' Stephen asked hurriedly – casting aside intrusive thoughts of his own fun-starved existence.

'You've spoken to him, lad? What do you think? I'm sure that you don't know much about Austin if you think that. He had an altogether different quality. There was something fine about him, something natural. Maybe it's wicked for a mother to say but he was much too good for Philip anyway; he was much too magnetic, it would have been impossible and illegal too anyway – not that breaking the law would have worried Austin. But Philip wasn't the only one to love him. Everybody loved Austin. I did too of course. Dearly. I still do.'

Her sparkling eyes moistened, she stretched over to a small occasional table and picked up a framed photograph, passing it to Stephen. In elegant monochrome, the young Austin Randolph was mounted on horseback, his head thrown back in laughter. He was, in the picture, a dark-haired, athletic young man shining in his own self-confidence, fully engaged and celebrating his own machismo.

'That's how I want to remember him,' she said with a growing deepness in her voice. 'I live here in the past – that way we can all stay young. Not just young, my dear, but beautiful too.' She tapped her forehead. 'You never get ugly up here you know. Even Austin stays the same. He was so like his father. So handsome! But his father never got old. Austin won't either. He will always be there sitting on that horse and laughing. Always laughing! That wonderful laugh! I hear it here in this room. Every day.'

Stephen returned the picture and she patted it lovingly before putting it back in its place.

'Is he well, do you know?' she asked in a calmer tone. Now Stephen was to be her informant.

'I don't know. He's living in Hong Kong.'

'Always the exotic for Austin!' she exclaimed delightedly. 'He'd be just fine in Hong Kong! So tall too amongst the Chinese. They are not a tall race you know.'

'Your son said that you practically adopted him,' said Stephen, trying to get back to the plot.

'Practically adopted him! We did adopt him. And if anyone was the country gentleman it was Austin. Best horseman in the county – and the best pair of dancing legs I ever saw on a man! Oh, you would have liked him Mr Dearsley. He was born to it. As I said, he was a natural. It was the times that did all the harm. It wasn't his fault.'

'What wasn't?'

'Oh, I don't know. I get very muddled. I don't remember everything that happened later.' For a moment she had the look of a naughty schoolgirl, caught out and lost for words.

The sound of one of Philip's old records interrupted them; the tinny sound of the gramophone enhanced by the hollow box resonance of the house's acoustics turned Mrs Irving's bedroom into the perfect auditorium.

'Listen!' said the old lady. 'It's the foxtrot. I hear the music so well up here. It's like the old days when we had bands playing for our parties at least twice a month. You should have seen me dance the foxtrot! Everyone admired it. I taught Austin myself. Not that that was hard. He was a natural. Can you do it?' She looked at him eagerly. 'Can you dance?'

'No, I'm sorry. I never learnt.'

'Well, I'll show you. Come on! Stand up.'

For all his resistance there was a dreadful inevitability about it all. She was already on her feet, moving to the music and singing along with it in her croaky soprano. At first it looked as if she would fall but she found her balance and her confidence and soon she was almost graceful.

'It's simple,' she cried out laughing. 'Look. It's slow, slow, quick, quick, slow; left leg forward, then the right. Cassé to the right, like this then three steps and you start again. Look. Stand up! Come on!'

Nothing would help his embarrassment; she insisted and he refused a few times before she got him practising his cassés and fox-trotting with the old lady in his arms, whose bones, under the slippery silk, felt brittle in his hands, like a skinned rabbit. Her touch was barely perceptible; old fingertips unused to gripping. Any clumsy movement and she would break like a dry stick. He closed his eyes; subtle fragrances of powder and lavender enveloped him, mingling with the smell, he was sure, of his own rising sweat. Gradually the absurdity of the situation receded and, maybe it was the gin, but he began to enjoy the physical rhythm that the disciplined ballroom choreography imposed. No matter how unlikely the coupling, the movement drew him in, uniting him with his insistent teacher with a power beyond the farcical situation. He smiled easily at his partner. It's easy he thought... there's nothing you can do that can't be done.

'There you are! That's it! You're a dancer, my boy!'

She clung to him and guided him through the steps. Now she was enjoying herself, her eyes sparkled and her frailty dispersed. When the music stopped, they stood there wordlessly panting for a moment before returning to their chairs, like survivors in some long forgotten party game. Mrs Irving resuming her elderly pose as she settled back into her cushions, Stephen somehow lighter and looser than before.

'So, don't go hiding behind that stiff exterior again,' she warned mockingly. 'You are an attractive young man, Mr Dearsley, and you shouldn't conceal your talents. Do you hear me? You've got to let that wildness out; and don't pretend you don't know what I mean. I know that you have it in there.' She gave him a serious look before her distinctive laugh returned.

'I know – tell me I'm a silly old woman with nothing better to think about, but by the time you've reached my age you have seen a lot, you know. We don't forget the good times either, so don't let it pass you by, do you hear?'

'You're right,' said Stephen, now beyond embarrassment. 'But I find it difficult.'

'Well there you are then.' She was looking at him but no longer listening. She had remembered something else, some other time, he assumed.

He changed the subject back to Austin, but it was not yet time to escape her eagle-eyed analysis, because she came back from her reverie and began looking at him as if she was judging a stallion in the stables. 'Do you ride?' she asked with a knowing smile. 'I think you'd make a fine horseman. You've got good strong legs.'

'Having a pleasant chat?' said Philip, bursting into the room with uncoordinated bluster.

'We were until you marched in,' answered his mother with the sneer returning to her voice.

'I hope mother wasn't boring you,' Irving countered nastily.

Eighteen

The drawing room filled with rock music, 'It's started,' Philip announced unnecessarily. He pulled down the yellowing canvas blinds but could do nothing about the electric guitars screaming through their range, from growling bass to a piercing altitude, while insistent drumming made the floor and furniture vibrate. A singer's voice, muffled by the amplification, penetrated the room intermittently. Individual words paraphrased the meaning: LOVE... HIGH... FREE... IS THERE A REASON? Irving refused to be silenced and their conversation continued in shouts; more drinks were mixed and consumed, but sometimes the noise was so strong that they just sat mutely looking at each other, re-discovering each other like passengers on a train coming out of a tunnel.

'Take your jacket off if you're hot,' bellowed Irving. 'I'm sweating like a pig!'

'No thanks, I'm fine.'

'I don't know how you can sit there like that.'

He kicked off his shoes and removed his tweed jacket, adding an extra stale smell to the already stagnant room.

'You're very young to be a writer. How old are you?'

'Twenty-four.'

'You should be out there with the others. Not hanging around with an old fogey like me.' He gave Stephen an embarrassed grin and gulped down more gin.

'You won't be able to get back to London tonight you know. There's plenty of room here though if you want to stay the night.'

'I'll be fine,' said Stephen vaguely. Irving's hospitality was becoming more suspect with each drink.

'It's no trouble. After all, we're a youth hostel now. We're used to entertaining young men. Anyway, you'll have to stay, I've got another guest coming specially – she knew Austin as well as anyone. She'll be here for dinner.'

'Is that Emilia Jeffries?'

'You're very well informed. Extremely well informed; I must say I find you very impressive; you'll be a fine writer I'm sure. Exceptionally fine.'

The gin was winning the battle for Irving's mind and tongue and his stories of Austin became increasingly disjointed and prurient. Anatomical details were embellished with slurred re-emphasise as the conversation degenerated into Irving's personal piece of pornography.

'He was like an animal. Like a tiger! No one could resist him. I am telling you, no one. Have you known people like that?'

Stephen put his glass on the table; drunk though he was, he was still sober enough to recognise his cue to leave.

'Could I go and see what's going on outside?'

He was already standing up.

'Make yourself at home, old thing. You can do as you like here. Do anything you want.'

He was still muttering into his glass when Stephen escaped.

'We'll be having dinner at eight so don't be late. Dinner at eight. Don't be late. Dinner at...'

Irving's voice droned on until the front door had closed then, unable to hold back any longer, he began to cry, uninhibitedly, his face crinkled with grief.

Nineteen

Stephen closed the front door on the gloom within and remembered the biblical Lazarus, back from the dead, having to adjust to a new set of social priorities. The mid-afternoon heat, the unforgiving sunlight and the loudest music that he had ever heard blasted his senses. The smell of the grave lingered in his nostrils for one moment more then it dispersed; he was hurtled into a scene of vibrant human activity; instantly in a crowd, suddenly thrilled, he merged, or tried to merge, into the throng. No one stared at him — that was a surprise. He was just one of the multitude, part of a gigantic party at play. All he could do was whisper expletives under his breath. 'Shit…shit…shit. I don't believe it! Shit!' Was this it? Was this his coming out party?

Music weighed down the summer air; thousands of people, he had no idea of the numbers, moved to its rhythm, happily crushed together. On the distant stage at the top of the hill, four tiny figures with guitars and drums were communing with their massed fans, framed by elegant green rows of lime trees and a perfect cloud-free blue summer sky. Taking off his blazer and slinging it over his shoulder, he meandered, drunk but feeling ecstatically free, wanting to be wilder than he was ever likely to be but excited to the point of overload and suddenly in need of that space on a grassy bank. He threw down his jacket and sat on it. A girl in a tiny skirt and bikini top stretched in front of him offering her cigarette to a skinny young man with a golden beard and jeans rolled up to the knee. Raising his foot, he took the cigarette between his toes and pushed it towards Stephen.

'Have a drag,' came the ironically conspiratorial whisper.

Stephen took it and inhaled deeply — the effect was immediate.

'Not bad, is it?' said the bearded man with a knowing grin. 'It's home-grown.'

After a few more drags they were friends, a bonded circle of smokers. Stephen's smile spreading through his body and out to the others, binding him to them. He was enveloped in the music: guitars, loud, confident and more beautiful, he thought rhapsodically, than he had ever heard before — dramatic, romantic, and seeringly optimistic. Bands came and went, the afternoon

66

blazed on and, gradually, his tie, shoes and socks joined the girl's bikini on the ground. He unbuttoned his shirt and saluted the sun, unselfconsciously theatrical, while the others celebrated in a long, slow, ritualistic hippie dance. Then the cannabis and the heat and Irving's gin had their way and he fell into a deep sleep, lulled into a golden dream of happy dancing people.

The sun shed some of its intensity, the music grew mellower and, feeling languorously drowsy, he awoke to find that the bearded man and the bikini-girl had gone. He walked through the crowd – not looking for them but hoping that he might see them. A breeze cooled his chest and blades of grass refreshed his toes – Nature was introducing itself, welcoming him as he walked to the pond, where the air was invigorated by moisture and the shade of a voluptuous weeping willow tree. The sinking sun sent its burnished light across the water, drawing him towards it; he sat on the bank paddling his feet in simple, narcotic joy – delighted by the sensation. Ripples spread across the little lake and a young naked couple waded towards the centre, their skin glowingly white against the bronze of their small child. They stood, hand in hand, beautiful, in a silent triangle bathed in sunlight. Tears rose in Stephen's eyes as others, white, black and brown, silently joined them in the water, summoned into a prolonged moment of sacred spontaneity.

The sun was fading when he went back to find his discarded clothes. The music, if it were possible, was louder, the bands responding to the high energy of the crowd. The twilight was countered by banks of lights that sent kaleidoscopic colours onto the stage, picking up wriggling amoeba images on the backdrop. Couples settled down together, snuggling into each other as if they were hugging the music. Gradually the crowd fell into shadow; everyone was focused on the stage but Stephen felt removed, bereaved, as he laced up the shoes on his heat-swollen feet. He was lingering, about to go, when the others returned.

The bikini-girl, now in a long cotton shift, kissed him on the lips and laughed when he said that he had to go back to the big house. 'No need for big houses any more!' she intoned, as if she had seen a vision. A cigarette was rolled, he did not know or care what was in it; the circle re-gathered, welcoming him into its midst and keeping him there long after it was time for him to go. He knew that dinner was 'at eight and don't be late' but he chose to ignore his watch.

Unhurriedly, he wandered through the campsite, savouring these last moments of belonging; his smile lingered after he found the driveway again. He was heading towards the house when a black Rolls Royce came up slowly behind him, breaking his trance with its sleek urbanity. In the back, behind a uniformed chauffeur, sat an elegant middle-aged woman in grey. Their eyes met, Stephen felt undressed, disconcerted; the woman, beautiful, coiffeured and inscrutable, smiled formally as she passed. Reluctantly and with an involuntary shudder, he followed the car towards the house, furtively adjusting his tie.

Twenty

Philip Irving and Emilia Jeffries stopped what looked like an aggressive and intense conversation when Stephen joined them. Both were masterful in rapid changes of expression; Philip beamed his welcome and Emilia reverted to a pose of serenity.

'Stephen!' Irving called out, claiming old friend status. 'I would like you to meet Emilia Jeffries, one of my dearest friends.'

Emilia smiled coolly and offered Stephen her long-fingered hand but recoiled rapidly when he took it.

'You're very strong!' she laughed, looking at her hand and adjusting the large diamond ring that he had pressed painfully between her fingers.

'I'm sorry,' said Stephen, suddenly made to feel apelike. A comic dope-inspired voice inside him told him to swing off through the trees grunting and scratching his armpits. Emilia passed it off demurely but a short uncomfortable silence fell over the group; real silence was impossible as the music from outside never dropped its decibel level, forcing the conversation to an unnaturally high volume but also giving reluctant talkers somewhere to hide. Stephen needed time to adjust; with a sigh of recognition he was back struggling yet again in his accustomed social awkwardness. This time, however, he was strengthened by his recent burst of solidarity, anaesthetised by the gin against embarrassment, and bolstered by the marijuana to observe the comedy of manners developing in front of him.

Emilia had a frail delicacy, designed for beauty not strength; stylish in a timeless way. It was difficult to guess her age, which had to be somewhere between fifty and sixty, Stephen assumed, as he appraised the chic grey suit, the black court shoes, short geometrically cut auburn hair, and discrete but sophisticated make-up. The light French perfume that permeated the hall said more about taste than body. Perfectly packaged, Stephen found her impressive and intimidating.

'Well, this is fortuitous,' said Irving, filling the conversational lull while he ushered them into the drawing room. 'I have told Emilia all about you, she's bound to help. She knew Austin so much better than any of us.'

A fraction of a second passed, just a fraction too long, before Emilia smiled and, when she did speak, there was still an edge of hostility.

'Of course, I will help if I can…. We will have to see.'

'Well, here we are,' Irving flustered as he handed a glass of sherry to Emilia and replenishments of gin to Stephen. 'Here's to a merry evening. We've certainly got plenty of background music! I think you must have made a great impact on Mother, by the way, Stephen, because she's joining us for dinner. First time in ages.'

'I expect she has missed intelligent conversation,' said Emilia sweetly.

'Let's drink to Austin,' said Irving.

'I think we should toast our young guest,' Emilia contradicted. 'Here's to your success, Stephen!'

'To success!' agreed Irving. 'Well, I'd better see to dinner. I'll leave you two together.'

Stephen longed for a fix of nicotine; he needed a stimulant top-up and fumbled for his packet of untipped French cigarettes.

'Do you smoke, Mrs Jeffries?'

'I'm Miss Jeffries,' she said in a warmer tone. 'But call me Emilia, it doesn't sound so formidable.'

She accepted the cigarette and when, inevitably, his lighter refused to work, she produced hers, a slim work of art made from silver and mother-of-pearl.

'It was boring of Philip to involve you in our little problems,' she said, deeply inhaling and then gently expelling a narrow plume of smoke through pursed lips. Stephen watched the cloud disperse, happy to expand the pause. 'It's his idea of a joke.'

Stephen shifted awkwardly from foot to foot and took a sip of the foul tasting drink.

'I should dispose of that,' said Emilia mischievously, lifting up a large green vase. 'It's gut rot. Quick, put it in here.'

Stephen emptied the glass and was about to replace the pot when Irving returned.

'A man of taste, I see. It's Chinese, one of my favourites. One of the few good things we've got left. Do you like the Orient, Stephen?'

'Yes, I do,' said Stephen, putting it back on the table.

'Well, let's eat. Dinner is served!'

As they went into the dining room, Emilia squeezed Stephen's arm.

'Well done!' she whispered.

Stephen had found an ally.

Twenty-One

The dining room had once been very grand with its oak panelled walls, parquet floor and towering casement windows. These features now formed a seedy shell, filled only by a large refectory table, not more than forty years old, Stephen thought, with six chairs of differing designs from mock Jacobean to Fifties teak. Their footsteps – Stephen's steel caps, Emilia's black court shoes and Philip's scruffy brown brogues – clattered and echoed in the swimming bath acoustic, even minimising the ambient rock music from outside. It made Stephen laugh when normally he would have recoiled – it was the cannabis, of course; it would sustain him through the ordeal that was unfolding.

'It makes me want to tap-dance,' he said unintentionally. 'Not that I can tap-dance, of course, but you know what I mean.'

'I suppose so,' Philip muttered distractedly.

Stephen sniggered awkwardly when his eyes met Emilia's smile.

'We could certainly do with some entertainment,' she said.

An ideal acoustic for a chamber choir, Stephen guessed, mindlessly amused, but this echo chamber was an ill omen for the anticipated dinner table conversation that, he knew, would be sporadic and forced at best. The room, Stephen thought, trying to suppress the growing giggle, was more suited to a fraternity of monks eating in silence, listening to a sonorous reading from the bible or the chamber choir singing Bach. He would have preferred that, especially as he was beginning to feel nauseous – drunk, hungover and pleasantly stoned all at the same time. They were sitting struggling with their small talk as Stephen began to lose his battle against laughter when everything was altered by Mrs Irving's majestic, if slow, entrance.

'Good God!' she exclaimed in a surprisingly forceful voice looking at each of them in turn. 'It's like a church hall in here. What have you done to the place, Philip?'

'We're living through hard times,' said Irving irritably as he settled his mother in a seat at one end of the table.

'Lack of imagination, you mean?' she countered. 'If you'd used your brains you could have kept the place going. It was all Jacobean furniture in here once, Mr Dearsley.' She was pointedly turning

72

away from her son as she spoke. 'They were a depressing lot though, those Jacobeans; I disliked all that carving – much too heavy – but it would have been worth a fortune today. And how are you, Emilia, my dear? Are you here for the rock n' roll?' she said acidly with hardly a breath between thoughts. Emilia was sitting silently at the other end of the table. 'You've always been such a slight little thing but you look thinner than ever. It's not such a good thing being thin after a certain age, you know, and you could do with a bit of colour in those cheeks. Have we still got the horses, Philip?'

'No, Mother. They went years ago.'

'Pity. A bit of riding would do Emilia the power of good.'

'Well, mother, I'm sure Emilia could go riding if she wanted to,' Philip persisted.

'Yes, I'm sure you're right. She has obviously done very well for herself. Haven't you dear?'

Emilia just smiled. Mrs Irving's voice, unnecessarily loud because of her deafness, ricocheted round the room, giving her an authority that she obviously relished. Stephen was not going to become the victim of their mutual aggression; his spirit was still caressed by the festival and, whether it was the cannabis or the gin, he felt newly inviolable and, unintentionally and uncontrollably, his smile continued to grow. He remembered a phrase much used by Dys; he had the solution for these people with all their repressed anger, their unresolved issues with each other; they needed to 'chill out'. The table was bare except for cutlery settings of worn silver gilt, four plain glass wine goblets and a clutch of wine bottles. The old lady looked down the table disdainfully.

'Where's the meal then?' she sneered.

'It's coming now' Philip answered, sounding suddenly weakened.

Eventually the door opened and a bad-tempered woman in a dark green overall came in pushing a metal trolley.

'Here's the food. Bring back the things when you've finished,' she said uneuphemistically as she parked the trolley by the door and left.

'Excellent,' said Philip to the already closed door. He wheeled the trolley round the table unloading its contents – the set meal from the youth hostel kitchen.

'Shepherd's pie with extra portions of mashed potato and peas. Just what we needed!' He was struggling with his forced bonhomie. 'It would be perfect with some claret to wash it down.'

'I don't know why you pretend,' said his mother cruelly. 'This whole business with the hostel is ridiculous. You're a bloody fool and you know it.' Philip was now recoiling in defeat; he raised a fraternal eyebrow to Stephen who quickly avoided his gaze. Margaret Irving didn't notice; she too was looking at Stephen. 'Mr Dearsley and I had a charming conversation about dear Austin. I hope you've both been helpful too; Mr Dearsley wants to know everything. So that will be fun for us all, won't it?'

'I've already done my bit,' Philip said, looking to Emilia. 'I think it's up to you now, Emilia. After all, you knew Austin best, didn't you?'

'Maybe Mr Dearsley and I could have our little session tomorrow. I'd hate to bore you both with all those old things you both know so well. Why don't we just enjoy the meal and Stephen and I will sort things out later.'

The conversation died as they ate, their chewing and swallowing cruelly exposed. Stephen worked hard at controlling himself, hoping that he would not have to say anything; he was happy just to watch the gentile battle being played out in front of him with all the repressed civility of a vicious game of croquet.

'Anyone for apple crumble and custard?' Irving asked, looking plaintively at Stephen.

'Yes please.'

'Anyone else?'

'No thank you,' said Emilia.

'Nor for me,' agreed his mother.

'Well, it's crumble and custard for one.' he said, placing a heaped helping in front of Stephen. Beyond embarrassment, he ate in silence as the others watched. The unhappiness in the room was palpable and intense; he found refuge in the custard, its yellow creaminess took on an exhilarating zing and then quietened into a balm to his heightened senses. For a moment he was lost to his own indulgence.

'It was good,' he said, finishing at last, daring himself to smile at the assembled company.

'Then I'll wheel away the things.' Irving was already packing everything back onto the trolley.

'Austin would have known how to keep this place going,' said Mrs Irving when he had wheeled it out into the hall. 'He was the decisive one – Philip was always the victim.'

'You should know about that,' said Emilia aggressively.

'Well the place is a dump; that's obvious at least,' retorted Mrs Irving. Philip returned, followed by a scurvy-looking cat that sat in a corner watching them suspiciously.

'You don't mind shacking up in the hostel, tonight, Stephen, old man?'

'No, that would be fine, thanks.

'Don't be absurd,' cried Mrs Irving. 'He is writing about Austin and he should have Austin's room. What are you thinking of?'

'But it's all locked up, Mother,' Philip bleated.

'Well, I'm sure that it would be better than the barracks. Mr Dearsley deserves a bit more hospitality – especially after enduring the three of us – miseries that we are.'

She smiled encouragingly at Stephen. 'Now, I must wish you goodnight. I go to bed early these days. I shall enjoy lying back and listening to all these young people enjoying themselves outside. You'll tell me how you get on with the book, won't you, Stephen? I am so looking forward to reading it. Maybe we could have another little chat. Good night, Emilia. Come and see us again soon, dear. Don't leave it so long next time.'

Everyone stood up; the chairs sounding like an artillery salute that made the cat run hysterically from the room leaving a highly repugnant smell drifting through the air. The old lady looked over to the corner.

'The cat's got diarrhoea again,' she announced scoffingly. 'It would have been that shepherd's pie. We'll all get it now. Good night everyone.'

'I'll see you to your room, Mother,' said Philip, now thoroughly demoralised.

'That was edifying.' said Emilia when they had gone. 'Maybe we should talk tomorrow.'

'Sure,' said Stephen, his Cheshire cat smile still growing in spite of the smell.

Twenty-Two

'Tear it apart, Mother dear, tear it apart. I am not there. Your rage is wasted. I am not my picture; my reflection left the mirror. Break what you want, scream what you want, you'll not reach me. You took your pleasure, I learnt in your lap. Take pleasure in this: nothing will wash you away.'

Austin Randolph, Tung Ping Chau, July 1967

'I hope you'll be alright in here,' fussed Philip as he unlocked Austin's bedroom door. They had gone up two flights of stairs, beyond Mrs Irving's room, to a narrow corridor dimly lit by one naked light bulb.

'So, at last!' Stephen thought. At last he would make contact with his elusive subject; it would make the painful evening worthwhile; he would, intoxicated as he was, root out some sense of Austin Randolph from his discarded childhood room. When inside, he realized what he should have guessed: instead of being a museum to its former occupant, the room was a store cupboard with furniture, mostly chairs and tables, some of them broken, lying in disorder on the floor; a wardrobe stood in the middle of the room, its opened door exposing its emptiness; everything was covered in dust and decorated with cobwebs. Philip's hospitality was restricted to spreading a bright blue sleeping bag on the large brass bed with its mildewy mattress.

'I'm sorry about the state of things,' he said, trying to sound cheerfully phlegmatic but looking tired and defeated with dimly expressionless eyes. 'As you can see, no one has been in here for some time and most of the other bedrooms are completely empty.'

'It will be fine,' said Stephen, hoping that the evening could now end.

'Well, it's been a funny old day, hasn't it?' Philip continued, as if he was still trying to cover his tracks. 'I'm sorry that Mother ruined the evening; she has these mood swings, I'm afraid. Well, at least you saw us without any frills attached.'

He righted an upturned armchair and hovered by the door.

'Well, I'll wish you goodnight then,' he said with an exaggerated yawn. 'I'm exhausted – I expect you must be as well.'

76

As soon as he was gone, Stephen searched the room. The drawers and cupboards were all empty; the mirror over the mantelpiece was broken, with only a few pieces of silvered glass left within the frame; the curtains were hanging off their rails with only the corners connected to the window frames, and a large empty picture frame lay on the floor along with other pieces of broken bric-a-brac. Outside, a full moon sent its silvered light over the continuing festivities, intensifying the blue flashing lights from the stage, tiny in the distance. Between him and the musicians, the darkened middle ground moved in unison, indistinct shapes became an amorphous whole. Stephen's earlier companions in the sunlight were now separated from him, transformed by a time warp. He would love to escape to them, to become a part of that swaying shadow but he could not; he was trapped. He pushed at the old sash window and eventually managed to open it enough to put his head out and to take in the sounds with the clean night air. He stood there for a long time until the last of the partygoers out there in the night preceded him to their sleep.

Then, thinking of Irving's unwelcome gaze, he put out the light and undressed nervously in the dark, hanging his clothes over the bed but retaining his undershorts; nakedness had been beautiful in the afternoon sun but now it meant vulnerability. He crept into the sleeping bag and lay back watching the flashing lights from the festival illuminating the room. Drunkenly, he tried to steady the spinning room by imagining what it would have been like during Austin's time; the bedsprings squeaked, maybe as Austin would have heard them, floorboards creaked, as they would have done for centuries, and the lights sent shadows across the ceiling rearranging the remembered space. This was as close as he had come to Austin – lying on his bed sharing childhood's mysterious night-time world, fearing some unknown malignant force or unwanted presence and sharing, maybe, the same need to escape from the cloying atmosphere of this unhappy house. He could not feel the radiant presence of the horse-rider in the photograph; here was something less joyful, more fearful and distressing.

Listening for unusual sounds, he lay there unsteadily, near to vomiting, with a throbbing beat in his head as the long night drew on; the music had stopped hours ago and potential sleep was interrupted by every creak. Then the long awaited but dreaded moment occurred: the door opened quietly and, without knowing that he had been seen, the pyjama clad Philip stood in the doorway watching the bed. Stephen lay in feigned sleep until the intruder slipped discreetly from the room. When the house finally fell silent, he got up and vomited into the sink.

Twenty-Three

The bedsprings creaked in that sun-bright room. Austin and Philip, young teenage friends, brothers even and therefore also enemies, were playing boyhood games, with violence as the hidden agenda. Wrestling, for them, was the solution to every dispute, the latest taking place now on the creaking bed at the top of the house. For Austin, the fight was a fight, he needed to win, to see Philip squirm and give in as he always did. He could test his skills, his power and his strength and he would always win. For Philip, something changed; a lingering touch, a move too far, a look of realization. He was flung to the floor, thrown from the room, expelled from his childhood. Now he knew who he was and what he had lost. He would not go back.

'Go play with yourself! Little pervert boy!' he heard as he wept, as he left that room at the top of the house.

Twenty-Four

'You think you are close to me now, my young detective. Be sure of this though, you don't know anything, my friend. You know nothing yet, I promise you.'
Austin Randolph, Tung Ping Chau, July 1967

Stephen washed in the brown rusty water that had dribbled from the tap in his bedroom sink but its foul smell and taste did nothing to get rid of the after-effects of gin, dust, dope and depression that crowded his senses when he awoke the next morning. He doused himself, trying to wash away his nausea and the invasive smell of his own stale sweat that had soaked him and repeatedly awoken him through his restless sleep. Sensations from the previous day, intertwined and confused as they were, did nothing to make him want to go down to see his hosts.

He carried the household's tension in his muscles and its cries of agony still rang in that part of the inner ear reserved for silent screams. Frampton House had towered over his dreams like a Gothic castle and he could not shake it off now. Everything else had been ephemeral; his brief moment of hedonism at the music festival faded with the night, leaving him with a feeling of illogical guilt as if he had committed some act of forbidden immorality. Depressing as it was, he now felt safely but sadly returned to his own introspection.

He dressed hurriedly and began a more systematic search of the room, hoping to find out more about Austin Randolph in daylight, but there were no more secrets to reveal; Austin's old room had been ransacked and abandoned. It must have been many years since it had been visited, judging by the decades of dust that had been gathering there. Why, knowing this, had Mrs Irving insisted that he stay there? She had her reasons, he felt sure. For good or for ill, there was intent in her determination that he slept in this room, just as there was distress in Philip's reluctance in letting him do so. Maybe she had simply forgotten the effects of time and Philip was merely trying to be hospitable. Soiled and stressed by the experience, he made his way downstairs to what appeared to be an empty house.

80

No one was about, which came as a relief. He had no appetite for his job now and he was tempted to leave quietly and put the whole thing behind him. Through the windows he could see that the great crowds of last night were still sleeping – in tents, in their vans, in sleeping bags on the ground; a vanquished army, their conquerors, well actually the men in boiler suits, roamed through their ranks collecting sacks of litter. He remembered a poem from his childhood, 'The Destruction of Sennacherib', where the Assyrian army destroyed its sleeping enemy, descending on them 'like the wolf on the fold'. They were just as vulnerable to attack, these idealistic hordes from last night. They stood for change, Stephen thought, but in his hung-over ennui he suspected that they would not be left unchallenged.

Stephen, still nauseous and with the sweat rising on his brow, felt sorrow and rage as he walked into the grounds; somehow he felt that he was about to lose something important, something that he had only just begun to understand. He startled a cluster of scavenging rooks. They rose in a cacophony of anger, high into the three-dimensional blue of the sky before dispersing into the surrounding oak trees, their ancestral homes. As he walked around the park, some early risers began to emerge, and newly-lit fires perfumed the air. The aroma of burning wood and the smell of newly baking bread encouraged him to imagine the childhood he never had, camping in the woods with kids he had never known. It was an oddly hopeful thought. Tiny radios sent out their competing signals; soft breakfast voices and gentle guitar music mingled as this nomadic tribe came back to life.

He made his way down to the pond where two or three brave and naked spirits were swimming in its morning coolness. Removing his jacket and shirt and crouching down on his haunches, he submerged his head in the water. Down there, in the murky liquid, he was instantly awake, quietly excited again by his solidarity with the sleeping multitude. When he surfaced, one of the swimmers called out: 'Come on in, it's beautiful in here, man!' Yes, he would; he would grasp this moment. Stripping to his undershorts – he was not ready to go any further – he climbed in, electrified by the cold green water; he swam in circles and celebrated his release while the others splashed around him in companionable silence.

Refreshed, even baptised by the water, he dried himself in the sun as he dozed off into a deeper sleep than anything he had achieved during his long turbulent night. When he awoke, the pool was full of naked bathers: male, female, single adults and parents with small children, all using the water hole like it may have been used, maybe thousands of years earlier. Stephen dressed reluctantly; his clothes seemed inappropriately urban suddenly, any clothes seemed redundant, but he decided that he would go back to his task and fulfil his obligations, so made his way tremulously to the house.

He met Emilia in the hall; she had been waiting for him and immediately confided that she wanted to leave early, as soon as she could after breakfast.

'Come back to London with me. We can talk more freely in the car,' she whispered. 'I need to get away from here, I'm afraid. I will scream if I have to spend any more time here.'

'Well, it's up to you old things,' Philip said with forced indifference when he found out that they were going. 'I'm told the main rock and roll bands are on today but you've probably seen them all before. You seem like a young man with his finger on the pulse.'

Emilia was already in the car by the time Stephen had said goodbye to a frail Margaret Irving, who was propped up in bed struggling with a handful of pills and a tumbler of water. She was having what Philip described as 'one of her bad days' and she barely recognised Stephen when he approached the bed. She threw him a disconcertingly alien, even hate-filled, grimace before looking away to something deeply unpleasant that she imagined in a dark corner of the room.

'Goodbye,' she said, in a distant haughty voice. Philip lingered in the shadows with the look of someone trying not to say something significant, as conversation about Austin was suddenly strictly off limits or so it seemed to Stephen. Irving walked him to the car, but it was a fumblingly awkward experience with the older man only making feeble jokes about the festival and vague promises about staying in touch. Clearly it was time to go.

Twenty-Five

The chauffeur, behind a glass screen, drove them smoothly away from Frampton, out of the grounds, through acres of tents and a few vaguely interested faces amongst the crowds of music fans. Soon, they were in the countryside silently journeying down lanes where the low-lying sun flickered through the trees with exhilarating effect. Stephen gazed through the window feeling sad and disappointed, like a child being dragged home from a party; it was too early for courtly behaviour, so he sat in unembarrassed silence next to the faultlessly dressed lady whose sophistication seemed less awe-inspiring when the smell of toothpaste mingled with her perfume.

Her gloved hand covered a slight yawn and mechanically, but much less elegantly, he followed her example, stretching out his legs on the thick white-carpeted floor, trying to forget about his pond-dampened underwear and hoping that they wouldn't mark the seat. The luxurious cream leather upholstery, the gently tinted windows and the nearly soundless purr of the engine cocooned them as they speeded onwards, watching the splendour of the newly risen sun. A soft touch from her grey-gloved hand alerted him to a fine cock pheasant stretching its extravagantly coloured wings on the edge of a barley field. He acknowledged it with a smile.

'Have you got the letter with you?' she asked quietly. 'The letter from Austin. Would you mind if I read it?'

He took it from his case and handed it to her. She read it briskly then gave it back.

'Thank you,' she said, turning her face away to gaze back out of the window. She had grown impenetrable again.

'I hope you weren't too uncomfortable last night,' she said after some time.

'No, it was fine but it was a very strange room.'

'It was the old lady's idea. She wanted to upset Philip.'

'Why?'

'He destroyed everything in that room when Austin left. She wanted to remind him and to embarrass him in front of you; she always resented his displays of affection – especially if they were not directed towards her. Does that surprise you?'

'Not after the conversation at dinner.'

'I'm sorry you had to experience all that but I suppose it is part of your job; you wanted the whole story – the full exposé. Well, we'll have to see about that.'

For a moment, her seriousness was lightened by a gently mocking smile. There was another long silence; she was deciding whether to trust him or not; he said nothing; he was nursing the gently sedative remains of his hangover and mentally replaying his experience at the festival. Was it the alcohol and marijuana mix playing with his mind or had something in him changed forever? He was not sure; forever was a long time he decided.

'I suppose you realise that Austin just could not stand the old lady. She, of course, always loved him. It was more than motherly love – there was nothing she wouldn't do for him; she worshipped him – she probably gave him too much love. Can you have too much love? I think you can actually. That's sad, don't you think?'

'I liked her,' Stephen answered indirectly – he had not known too much love.

'She's my aunt. You knew that I presume.'

'No, I hadn't realised.'

'It's sad that we're no longer friends. Love divided us, I suppose. Anyway, she's my aunt, my Aunt Margaret; I thought you knew that. Philip should have told you. Philip and I are cousins; our mothers hoped we might be kissing cousins as we were raised in the days when children were considered eligible for marriage as soon as they were born. My mother was Aunt Margaret's sister and both of them always wanted Philip and I to marry. We were thrown together right from the beginning. But babies change. Nothing is so simple – we grow up and develop our own, quite different, um, desires.'

The morning sun gave the countryside an extra beauty, lighting it from below and adding a golden glow to summer's greenery. It nurtured the emotion in the car. Dew covered leaves swollen with the expectant richness of early summer were further impregnated by the low-lying mist with its shades of blue and grey. Tears come easily on such days and Emilia's eyes glistened as she turned away. Stephen was drawn into her sadness; the world, as they glided through it, seemed to sigh, but he had no vocabulary to express his sympathy; he knew that he was not qualified to comfort her.

'You know what Keats said about joy?' she asked.

'Yes, "in the very temple of Delight..."'

'".... Veil'd Melancholy has her sovran shrine". Keats understood what I'm feeling: going back to Frampton and seeing it like that was terrible; yet the joy was still there too; even now after a long time of sadness. It is difficult for me, Stephen; you will have to understand that. It takes a bit of getting used to, that's all.' She paused. 'What do those people want?' she asked, seeing a young man and woman standing at the side of the road with their rucksacks on the ground.

'They want a lift,' said Stephen.

'Well, they won't find many cars on this road. We'll have to give them their lift or they will be standing there all day.'

The car came to a gracious halt and the surprised and nervous couple ran up to them. They had not expected the grand car to even notice them.

'Where are you going?' Emilia asked, opening the electric window.

'We're heading for London,' the boy answered in an American accent.

'Well, jump in! We're going there too. The driver will put your bags in the boot.'

Incredulously, the young Americans climbed into the car and sat on the pull-down seats in front of Emilia and Stephen. Their ex-army combats and heavy hiking boots were dusty from the road but Emilia seemed unconcerned about her white carpet or the pale upholstery. The man, who had no shirt on under his jacket, instinctively covered his stomach when Emilia spoke to him.

'You're American I see,' she said brightly.

'Yes. We're touring Europe,' said the girl who, except for a crudely dyed T-shirt, was dressed identically to her partner.

'You've got a lot to see then.'

'Yeah,' grinned the boy. 'We started in France and so far we've been to Germany, Switzerland, Austria and Italy.'

'We're going on to Scandinavia when we've done England,' added the girl.

'What do you think of England?' Emilia asked.

'Great!' said the girl. 'It's so green.'

The boy gave Stephen a comradely nod.

'Are you hitching too?' he asked.

'No,' Stephen answered awkwardly.

'Uh huh,' the boy grunted, expecting more.

'Why do you have Love written across your blouse?' Emilia asked the girl, now revived and instinctively fluent in her conversation making.

'It's cute isn't it? Well, you know. Love and Peace,' she said, looking at Stephen.

Stephen smiled, embarrassed for her, but he looked to Emilia for a reply.

'So are you hippies?' she asked.

'Everyone can be,' said the boy earnestly. 'We're on holiday from college but we like to feel that we're part of the movement, yes. We're really pleased to see that it's beginning to happen over here as well.'

'Isn't that just the drugs?' Emilia countered, clearly enjoying herself.

'Well, that helps!' laughed the young man. 'But there's a lot more to it than that. We're all changing; the world is changing. You can feel it everywhere ma'am, I suspect you could too if you thought about it.'

'Well I certainly hope so. We need things to change. We're relying on young people like you to make things better. You're the future, you know. We're relying on you now that we know that we failed our time round.'

The thought hung in the air, silencing them all with their own interpretations of her remark.

'So what are you studying at college?'

'Marine Biology, ma'am,' he answered awkwardly.

'And I'm doing Design Technology,' said his companion 'I hope one day to work in the theatre.'

'Well I wish you both success and a lot of peace and love,' Emilia said with no hint of irony.

As they sped on to London, Emilia asked about the hippie movement in the United States; she wanted to know about those young people that she had read about who had vowed to give up possessions and gone to live in the communes in San Francisco.

'It's all possible,' said the boy. 'All over the States people are giving up material things. We want more than that of course, but it's not utopia, ma'am, it's reality. Everywhere people are seeing how bad the old ways are; how we've been imprisoned by money, possessions, unimportant things.'

'Bless them!' Emilia said when they had been dropped off to continue their grand tour. 'They made me feel quite decadent. But I'm sorry, Stephen, I just couldn't help quizzing them; they are so innocent, so full of hope. And now we're in London and we haven't really had our chat, have we?'

'No, not really,' said Stephen, knowing that she had done it deliberately. There was an art to getting these interviews, he thought, maybe one that he would never master.

'Well, you'll have to come back to my house, have dinner and stay the night. We can talk as much as we like then.' She squeezed his arm and laughed. 'I have promised to help,' she said. 'I know you think I'm avoiding the issue but I want you to know you can trust me. I wasn't sure that I could talk to you about these things at first, but now, somehow, I feel that I can trust you too. In fact, my new young friend, I want to tell you everything.'

Twenty-Six

Two German women, in floral dresses, sit on sun-blanched colonial teak chairs, drinking tea on an English lawn, watching tennis. Butler and maid fuss with delicate china, slices of lemon and subtle crustless sandwiches moist with locally gathered watercress. Two German sisters with perfect English husbands – Margaret Irving and Julietta Jeffries, Margrethe and Juliette, beloved daughters of General and Frau Gottlieb von Öchen, residents of Berlin. Now they are perfect English ladies: Mrs Irving, mistress of Frampton, and Mrs Jeffries, London widow; nationality conveniently swept aside on those summer days of tennis and tea between two World Wars.

Austin Randolph Irving, a firm muscled youth now and an English gentleman, born and bred, lowers his guard, weakens his power in a game of social tennis. His opponent, his new cousin of sorts, newly home from Berlin, girl turned woman, the German general's English rose of a granddaughter, Emilia Jeffries, young, fair and athletic, her blossoming body moistening to meet Austin's challenge; a game of seduction that both sides will win.

Emilia's victory is celebrated; the players exchange unspoken vows, clinking their crystal glass tumblers filled from the plain porcelain jug of iced barley water. Their audience observes, knowing what is happening but hoping for some other outcome: Mrs Jeffries, embarrassed, Mrs Irving, dispirited and, at their feet, Philip, sitting sullenly cross-legged on the grass, a white-flannelled, ginger-haired man, face reddened by more than the sun.

The summer of 1933, long and idle for those two German ladies within Frampton's protective walls; Margaret Irving issuing orders to perfectly drilled servants – autocratic quality control; Julietta Jeffries, recovering widow, the withered image of her radiant daughter. She passively observes; easel set up under a tree, week after week she paints, pure white and deep green, Frampton House, then a thousand shades of green, the immutable shelter, purring limestone in its leafy glory.

Elsewhere, on starched sheets, in butterfly-frequented meadows, golden, blue and scarlet with flowers, on barn loft straw or silently stolen at the top of the stairs, anywhere and everywhere, Emilia and

Austin submit to their fate, continually consummating but never satiating their desire.

Twenty-Seven

'Find the woman, my friend; if you understand her, you might find me. Tread carefully and you will get there. I see you on my trail, sniffing me out. Cherchez la femme.'

Austin Randolph, Tung Ping Chau, July 1967

The journey ended in Richmond, Surrey – a leafy and respectable south-western suburb of London, sitting comfortably in its own affluence on the banks of the River Thames. The Rolls Royce stopped outside a solid Victorian semi-detached house that looked over a neatly clipped privet hedge onto common land – once used for grazing cattle and sheep, but now the natural habitat for parents with young children or unadventurous dog walkers and under-sized dogs and, Stephen suspected, cricket.

'Thank you, ma'am,' said the chauffeur when he had deposited Emilia's cases on the pavement. 'If you need us again just give us a ring.'

'Yes, thank you. It was fun.' She was smiling at Stephen as she gave the man a tip.

'I thought it was your car,' said Stephen, immediately the car had gone.

Emilia was already letting them in at the front door of what was a substantial Victorian villa and laughed. 'Good gracious, no! I couldn't afford anything so grand. Now come in and we'll have a cup of tea.'

Instead of the elegance and luxury that he had expected, the house was cluttered and attractively, to his eyes, down-at-heel. The old-fashioned cosy furniture had home-made chintzy covers; there were porcelain ornaments, shepherds and shepherdesses, collectable pieces, Stephen realized, in rows on every available flat surface; and pictures, oils and prints, early twentieth century, mostly naturalistic landscapes, were crowded over all the wall spaces in the cluttered style of a Victorian art gallery. It had a friendly, careless atmosphere – a place for relaxation – yet again, it was not what he had expected. At every turn he had been wrong; his powers of analysis had misled him, and just maybe, he thought dispiritedly, this whole project was beyond his capabilities.

'Go into the sitting room while I put on the kettle,' Emilia called cheerily from the kitchen.

He removed a pile of newspapers from one of the two different-coloured, floral sofas that dominated the room – homemade loose covers on Edwardian originals, he thought, cheekily looking underneath. Adding the papers to an even larger pile on the oak coffee table that was already crammed with books, magazines and dehydrated potted plants, he sat back and, without his customary politeness, lit a cigarette. The room welcomed him, promised him instant comfort, telling him to make himself at home. He was looking for an ashtray when Emilia returned with a large tray of tea things and cakes.

'It's the one thing I miss on the Continent,' she said as she officiated at her own tea ceremony. 'I don't understand why no one can make tea like we do. I can't live without it.'

Stephen took his cup and saucer with a smile. This was the way of his own childhood – long dull summer days punctuated with cups of tea and superficial pleasantries, genteel England frightened of its own shadow, the half-understood adult world of the only child.

'I suppose you're right to laugh,' she said. 'Maybe I'm a tea addict. It's a drug just like the LSD or the marijuana that those lovely Americans in the car smoked. What are you smiling about now?'

'Oh, I was just thinking what a surprising person you are,' he said, emboldened by the comforting qualities of Dundee cake. 'First the car and then this house. That's all. It's not what I expected.'

'I'm not as posh as you thought. Is that what you mean?'

'Well, yes,' he laughed.

'As Philip says, times are hard. I'm luckier than most, though. This was my mother's house and now it's mine. The car was another thing altogether; when you're an ageing spinster, like me, you have to get your kicks whichever way you can. I need to keep the Irvings at bay too; they would eat me up if I showed any signs of weakness. Is that so undignified? Playing games?'

'No, not at all.'

91

'Well, my pupils think I'm decidedly eccentric. I know that they laugh about me behind my back.'

'What do you teach?' He was trying to be professional now.

'Oh, German, of course. You know that I'm really German, even though I mostly grew up in England. So I teach rather solid middle class English girls my native tongue. I help them with their A levels at a nice undemanding private school here in Richmond.'

'But you don't sound at all German.'

'It's still not a very good idea to sound too German in this country.'

A rumbling noise interrupted the conversation; the house shook with the vibrations but Emilia was unconcerned.

'It's the train,' she said. 'It practically runs through the garden on its way to interesting places like Waterloo. Unfortunately it doesn't stop. Austin said that we should build a platform in the garden but that was typical of him; full of mad ideas, so full of life.'

She laughed weakly but the mention of his name darkened her mood.

'So he came here?'

'Oh yes. We used to sit here, on this sofa… In those happy days.' She was speaking quietly, her eyes focusing somewhere beyond the room. For Stephen, the sofa was instantly transformed; its cosy chintziness was electrified, eroticised, and he withdrew his fingers from its comfortable softness.

'Do you mind talking about him… Austin?' he asked clumsily, covering his thoughts.

'It's marvellous talking about him!' She said brightly, with vehement passion, returning from her private place. 'I've had to pretend that he never existed for so long. I loved him, you see. I still do. When you have to keep a great love secret it grows even greater inside you. There is nothing there to inhibit it. Have you ever felt like that?'

Stephen was caught without an answer – the question was too near to his thoughts, his own distractions.

'Well, one day you will know. Enjoy yourself before it happens to you too. Have you got a girl?'

'Yes,' he lied, fumbling in his jacket for another cigarette. It was less than a week since he'd seen Dys and he had hardly thought of her. Yet, having this conversation, sitting on this sofa, Austin's sofa, Dys came back to him – unsettling and annoying as she was. He missed her.

'I'm not sticking to the point, am I? You want to talk about Austin and all I do is talk about everything else. Well, we have the whole evening with nothing to distract us – except making dinner.'

'Do you like cooking?'

'I loathe it!'

'I could always get us fish and chips,' he said, surprising himself with his own spontaneity. 'You do have fish and chip shops in Richmond? It's not too posh I hope.'

'What a good idea! Yes of course we do. I'll come with you and we can eat them in the street with lots of salt and vinegar. Then, I promise, I will tell you what you want to know.'

Unwittingly, she had begun to do that already.

Twenty-Eight

Discovered, exposed, naked on the bed; pulled apart at the height of their joy. Emilia dragged off by her hair, thrown to the floor, spat at in rage. Margaret Irving, dried up, screaming, cursing, aiming scornful hatred at her son's betrayal – his father's boy after all. She knew she was wrong, she knew she was out of control, but still she shouted. In her rage she still could not keep her eyes off him. He was and would always be the focus of her passion: so beautiful, so naked and proud. Now defiant, immodest, uncovered before her. He knew her, knew what she craved.

'This is what you wanted but you'll never have it, mother-whore!'

'How dare you speak to me like that! Standing there, not even covering yourself up – shameless in front of the one person who has always loved you. Loved you more than I could even bear. So typical of you to betray me just like the bastard son that you always were! Get out of my sight, you upset me too much. I can't live with this, go on and take her with you.'

Her sentence could not find its natural ending. The more she spoke, the more destructive she became and the more damage she did, repeating herself, shrieking in her pain and out of control in her anger.

It was over. No pleading would help. No words brought him back, no matter how much she begged him, screaming her guilt in her agony as they hurriedly dressed, Emilia sobbing, Austin defiant.

'We'll go,' he said calmly, almost serenely. 'I don't want anything from you.'

She had knelt on the drive long after they had gone, blinded with tears, paralysed, gasping for breath. It was over. Nothing would help.

In the room at the top of the house, Philip sat alone in the rubble. Exhausted, shaking in grief, he had done all that he could; he had broken the furniture, shattered the mirror, destroyed everything that he could destroy. It did not help. It was over.

Twenty-Nine

'She was fine. Emilia, volcanic under her sang-froid. We stripped back the layers, exposed the fruit, to celebrate the moment, our moment, our glory. Don't underestimate it, my innocent young friend. When you taste it then you will know.'

Austin Randolph, Tung Ping Chau, July 1967

Emilia talked into the middle of the night with Stephen sitting just far enough away for her not to be able to see his notes. Once she started to unburden her grief, he put down his pen. He would have no trouble in remembering what she said.

When he finally got to bed, a large but elderly king-sized affair which could well have been the scene of Austin and Emilia's passion, his sleep was disturbed with images, ungallant no doubt, of Austin, of Emilia, or was it Dys, he was not sure; they kept interchanging. He awoke exhausted, a sinner in need of penance or a novice with his first vision through the veil.

Early morning exercises usually worked for him. Brisk and business-like as always, he did his military style press-ups, sit-ups and jumping jacks before shifting to various very non-military yoga inspired stretches, and then his first cigarette – the best one of the day.

Today his automated routine felt different. He was transplanted, out of place, awkwardly masculine in just his shorts, finally dried, in this distinctly feminine bedroom with its thick pile carpet of rose pink and its delicate Maplewood furniture; a perfect example of middle-class decor from almost forty years ago, he thought, elegant but emasculating and definitely not the place to build up a sweat.

Putting on his glasses, he noticed the oil painting over the mantelpiece; Emilia's mother's view of Frampton House – the one that she painted during that fateful summer stay. It was an amateur landscape, painted in clumsily bright oils and showing none of the passionate emotions that Emilia had described in her stories about that summer. It was just an idyllic English pastoral, all the more poignant for its simplicity – an unwittingly innocent memento of Emilia's sexual awakening. Hung discretely in the spare room,

95

Stephen guessed that it had been placed there, out of sight, as an occasional reminder of lost happiness only to be seen when Emilia needed it.

Last night Emilia had created her own vivid portrait of that year and the man that she loved. It was the first time he had felt any sympathy for Austin Randolph, the object of so much passion. Until now he had been more of an employer, a benefactor rather than an imagined human being, but now Stephen was being forced into making comparisons with his own life. Biographer and subject – they should become intimates or enemies. Randolph was everything that Stephen was not: man of action, object of desire, natural force and creature of impulse; he was like a cinema legend and similarly unreal – the Errol Flynn and Humphrey Bogart to Stephen's box office clerk.

Maybe there was no comfort in the comparison, but its irony was no longer lost on him. As he shaved the lather from his face with his studiously old-fashioned cutthroat razor, he contorted his face comically. He was emerging from his cocoon, beginning to enjoy a sense of his own physicality, losing his inhibitions, even beginning to feel happy. He might never be Errol Flynn but he could try Bogart; pushing out his chest, he let his shoulders sink and pointed the blade at his reflected image, his face an image of mock gangster cool.

'OK, kid.' He could do Chicago too. 'You'd better turn your act around.'

'Stephen, would you like breakfast?' came a bright voice from outside the door.

'It's another beautiful day,' said Emilia, once again hiding behind platitudes after the previous night's intensity. An image of domesticity, she was wearing a simple pale yellow cotton dress in her pale yellow kitchen; making toast under the grill while percolating coffee and setting the small breakfast table with striped blue and yellow breakfast crockery. The sight of Stephen unnerved her, well something did, and she turned away from him in tears. 'Forgive me, Stephen. Just a few girlish wobbles, I'm afraid!'

Controlling herself, she settled everything chaotically onto her perfectly arranged table, toast spilling onto the cloth, and the coffee pot and cups clustered awkwardly out of reach. She joined him at the table and immediately started rearranging things.

'They say it's good for us to cry. So I must be getting some benefit from your visit. I haven't cried for years! I've enjoyed it actually – funny though that sounds. When Austin and I split up in London all those years ago, it was not just us who had changed. The whole world was changing. It was never the same again.'

'When I was talking to the others, I kept thinking that there were things they didn't want me to know.'

'They would like to bury me and shut me up for ever but they know that they can't.'

'What did Austin do after you stopped seeing him?'

'I lost contact completely – until you brought him back into my life the other day. I don't know what happened, neither do the others as far as I know, but I've often wondered if they know more than they say. We knew that he had dropped the Irving from his name, that he became just Austin Randolph, but I'm afraid that's all I know. You will be able to tell me the whole story one day, I hope.'

'Would you want to see him again then?'

'I don't know.' She paused, controlling her feelings. 'Ask me again some other time. I guess that part of me would like to.'

Yet again she had to look away to gather her emotions. Stephen sat and waited patiently for her to return.

'I can be dreadfully soppy, you know,' she said, brushing away some tears and laughing. 'Sometimes I play an old record, one that we used to play, and it makes me cry. It always makes me think of Austin. I'll play it for you now – what the heck, I'm crying anyway.'

They went into the sitting room and found the record; the melody had the lyrical passion of a typical crooning song from the thirties – a woman's voice supported by a mellow band of muted trumpets, saxophones and a lilting rhythm section that told the audience to dance away their sorrows. It matched the moment; its sentimental lyrics were turned into momentary poetry allowing Emilia to share her emotion.

'We are romantic fools, and the gods of love really must look down at us and laugh. I love that! Love does seem foolish when you look at it objectively, doesn't it? I expect you think I'm a silly old fool, though – all that emotion, the uncontrollable tears. It's like an illness, Love... It leaves a scar too; a long jagged line behind our eyes that is always there wherever you look. No, I don't think I could meet him now, even if he wanted to meet me. I heard a story about some water creature once – a larva or something. I was never good at biology. It grows at the bottom of rivers, always preparing itself for adulthood when it will rise to the surface. All that energy is devoted to its journey to the top, but you know how long its adult life is?' There was a break in her voice, but she answered her own question. 'Just one day. I wanted it to be like that. Everything was so perfect, I wanted some heron or kingfisher or something to swoop down and kill us while we enjoyed that brief moment of perfection. It didn't of course. I'm still here all these years later. A very mature damselfly no doubt!'

Skilfully and imperceptibly, she drew the conversation away from Austin and back to the business of breakfast and the day in hand. Without feeling in any way unwelcome, Stephen found himself walking away from the house. They had exchanged addresses and promises but the interview was over; Emilia had resumed her life as an inscrutable English lady of a certain age.

Thirty

Stephen was reclusive by nature and he had never spent so much time with other people, being polite, attentive and trying to be sensitive to their feelings. He could feel the muscles in his face relax as he fastened the latch on the gate. Even though he liked Emilia Jeffries, she had made him feel clumsy and ox-like in her genteel presence. She made him want to do all those things forbidden in polite society: burping, groin scratching, ear picking and worse, but it was only an impulse, he knew he could never be that vulgar. Now he could do as he pleased; he had a case full of notes suggesting that his planned book was on its way and, something he had never quite appreciated, he had Austin's money in his wallet.

This summer had been a new beginning, with Dys as the catalyst. She was annoying, challenging and beautiful: the sort of female that he would never have thought that he could interest but she had begun this awakening in him. The Frampton Festival and all the talk of love that Austin Randolph had inspired brought Dys back into his thoughts. If he wanted to start a new life, and he could see her now, urging him on to do just that, then this was the perfect moment and the perfect place. On his own in a town where no one knew him, and away from her mocking gaze, he was free to do whatever he wanted if only he was brave enough to want things that he had never even considered before. He was free too, he thought wryly, to do just what she wanted him to do.

He had to smile and admit that it was typical of his unambitious nature that he would choose this pleasant suburban street on a sunny morning as the unusual starting point for a revolution. Among the orderly flowerbeds and neat little squares of lawn, home to platoons of chattering sparrows, he decided to take the plunge. The milkman, whistling show tunes, aproned and intense with his crates of clinking bottles, nodded politely on his way back to his milk float, oblivious to Stephen's internal metamorphosis. It was hot and his clothes were dirty; he wanted to change, not just his clothes, he needed to change himself. The twentieth century was already over halfway spent; he would join it, he decided, before it was too late.

He walked along the riverbank inspired, moved. The Thames at Richmond was at its most benign, punctuated with urbanely floating swans and long-limbed rowers racing towards Hampton Court. Weeping willows combed its surface; the water shone in the sunlight, its underlying sludge turned to silver. It was a bittersweet experience, walking alone in a truly romantic setting. He watched a young couple, lovers in a landscape, then he saw more of them: there were young lovers all around him or so it seemed.

On a day like today, he thought, Emilia and Austin must have lingered here too. Shaken by their personal dramas, he knew they were at least allowed those moments of intimacy together, even if their love had to be condensed into the shortest of moments. Some of that love hung in the air as Stephen watched other couples strolling in front of him. Although the young had always walked thus, arm in arm, on riverbanks, on summer days, he thought these, mankind's latest lovers, must be different. Body proud, sensually liberated, both male and female, everyone was dressed for display; their clothes colourful, individual and body revealing, yet nevertheless a uniform, an acclamation, an acknowledgement of a new age. An age, maybe, when love, sex and sensory pleasures were not to be hidden away any more.

Richmond's new generation, admittedly, were that much better dressed and decidedly better groomed than their Brighton contemporaries. They were growing their hair long, both male and female, but it was still scissor-trimmed and shampoo-shining. To join, it seemed, one had to buy the clothes, buy into the look, superficial as it was. Stephen, more than anyone, knew that he needed to make an effort to join the new culture. He must try to look the part and, fond of his new blazer as he was, he had to be more radical about his appearance.

Clothes boutiques for men as well as women, selling the ultimate in new disposable chic, had been opening in every town in Britain and, even though they were just shops like any other, run to make a profit, they were also part of this surge of social change. Boutiques, under-estimated by the establishment, championed the new democratic spirit where anyone, but mostly the young and fashionable, could buy cheap cutting-edge clothes, wear them today then discard them, clearing their wardrobes for tomorrow's ideas.

It would be the end of Savile Row suits, tweed jackets, flannel trousers and all the traditional symbols of the successful man, where clothes were a way of asserting social superiority. Not any more. Now fashionable clothes would be made from disposable materials, designed by bright young psychedelic art graduates whose ideal was the boldly-patterned paper shirt worn once and thrown away. It was also a democratic reawakening of the peacock spirit in the young Western male, who could reinvent himself every day and make himself every bit as ornamental as his female mate. This was a concept that Stephen had found threatening and alien at first because he always regarded himself as more dodo than peacock. Before fading into extinction, however, watching as he walked, intoxicated by what he saw, he recognised that this was not just about trousers and shirts, bangles and beads, or whether or not to wear a tie. Clothes and hair length had become not only newly eroticised but also politicised like never before. Things were moving so fast that Stephen Dearsley would have to move too.

He had always distrusted fashion-conscious people and, even if he had wanted to, up until now he would never have dared to enter their territory. He had made a point of preferring the solid comforts of department stores or gentlemen's outfitters; by choosing the past over the present, he had intentionally made a public statement: he was interested in fashion if it was unfashionable. Unwittingly, he had had a touch of the peacock all along. Here, walking down Richmond High Street, trendy boutiques to the right of him and even trendier boutiques to the left, it was time to make the change; if he was to make a fool of himself, he might as well do it here.

He came across a small shop, its original Victorian frontage painted pink and mauve. It was relaying sitar music into the street through loudspeakers, musty smelling kaftans hung in rows around the door, and strings of little bells jangled in the breeze. The window display starred two exotic male dummies dressed in rainbow-coloured shirts with tight red-and-yellow jesters' trousers, long curly orange wigs and tiny round sunglasses. Inside, the kaleidoscopic rows of shirts, jackets and trousers brought their own light into the tiny but dimly lit emporium. The strong smell of incense made him sneeze as soon as he entered.

'Hi!' said a pale girl in a floor-length purple dress who was sitting on a stool flicking through a woman's magazine, licking her fingertips for speed. 'Can I help you?'

'Uh, yes. I want to buy some shirts.'

'Anything in mind?'

'I'm a size fifteen collar.'

Barely registering his statistics, and without getting up, she showed him the nearest thing with the limp wave of an arm. Some collarless cheesecloth shirts that looked like shepherd's smocks hung in rows next to some satin ones, scarlet and blue with voluptuous sleeves. They were all much too extrovert for his first dip into the world of fashion.

'What about these?' he said, pointing out a row of garments that at least had recognisable collars and cuffs.

'They're great. Do you want to try one on?'

He took a shirt, made from a shimmering pink and orange fabric, and looked for the changing-room. All he could see were clothes racks.

'We haven't got anywhere really private, I'm afraid,' she laughed. 'But don't worry about me. I've seen all sorts.'

This information was no encouragement to him but, fumbling out of his jacket and shirt, he changed into the flimsy new one. As he was buttoning it up, three girls came in shouting loud greetings to the assistant but they were silenced by Stephen's reluctant and impromptu fashion show.

'Oh, that's really great!' one of them said. Stephen smiled through his embarrassment. Rather than take it off, he bought it and kept it on, but he wasn't allowed to hurry away until he was persuaded to buy a cheesecloth shirt and one in purple satin.

'That will look really good with your blazer,' said the assistant when the others had gone giggling out of the shop. 'But you can't really get away with those trousers. Look we've got these great flared loons. Why don't you try them on? I won't look!'

Surviving the ordeal, he looked at himself in the mirror: they were skin tight from the waist to the knee and then flared out to cover most of his shoes. He had not only ridden his embarrassment but he felt good, a newly-hatched peacock in full display plumage.

'They really suit you. They're very sexy,' the girl said, looking at his crotch. Her surprised approval marked his coming of age.

102

'I'll buy three pairs,' he said. 'The blue, the black and the red.'

It was only when he got outside and was looking at his reflection in the shop windows that he realised that his tight new shirt was totally transparent. He dared himself to carry on, to flaunt himself just for once, so he unbuttoned his jacket and carried on down the high street feeling broader and taller and, somehow, more physically substantial all over. Simultaneously, his walk took on just the slightest hint of a swagger.

'OK, let's go!' he whispered out loud, grinning at his reflected image and tousling his hair. Bogart had come back to lift his spirits.

Thirty-One

London's Victoria Embankment Gardens: a grassy thoroughfare on the banks of the Thames; a pleasant walk for a man in need, from Charing Cross to the Savoy and back again; a place to rest, to feed the pigeons, to sit on a bench, beg for some coppers; and all he is asking for is the price of a cup of tea – but it is not so good at night.

Begging for coppers is not his style, the fresh-faced tramp with a suit in his case. He sits on a bench with scar-faced Stan – the gentleman and the gentleman's gentleman; master and servant, Don Giovanni and his Leporello. They talk of getting away.

Stanley Finch, scar-faced Stan, fell on hard times in those Depression years. A scar is not good for a gentleman's gentleman, now dirty and ragged in 1934. They are not having much luck with that cup of tea.

A wash and brush up in the Gentlemen's convenience, conveniently placed for Charing Cross and perfect for the Savoy Hotel. No longer a tramp, the fresh-faced man in the light brown suit earns banknotes for favours, better than coppers, making use of his talents. It makes sense if you're a fresh-faced man.

A drunken starlet staggers home from the Savoy in her white fox fur and precipitous shoes. 'Is this the way to Charing Cross?' She's a platinum blonde – well she has to be these days. A musical artiste with a taste for the boys and a weakness for gin, but a good enough singing voice.

Ivy Cooper finds her man: she pays handsomely for the handsome, especially if he is not too discerning. She takes a fancy to fresh-faced Mr Randolph, the nice, physically gifted young gentleman down on his luck.

Thirty-Two

Stage one of his transformation was complete. The new Stephen, or so he liked to think, boutique-clad and feeling puckish, sat at the back of the upper deck of a bus travelling through central London in the middle of a dusty metropolitan afternoon. It was easy – there was that song again: its message was insistent. His new clothes brought enjoyable new material sensations, different textures against his skin, the unfamiliar smell of new fabric, a new definition to his body shape, perceived if not actual – they combined to make him feel different. He exhaled smoke from his latest cigarette into the stale tobacco fumes hanging in the air and avoided looking at the only other passenger, an old man sitting at the front who was coughing convulsively. Below him, in the street, no one looked up. It was as if no one knew that a revolutionary change had just happened and that they were missing the opportunity of seeing the new Stephen in his full splendour. The bus conductor came and asked for his fare; he had already paid and he showed his ticket to prove it.

'Sorry, mate. I didn't remember you.'

He had made no impression, even on an empty bus. He was moving through the centre of a great city familiar to more significant people than him. He was no Dr Samuel Johnson, Horatio Lord Nelson or even Jack the Ripper, and he was certainly no Austin Randolph. Stephen Dearsley was merely the forgotten holder of a bus ticket. Maybe nothing would change; he had got carried away, over-influenced by Emilia Jeffries' story that had made him feel that even he could make his mark somehow. Just as he had been as a child when reading a novel by Dickens or Tolstoy, he could become totally absorbed in other people's lives, other worlds, losing himself to his own life.

That was where his ambition to be a biographer had been born. After reading the final page, shutting the book for the last time, he was always shocked, bereaved even, disappointed to be just himself again, unchanging, already defined in an existence that he found bleakly unsatisfying. Now he was determined to do something about this, to lay claim to his own life. It was not about Emilia or the bus conductor, or the pedestrians below. It was Dys who had made the difference; she had noticed him, opened his eyes. She would see the change and help him to grow beyond it – he was doing it for her as much as for himself.

He was on his way to visit Stanley Finch. Now that he knew more about Austin Randolph, even though no one was telling him the whole truth, he wanted to try Finch once more, to persevere this time and prove that he could do this job. In the canteen, the Spanish woman was cleaning the tables; she did not notice him at first.

'Excuse me, is Stanley Finch in today?'

'He's gone,' she answered, wearily looking up from her work.

'Do you know where he went?'

'No. He just stopped coming in. Sometimes people are like that. If you knew him you would know he wasn't a happy man.' She stopped wiping the table and smiled sympathetically.

'I came to see him a few weeks ago. You pointed him out to me.'

'Oh, I don't remember. Sorry, love.'

She went back to her work with that same vaguely sad smile on her face. He left defeated.

As a private detective he was useless. He went into a pub for a beer and shepherd's pie, sitting in the darkest corner of the red-curtained, red-upholstered bar, with red plastic barrels decorating the beer pumps. A Watneys pub: bright, modern red right down to the beer mats and ashtrays. Branding more important than charm, Stephen thought. Trying to put the story together, all he could see were the holes – nothing, so far, justified the writing of the book, even though he knew that there was more to tell. The witnesses: Irving, Finch, even Emilia had reacted nervously, suspiciously; he was sure that they had all lied to him or not told him the whole truth.

A dozen young men came in, instantly filling the bar. They wore dark suits and incongruously bright ties in psychedelic pastels. They had that wild, freed from work look and were obviously on a pub-crawl celebrating a birthday with beer and whisky, daring each other on. They activated the jukebox and filled the pub with music and laughter, cracking jokes, vying with each other in their playground crudity and measuring up against each other's masculinity. Stephen realized that he was staring, unintentionally sending icy vibrations into the party. He looked away when one of them, momentarily unsettled, met his eyes in mid-laughter. Gulping down his drink he left but, when he got outside, he heard that song starting on the jukebox: love, love, love – the words repeating themselves like a mantra. It was too late to go back.

Then he realized that he was crying; tears welled up in his eyes without warning and for no clear reason. He ran, rushing down into a subway with an overwhelming need to hide. He found a public lavatory, locked himself in a cubicle and sat with his head between his knees trying to clear the pounding in his brain. In blue-tiled isolation, he regained control and leaned back against the water pipes. He sat there for some time, regulating his breathing, clearing his sinuses, frightened by his emotion. The blue Formica door was covered in graffiti: 'Mark is Queer', 'Manchester United Rules OK'; 'Harold Wilson is a Shit'; or, more simply, 'Fuck Off'. One message asked, rather passively, for the meaning of life; there were various explanations, ranging from the obscene to the absurd – he was not alone in finding solace behind a locked door. He took out his pen and, avoiding the crudely sketched diagrams of male genitalia, he wrote in bold large letters: 'There's nothing you can do that can't be done.'

As if on cue, as he finished writing, he heard the sound of a strummed guitar accompanying a pure high female voice. It was coming from outside, but it was caressed by the cavernous cathedral acoustics of the lavatory. Securely locked in, he felt no need for restraint so he opened himself to the music and allowed those tears to return, to flow freely like never before, purging him of his grief.

Outside in the subway, a small long-haired woman in a scarlet kimono sat cross-legged on a blanket. She played her guitar and sang, looking up at the ceiling. A few coppers and a half-crown lay in the small velvet hat on the ground next to her. Stephen wanted to thank her so he threw five shillings into the collection. She smiled but could not see him – her white pupilless eyes gazed into space. 'Thank you,' he said as he walked back up to street level.

Thirty-Three

'The bath is ready, luvvie.' Ivy Cooper issued orders, her pearl-coloured satin dress cut tight – her body on display. At home in Piccadilly meant white furniture, silver curtains, and large mirrors on the walls – no room for pictures, colourful décor or personal style because home meant the latest style and the latest style was a Hollywood set.

'Drinks come later.' There was harshness in her laugh – a touch of desperation too.

'Fussy, aren't you?' His voice was sullen.

She brought him bourbon on a tray, in the chrome and marble bathroom where she sluiced her men before taking her pleasure with them. She watched and drank while he scrubbed away the street – unembarrassed by her lascivious curiosity. His body was on display too.

She will keep this one, this arrogant beautiful man.

She threw away his clothes and she dressed him for his part in her life.

Austin Randolph, body clean, in West End clothes, now she will wear him on her arm.

Thirty-Four

Cogito ergo sum – I think therefore I am. Stephen had always liked it: the introvert's motto. It emphasised the cerebral and minimised the physical, in his interpretation of the phrase, and it had been a magnificent justification for his retreat from the world. All you have to do is think. He had been reading Descartes before going to Frampton; the great seventeenth-century French philosopher had been one of the pillars of his carefully constructed persona.

Thinking about him again, now he was back in Brighton in the familiar surroundings of his dowdy little room, he realised that he had ignored the more concrete realities of Descartes' life. If he had been so cerebral, how did he sire an illegitimate daughter? His journey away from Brighton really had made a difference; he had learnt to at least acknowledge the physical world and connect it with his own flesh and blood. Pulling back the curtains, he said, just to convince himself that it was true: 'I am a living body, therefore I am. Repeat enough and you might even believe it.'

He sorted through his notes at his desk in the window; he was struggling to focus, to retain his interest in Austin Randolph. He had a job to do but his pent-up energy wanted more than work; he was hungry for other things – unsatisfied, bored even. He fidgeted, clicking his pen until it fell apart and then, with nothing better to do, he began emptying his pockets as a distraction from his ennui.

He found the small package that he had bought at the station on that first biographer's trip – his first illegal act. Dys would have liked that. He could see her laughing, hear it as well. He put it away at the back of a drawer, saving it until she came back, hoping that she would come back, feeling that she had to come back now that she had got behind his defences. The thought of her only rekindled his restlessness: living bodies need other bodies, and even Stephen knew that; she haunted his room. It was no good, he couldn't work there; he would have to go back to the library.

He found his usual seat by the window; the old regulars were in their places too but no one acknowledged him. He wouldn't have expected them to behave any other way. He unpacked his documents: his notes; letters from Austin to Emilia and Philip; photographs from their childhood, with Austin as the dominant

109

figure amid scenes of the unchanging country life of the English middle classes – tennis parties, drinks on the lawn, fancy dress parties and horse riding. Always, it was Austin in the centre: handsome, confident and effortlessly magnetic. Old papers concerning Frampton and Emilia's German family were mixed with Philip's father's estate reports.

There was a lot of work to do and now Stephen was in his natural habitat – he came alive when he had papers, letters and statistics to rationalise. He was now inspired to add to his workload too, wanting to access various old regional periodicals from the Huntingdon area. He went up to the assistant librarian's counter, and even the normally unobservant Stephen noticed that she blushed when he spoke to her – she was hardly able to look at him.

'Are you writing a book?' she asked in a hushed tone, the blush spreading to her neck and staying there. When he told her that he was working on a biography, she blushed an even deeper red and started to straighten her light brown pullover, nervously drawing attention to the firm breasts that still took him by surprise. For some time, locked in close proximity, they pored over the indices that she kept behind the counter; she pushed her hands through her limp hair, creating static electricity and filling the space between them with nervous tension.

They had to speak in intimate whispers, obeying the library's rules. Stephen tolerated her characteristically stale smell and shivered when her breath tickled him on his face. She promised to order in whatever periodicals they didn't have but it would take a few days – library things take time she told him. When he returned to his seat he couldn't concentrate, he wasn't in the mood for patience and, in a moment of private exhilaration, freed by the imposed wait, he declared the day a holiday and left hurriedly, not noticing the assistant librarian's look of disappointment.

Next to the library were the gardens of Brighton's most eccentric building – the Royal Pavilion. Built by the future King George IV as a voluptuous retreat where he could act out his sexual fantasies away from his father's disapproving eye. The building was designed as an oriental fantasy of domes and turrets – known whimsically by architects as Hindu Gothic. It was the founding inspiration for seaside architecture everywhere and had never quite lost its ability to shock, standing in the centre of Brighton, celebrating sensuality and individuality, and daring onlookers to let go a bit too.

Here, as one of his minor traditions, Stephen often came to the small outdoor café established in the grounds. He would sit at one of the scruffy metal tables, ignoring the marauding pigeons while reading the daily newspaper over a cup of tea and a piece of ginger cake. Today, though, he had done enough reading; he was sitting back, wondering if the Prince Regent would have approved of the Summer of Love. The old roué's former gardens were full of elderly ladies taking tea, vagrant drunks sleeping off their habit, and sunbathing would-be hippies delighting in their own sensuality. The Pavilion smiled tolerantly. So did Stephen.

A young man in a kaftan sauntered in a slow zigzag towards Stephen's table with a friendly but stupefied grin. He had a string of Chinese bells around his neck that chimed with his every jerking movement.

'Cool, man,' he said. 'If you like tea, you have it. Yeah. Do yer own thing!'

'Do you want some?' Stephen asked.

'No, man, but I'll join you. I prefer these things,' he said, producing a half-smoked joint. 'You have some of this.'

'You won't be able to do that here,' Stephen warned, looking at the deckchair attendant and wanting to protect his new companion.

'I'm doing it anyway. Here, have some.'

He did. Tea and ginger bread were the perfect camouflage; no one noticed and the Pavilion definitely did not care.

It was possible to live in Brighton, maybe Britain's most famous seaside town, without ever going to the sea. The beach was the preserve of the holidaymakers and, until today, Stephen had always left it to them, preferring more cerebral pleasures. He was not getting much time to think here at his table, however, as his visitor had decided to tell the story of his life with a blow by blow account of every 'hit' he had felt.

'It was amazing, man,' he said after each anecdote, but Stephen was not so sure.

After trying all his, admittedly few, social skills in getting rid of his increasingly intrusive friend, Stephen decided that the only way was to abandon ship. Unfortunately, getting away from his spaced-out companion was difficult because the man decided to follow him down every side street, and Stephen only lost him by running down the steps to the beach.

Sunbathers lay on the shingle like corpses washed ashore while the survivors splashed around in the sea, or so it seemed at first. The beach was alive with excited sounds: children's screams were barely distinguishable from the harsh calls of the seagulls, while parental commands competed with the crashing of the sea breaking onto the pebbles. Laughter, shouting, screeching and crying – English reserve had been jettisoned for the wild world of the seaside. Stephen clambered over the sloping shingle beach, past the oily sweating bodies of the sun worshippers, the naked toddlers with their buckets and spades, and the occupants of precariously balanced deck chairs – older holiday-makers indistinguishable from their parents and grandparents who had also sat here years ago. The women in flowing floral frocks bellowing round stockingless legs, their men folk with vested beer bellies and grey trousers rolled up to the knees. There was still, in 1967, a strict uniform for anyone in their middle age or older.

Stephen, as excited as a child, changed into his new, daringly minimalist swimming trunks inside a voluminous towel: new essentials he had just bought for the occasion with the unwelcome help of the spaced out kaftan wearer. He abandoned his clothes and glasses in a pile on the stones and, feeling very white and naked, his vision now soft-focus, he made the painful journey over the pebbles, oblivious to faces and their expressions and therefore free from their gaze. After some tentative wading, he plunged, cannabis-inspired, into the cold salty water. The impact crashed in his ears and he was momentarily deaf to the world, and then he was floating in murky silence, taken out of time, his body supported in a new dimension.

When he surfaced, gasping for air, his vision was filled with red and blue – a large beach ball hit him in the face.

'Hey, sorry mate!' came a laughing voice.

He had surfaced in the middle of a game. A group of young men and women swam over to him to retrieve their ball and, when he threw it to them, he found he had unwittingly joined in. It was easy – there were no rules, only swimming and laughing and, sometimes, catching the ball. He had never felt so uninhibited. Without his glasses, his new friends were reduced to white teeth, brown shoulders and flailing arms. Their language was a vocabulary of screaming laughter and raucous shrieks. A large wave broke over them, signalling game over, and then they were gone – running up the shingle and disappearing into the crowd. Stephen stayed behind, floating on his back absorbing the sun as it transformed the sea into a million sparkling dots.

On the next day, his next visit to the library was brief; just enough time to check on the periodicals with the now very attentive assistant librarian. The summer drew him from his work and promised other pleasures. In half an hour he had left and, after visiting a camping shop, he was soon walking onto the beach armed with his briefcase, a portable typewriter, a camping chair and a small collapsible table with an incongruously striped top – in Stephen's opinion, the bright yellow was an unnecessary addition to the blue and red. Essential too were his swimming trunks wrapped in a towel.

Days later he had become a regular here, just as he had been in the library; working quietly at his book in his position by a wind-sheltering breakwater, relaxing with excursions to the sea. Over time, his body turned a fashionable brown and the Randolph book started to emerge on pieces of paper weighed down by flint pebbles.

Thirty-Five

Lulled by the beach regime, Stephen's idea of time came to mean the rhythm of the tides and the rising and setting of the sun. As summer reached its height, each day repeated itself with identical blue skies and relentlessly high temperatures. If there had been bad weather then he closed his memory to it. He became a sea creature, swimming until his muscles surrendered, then basking on the beach before returning to his notes and, unavoidably, to sun-baked, restless thoughts of Dys, wondering what she was doing on these breathless days and restless nights.

One day, he stayed on the beach until nightfall, held by the liquid gold of the sunset as it spread over the still uncannily bright blue sea. When the sun finally faded, a full moon sent its replacement silver light onto black wavelets: a rippling, sparkling line that stretched towards the horizon with moon and stars resplendent in three-dimensional purple space. Stephen was an unusual sight – a touch of noonday in the darkness when he did eventually walk back to his bus stop – incongruous camping equipment protruding from his rucksack, past night time revellers on their way from pubs to clubs, couples stealing last furtive kisses before the last bus, for some their first sexual encounter, and young drunks urinating against any available wall.

At the bus stop, he breathed in the girls' kiss-me-quick perfume with his evening cigarette and, as he watched the vivid changing colours on the floodlit Royal Pavilion moving through the rainbow spectrum – some town-planner's unintended psychedelia – he smiled at the obscene jokes shouted between groups of young bucks. Midsummer had touched them all with the spirit of carnival; Stephen was intoxicated, in love with humanity, and his yearning grew more intense for the absent Dys.

He clambered aboard the late night bus, willing on the young limbs that raced along the pavement, leaping onto the moving vehicle with extravagant cowboy whoops. Then they were off to distant Hove, leaving Brighton to the frivolous and the romantic. They passed lovers in shop doorways pressing their bodies together with a sensuality that owed nothing to love, while around him, on the top deck, partying passengers prolonged their evening with tales of their outrageous adventures and drunken misdeeds. Stephen immersed himself in their experiences, watching their reflections in the dusty windows and wishing them all well with real affection. When the brightly lit bus dropped him off, he watched the image of the revellers, an illuminated box, retreating into the darkness.

On the wall by his gate a small shadowy figure sat, legs tucked up under her body, staring at the night sky. His eyes drifted over the dark figure abstractedly and, as he passed, it spoke.

'Christ!' came a soft female voice.

'Hi,' he answered, calmly carrying on through the gate and into the house. It was only when he was walking up the stairs that he realised what he had done. The moment that he had been anticipating for weeks had arrived and he hadn't even noticed it. Somehow, he couldn't go down again: he wanted to, he nearly did, but he was scared of the probable disappointment. He was too happy to risk it. If his dream had to shatter, let it not be tonight. He would wait until tomorrow before speaking to Dys.

The next day, perversely, he hoped that he wouldn't see her. In the morning calm of his room, she gave him vertigo; as if he had awoken on the tip of a spire unable to move, terrified of falling through space. He wanted to perpetuate this moment of fragile happiness, the moment before he confronted his hope. He could hear his pulse as he lay in bed; it accelerated and frightened him with its irregular rhythm, accompanying his fear like the melodramatic music to a film.

His breathing was effortful and his limbs tingled, lightly trembling as he stumbled through his thoughts, looking for a plan somewhere in the chaotic muddle of his brain. He would go out as usual, that was all he could do; if he came and went as he always did, he would be bound to meet her eventually, bound to have that moment that he had longed for but now dreaded. He was very aware that she had never promised anything more than casual friendship and she was, as anyone could see, far above his status in the pecking order. He knew all of that but he had a dangerous ability to ignore his own warnings.

115

He crept down the stairs, carefully controlling the sound of his own footfall, but when he opened the front door she was there, inches from his face, standing in front of him.

'I was just coming in,' she said with her quick laugh.

He laughed too. 'I'm going out,' he said, as calmly as he could sound.

They gave way to each other, paused, laughed and gave up.

'Did you have a good time in Salisbury?'

'Oh, yes.' Her eyes opened wide with enthusiasm but she said nothing more. Laughing again, she pushed past him and dashed to her room. His face was burning with excitement at her physical proximity; he had felt her warmth, sensed her breath. In her absence, she had begun to become a disembodied idea to him, an idealised vision, sometimes even an unreal or misremembered mistake, but now she was flesh and blood again. She was so alive, so vibrant and tangible, he wanted to run, to leap in the air, to do all the things that young lovers do and he had never tried. Without being sure whether he had done any of them or just imagined it, he was transported across town, his journey a total but joyful amnesia until he found himself in his usual place on the beach.

He set out the table and chair, arranged his papers under large stones, and sat back to the sound of his own deepest sigh. He may have looked industrious but he couldn't work. He changed into his swimming trunks and lay down on his towel, closing his eyes to the sun and thinking very physical thoughts about Dys. He dozed off in his warmly erotic reveries and, sometime later, he was unsure how much later, he was startled awake feeling the cold pressure of what was a bare foot on his stomach.

'You've got quite a tan,' said Dys brightly as she mockingly pretended to stop him sitting up. The sun shone over her shoulder and he had to shield his eyes to see her face.

'Can I join you?' she asked, already sitting next to him on the towel and all too obviously scrutinising his body as he pretended to look out to sea self-consciously curling his toes. 'I only went to get my things,' she said. 'I thought you would wait for me.'

'How did you know I was coming here?'

'I followed you.'

She laughed again, that same sudden bright sound, a joyous ring in her voice that he had carried with him while she had been away.

He had missed her, he decided, much more than he had even realized. They watched a fat elderly man changing beneath a billowing towel and laughed benignly, almost like lovers, intimately at ease with each other at once.

'I'm going in!' she said, pulling off her muslin dress and running down the beach in her bikini, a tiny affair made from bleached denim, emphasising her elfin lack of curves. He ran after her, catching her up as they splashed through the shallow water, and dived into the sea. They swam in silence, plunging below the surface and bursting up through the waves with a flourish of spray, laughing when they found each other. Weightless and short-sighted, and astoundingly uninhibited, Stephen felt that they were miles from land, freed from its rules, and that the water was electrically charged and life-giving as they circled each other, still reconnecting like old friends. In a moment of daring solemnity, he swam towards her, almost the predator now, but she shouted that she wanted to go ashore.

'I'm thirsty. Let's go for a drink.'

He collected his money and passed Dys the towel.

'Don't bother about that. The sun will dry us.'

They walked onto the promenade, their bodies glistening with seawater and their hair clinging damply to their scalps. They were dry before they reached the ice-cream kiosk, and hot by the time they were sitting on a bench with their cartons of orange juice.

'You've changed,' she said, after a long and noisy slurp.

'Have I?'

'Yes,' and then, after a long pause, 'it's good.'

They sat there in the sun: Dys looking at him, his heart pounding though he didn't yet dare to return her gaze. She was offering herself to him, he knew that, because, without looking at her, he could feel the glow of her body, her heat warming him, driving away his inner melancholy.

'So you've kept my bracelet I see,' she said, fingering the plaited hair that encircled his wrist – it was still damp against his skin but her touch was dry and hot.

She asked him what he had been doing and, reluctantly, he told her about his book. She listened for a while then interrupted him. 'That hasn't done it.'

117

'Done what?'

'Changed you. I think the sun has done it – has freed you.'

'Maybe,' he said, delighted by her attention, but instinctively changing the subject. 'What about you? What did you do in Salisbury?'

'Oh, I just stayed with some friends. We talked a lot. It was fine.'

He was expecting her to explain but, instead, with characteristic timing, she stood up.

'I must go,' she said. 'I'll see you later.'

'But what about your dress?'

'Could you bring it back for me? Bye.'

She ran off leaving Stephen, once more, in disappointed confusion. Looking for comfort, and needing to hide his excitement, he went back into the sea.

It was late when he returned to the house. Dys was not there. He took her dress up to his room. It felt so small and delicate, this tiny bundle of cloth – so easily crushed and so insubstantial. He draped it carefully over his chair as if it were a holy relic. It spoke of the moment in the sun when he had discovered that he needed some of this delicacy and warmth in his life. Entranced, he lay on his bed staring at the ceiling, but sleep only came to him as the dawn broke. It was then that the door opened and Dys crept under his sheets, waking him gently with her touch.

Thirty-Six

'Miss Ivy Cooper, the singing star, marries Mr Austin Randolph. Yesterday's celebration was one of the year's most glittering occasions. Stage and radio stars add glamour to the day. The couple leave on mystery motoring honeymoon.'

Emilia Jeffries is tearful in Berlin's Schiller Park, an English newspaper on her lap, sitting on a bench on a summer morning in 1934. Perfidia! That was the song: a sultry voiced gramophone hit. It spoke for her, condemning the grinning hero in the photograph – posing, Hollywood-style, with his shining blonde-haired wife.

Doubly duped Emilia Jeffries, an English rose, the severed half of an incurable passion, sitting in the park, sensible-looking in pleated tweed skirt and folded, silk-stockinged legs, reading the morning paper. Then, most unladylike, she lights a cigarette with trembling hand and inhales enough smoke to fumigate her grief.

Margaret Irving, vengeful aunt, smiles; or is she flinching? Fly swat in hand, remembering her sister's letter, she takes aim. Emilia and Austin separated, tricked; Emilia lied to, whisked off to Berlin, and Austin deceived, cast out onto the streets. No, she is not smiling. The bluebottle settles, black blot on white paint. Margaret Irving strikes, aim deadly; so much juice in one so small.

Thirty-Seven

They moved down to Dys's room in the morning. It was larger than Stephen's; cell-like in its whitewashed bareness, but with a large double mattress on the floor in the centre. Stephen not only moved into the room, he moved into the bed – seldom leaving it, or Dys, over the next few days. Apart from hurried, towel-covered forays to the lavatory, hoping not to meet anyone, he remained where he was happiest and, among white sheets, he was encased in the white environment that she had created for them. Everything was white – the walls, woodwork, floorboards. Even the curtains were made from large white sheets.

The only contrast came from the purple, cream and scarlet dresses hanging from nails in the walls, and from a deep cobalt blue pot of giant red paper poppies standing on the floor. Otherwise, they supplied their own colours. The white intensified the green of Dys's eyes, the auburn in her black hair, the golden brown of her skin and the vivid, almost angry red of her mouth. Stripped of his camouflage, Stephen, over-awed by its ease, grew fluent in his sensuality but decided not to tell Dys that this was his first time. It was much easier than he had imagined.

'I saw you hiding there,' she teased him. 'Mr Professor is not so studious now, is he? Not when his lady friend comes to call! I knew I would break through one day.'

'I thought you were laughing at me.' He was feeling pleasantly sensitive after shedding more than just his clothes.

'I was. But I was sent to save you. To save you from yourself.' She was laughing again. 'And I wanted to find out what you were hiding down there!'

She became more beautiful to him now that he knew where each mole or so-called imperfection hid. He learnt to lose himself in her, so that sometimes he wouldn't know which leg was his, which arm hers. The two bodies together became his total experience. Often, she would sit on the floor, cross-legged, hands on knees, eyes closed, meditating. While she did so, he meditated on her – so physical and yet so ethereal, now temporarily separated from him in her own aura. By surrendering himself to her, part of him entered into her own transcendental experience. It was, he knew, the first hint of what it would be like to lose her. He would be losing part of himself. Then her eyes opened and she returned both to him and their bed.

Dys boiled up hastily prepared meals of beans and rice on her little electric stove; she made iced tea, brewed on the sunlit windowsill and stored in her toy-sized fridge. They ate and drank, obsessed with each other's bodies; tongues and teeth wonderfully revealed, their swallowing studied, their anatomy shared, nothing hidden from view. They stayed on the bed for days tracing the course of veins, exploring muscle shapes, feeling the bone beneath the flesh and comparing skin texture: hers soft, brown and downy; his newly tanned, dark hair shaded on chest and limb. They explored, analysed and memorised each other alone in the room, communicating non-verbally in ecstatic isolation.

'You stay there,' she whispered tenderly in his ear one morning. 'I must see my friends. I won't be long.' She slid from their sheets, smiling at him all the while. He watched from the bed as she slipped naked into the long purple dress and disappeared from the room; her clothes had never really covered her. He pulled the bedding around him, chilled by the physical bereavement. His body withered under the sheets and he found no comfort there, so he too finally got up too.

Finding his dressing gown, pleased with its old familiarity, he went back to his own room. As he climbed the stairs, he was going back through history, many years longer than the week he had been gone. It should have faded away like an ancient monument but, startlingly, the room had not changed since those first moments with Dys. The bedclothes were scattered: her dress was still on the chair, his pyjamas crumpled on the floor. A shrine to that first act of love, it could have been the scene of a murder; of course it had been the scene of a death, a welcome one too.

For a while he stood frozen on the threshold and, when he went in, it was as a visitor, nostalgic but objective, smiling wryly at the symbols of his former life. He washed standing at the sink but she had made him superstitious – he was frightened of washing her away. For a long time he looked into the mirror, trying to find himself in the reflected image; his face, with a week's growth of beard, was new to him. He had become a man but not a stranger.

121

He was happy, happier than he had ever been before; tears glistened in his eyes and he decided not to shave, not to tamper with the changes sprouting from his mind and body.

Thirty-Eight

Stephen's cheesecloth shirt and new blue trousers that had felt so significant when he bought them now seemed superfluous as he clambered into them. He felt no need to cover up, to put on camouflage again. His body had been given its freedom and it had responded with a suppleness, an athleticism even, that had taken him by surprise, revealing to him his natural state. He was not ready for the world beyond Dys's bed, where human nature still had to be hidden from view. He went back to see if she had returned, but the room was empty; its whiteness, now comfortless and harsh, forbade him from settling there to wait for her. Through the open door, from a room on the ground floor, came the often-heard sound of sitar music. Shoeless and unaware that he had been propelled subconsciously, he went down the stairs and found himself knocking on the door and entering the room before he knew what he was going to say.

'Hi there,' said a serious young man sitting on the window ledge. 'Is the music disturbing you?'

'Uh, no,' Stephen replied, looking at him and then round the room, taking in the sitar player, who was sitting on the floor seemingly unaware of the interruption. The room was barely furnished in the European sense: its walls were draped with intricately patterned Indian sheets, and the floor had a generous covering of faded oriental cushions and, instead of a bed, here too was an old double mattress covered in tousled blankets and sheets. A joss stick was burning on the mantelpiece and a jangling brass ornament hung in the window.

'Sit down,' said the man in the window, indicating one of the cushions.

'I was looking for Dys,' said Stephen, settling onto the floor with new-found yogic ease. 'Have you seen her?'

'Not really, but I think she's around,' came the helpful but whimsical reply.

The music compensated for the pause in conversation. What had been an irritating noise in the distance was impressively eloquent at close quarters. The player, not Asian as Stephen had assumed, was a long thin man, about the same age as the other tenants but with a

123

pale seriousness that made him look older. He wore a simple white shirt and jeans and crouched on a pile of cushions, rapt in his playing.

'So, how's our very private neighbour?' said the first young man with a gentle laugh. 'We've all been wondering how long it would be before you said hello.' He laughed again: it was a knowing, thoughtful laugh, and he looked out of the window; the look was to an idea and not to any view outside. He was, like the sitar player, about Stephen's age, with thick black curly hair framing a handsomely structured bony face that was ornamented with round gold-rimmed glasses. He wore old jeans, an open-neck shirt and an old grey cotton jacket that was too big for him and hung limply from his shallow shoulders

'I'm fine, thanks,' Stephen replied, ignoring the hint of provocation, and then he relaxed enough to let the music fill the gap. The private, unsociable neighbour who was being mocked was no longer him; that was the Stephen from his previous existence. He could not take offence at any personal comments directed at his old self.

'You're Steve, aren't you? Dys has told me about you. I'm Mark.'

'Hello.'

'I hear you're writing a history book.'

'Well, I suppose you could call it that.'

'Do we need any more history books? Don't you think we've had too much of all that already?'

Already their conversation was accelerating towards confrontation. Mark had been waiting for this it seemed.

'No, history is important,' Stephen countered. He was not going to be put down so easily. 'It's our way of avoiding past mistakes.' He bounced back with the first cliché that came to him. He had found the well of aggression inside himself that Mark seemed so keen to provoke. 'I'm really writing a biography. Do you disapprove of that too?'

'It's not a matter of disapproving,' said Mark grinning. 'I don't know what biographies are for. What are they? Just another way society keeps us down. Telling us stories of the great and good. Giving us heroes and villains. I don't need that, man.'

'What do you do, then?' asked Stephen, backing down.

'I suppose you could call me a student. Me Mark, you Steve. Isn't that enough?'

'I suppose so.'

Mark leant forward and proffered a long arm to shake Stephen by the hand. The grip was weak and relaxed, and the shake perfunctory.

'Don't think I'm getting at you, man. You're cool. OK? We've all said that you're cool. You do your own thing and that's just fine. So no bad feelings, uh?'

He grinned again and started to roll himself a cigarette. When he finished, he passed over the papers and tobacco as a gesture of peace. When Stephen failed to secure the tobacco into the paper, Mark even offered his help. Stephen enjoyed the human warmth when Mark bent over him and took the papers from his fumbling hands. They were both smoking in calm fraternity when Dys and another girl came crashing into the room. They were in the middle of a semi-serious but highly animated row.

'Dys won't let me use my tarot cards,' said Rosalie, in a deep chesty voice that was characterised by an infectious and maybe permanent laugh in its tone. She changed the ambience of the room with her easy informality and found herself a cushion at a distance from the others. 'She's frightened to know what the future holds for her.'

'I don't need to know,' Dys said, joining Stephen and lying across his lap.

Rosalie backed off and began to shuffle the cards. Totally the opposite of Dys, she was tall and heavy boned – too young and strong to be called fat – with wild straw-coloured curly hair that she allowed to spring out in all directions. She was wearing a long tent of a frock that opened at the front revealing a voluptuous cleavage. In spite of all these new people, it was enough for Stephen to see Dys again. He tried to merge her into this new group, wanting to take in these new friends, but all he could do was look at her, smile at her. They sat there for some time – four silent listeners and the sitar player – then Dys got up.

'Can't you stop that for a bit, Paul?' she said. 'I want everyone to meet Stephen.'

Paul abandoned his raga, shrugged and lay back on his elbows.

125

'This is Stephen,' she said, solemnly and generally to the room, squeezing Stephen's hand as she raised it in the air. 'He is my friend. This is Rosalie – she's a witch. This is Mark – who'd like to be our leader but doesn't believe in such things so he can't be, and this is Paul, the mystic minstrel. So there we are. Now we're all friends. OK?'

Paul smiled and everyone else said 'hi'.

'And who are you, Dys?' said Mark mockingly. 'Who is the real Dys?'

'Who cares?' she answered breezily.

'We all do,' said Rosalie. 'You're the only one who doesn't. You're frightened of knowing who you are but you don't need to be. Nobody should – you hide from it because you're frightened of life.'

'I don't want to think about it that's all. Why does everyone have to keep planning the future? Why can't we just enjoy now?'

'Yes,' said Mark, seizing the opportunity. 'We're victims of our fear of the future, I agree. Ambition is one of the ways we try to control our fear; we dream of all those wonderful achievements and possessions but they really just keep us down, keep us away from now. We're not meant to be happy with our own present tense – it would make us ungovernable.'

'But the times they are a'changin'!' Dys sang – her joy returning. Stephen did not know the words but he was happy to be a part of it when all the others joined in, and he laughed when Paul orientalised Bob Dylan on his sitar.

Thirty-Nine

'I think we should join the others at the pub,' said Dys. They had returned to bed, night had turned into day, day into early evening, and they had been lying next to each other, trance-like. It had been over an hour since they last spoke.

'Must we?'

'No, but I think we should,' she said, gently climbing into her dress and tossing his trousers onto the bed.

They went into The Bear as lovers. Stephen, proud and enjoyably embarrassed with his woman on his arm, struggled to conceal the whole body smile that spread from his pounding heart through all his veins. Dys was wearing her musk perfume, exoticising their body-space, filling his senses with her presence. Feeling her joyful grip on his arm, he flushed with excitement; they were taking their boudoir with them and their bodies had not really disengaged.

Mark was sitting with Rosalie and some others at a round, baronial table in a darkened alcove; smiles and greetings were exchanged, knowing looks were given and space was made for them.

'We thought you would never speak to us again,' laughed Rosalie. 'But you've come back to Earth again now.'

'Kind of,' said Dys. 'We've been living anyway.'

Stephen smiled shyly and she squeezed his hand as Rosalie, her hair even wilder than before, introduced the others. Hidden beneath his shyness there was a rush of excitement. He had never thought he could be friends with people like this. Would he dare? Could they really be friends? There was José, a Puerto Rican American in his late twenties with thick black hair and an impressively dense moustache – by far the most macho facial hair in the group – and a laugh that disguised his seriousness. Mick, an older man with long thin hair that was speckled with grey, and a jaundiced face lined with wrinkles that recorded many of the good times he had undoubtedly enjoyed. Jo and Viv were a young couple with identical mid-brown Beatle-mop haircuts; each wore a daisy-bloom ear-ring in one ear and they dressed alike in crisp new denim jeans and white t-shirts. They were identified by Rosalie as an indivisible couple and Stephen had difficulty deciding their gender.

'Don't worry about them,' she said. 'They're in love! Mick is an artist – he does really interesting things – and José is on the run. He's dodging the Vietnam draft. They all live in a squat near here.'

'It's a house commandeered by the people,' Mark explained without irony. He had already gathered that he needed to help Stephen out with modern terminology. 'No one else was living there so Mick and the others broke in. Now it's their home.'

'Until the council chucks us out,' said Mick.

'It's a cool house. We're gonna go there later,' said Rosalie 'It's called The Toadstool.'

'Can I get anyone a drink?' Stephen asked inconsequentially. He would never be good in crowds. Everyone looked blankly at him.

Mark grinned and said that none of them ever drank in pubs. 'It's a reactionary vice, the opiate of the people, but don't let that stop you. You have one if you need it.'

'Doesn't the pub mind if no one drinks?'

'No,' said Rosalie. 'The landlord's cool. He never says anything.'

'Well, I don't think I'll have one either,' said Stephen, pleased to forgo it. He had only just discovered alcohol and had already found it a depressant.

'Can you get me a Guinness?' said Dys. 'I never drank the last one you got me.'

'If you're going,' added Mick, 'I'll have a whisky.'

The Toadstool was a shabby five-storey terraced house in a rundown street behind the pub. Stephen, who had been persuaded to have a Guinness before they all left for the party, deduced its age as early Victorian, probably built in the eighteen-thirties. Drab on the outside, its inside was a startling contrast. The apparently dour Mick had used all his pent up exuberance on its decoration. Using primary colours he had been through every room creating the imaginary interior of a Disneyesque mushroom. The hall was pink with large purple spots; the stairs were yellow and green. Every room was a different combination of colours, with dramatic stripes and zigzags deliberately brought together clashingly from the opposite ends of the rainbow. Garden gnomes, stolen in profusion from the suburban gardens of Hove, were repainted in psychedelic patterns and placed on window ledges and tables throughout the house, often in pornographic positions. Stephen saw none of this when they came through the door because the squat had no electricity. Everyone took matches and went through the building lighting candles until the extraordinary colours were all illuminated in flickering light. Definitely Byzantine, Stephen thought approvingly.

Then the others arrived. Stephen was introduced to them all as if he was the guest of honour: Thomas, the dope man, and Roxanna his partner, who had decided to run with her sallow complexion and jet black hair, so she dressed in layered and faded gypsy-like clothing; Mary, the busker, with her open-air skin the colour of nutmeg; and Cadmus, the juggler, who was either very brown or very dirty; Phil and Maeve, and Simon and Maude – young couples who knew just how young hippie couples ought to look and strived not to disappoint; Martin the Redhead and Martin the Flautist who had brown hair; Traveller Will with Autolycus his dog, who made the crusty Cadmus look positively laundered. Bilbo and Frankie and Barnaby and Florence were resplendent in primary colours – red or yellow loon trousers – and they all competed with multiple rows of glass bead necklaces. And then there were the members of The Id, The Toadstool's resident acoustic folk rock band, made up of the androgynous twins Jo and Viv on guitars, and their friends, who were definitely both male: Rocky on drums and Bev on the violin.

They had begun to play – a mixture of Californian folk rock and experimental jazz – when the last visitor arrived. Dressed in a black frock coat, white Byronic shirt and black knee-length boots, a tall, longhaired man with an anaemically pale complexion went straight to the table and chair that had been placed in the middle of the hall especially for him. Sitting down, he pulled a pouch from his pocket and took out two packets of cigarette papers – one white, the other black. Solemnly and without a word he stuck them together, alternating the colours. Everyone watched in silence – they were in the presence of a master. The black-and-white construction grew until it was a foot in length. Then the cigarette maestro took out another pouch and, with studied care, spread a line of tobacco and another substance before the papers were rolled and a long black and white joint was held up to the audience's applause. Striking a safety match against his boot, he lit his creation, inhaled and passed

129

it on. To cheers and applause, he bowed for a moment, grinned and, as silently as he had arrived, he left.

'Consider yourself among friends,' said Mark, passing him the joint. Taking it, Stephen remembered Emilia Jeffries' remark about Keats. In the temple of delight, surrounded by friends, he was looking for Dys. Veiled melancholy ascended her throne: Dys had gone.

Forty

Austin Randolph, brown eyes burning: his black shirt sits handsomely on his puffed-out chest. Hatred brings back his energy, brings back his pride. He remembers Frampton days, riding to hounds, that taste in his mouth, the excitement of blood, the fox and him, both predators, both hunted, breathless, eye-to-eye, sharing a truth.

Mosley's fascists, British fascists, out on the streets stoning the Jews: British Jews in their East End homes. Austin Randolph punches straight to the face. He is one of the best – fearless, committed, easily roused even though he knows no Jews and doesn't hate them or even know who they are. It is that same old feeling – the excitement of blood, that taste in his mouth. Hatred for something other than himself: the hatred of an angry man. Austin is angry and full of hatred.

Arrested and locked up in an East End cell, his knuckles bloodied, his lips split, Austin Randolph, a hero for some but an enemy for other more innocent folk. He is running with hounds, unthinking, thrilled to have found his role.

A loving wife bails him out; she signs the cheque with a white-gloved hand. They kiss on his bleeding lips; she devours him, loving his anger, bursting his wounds. The pain is his price and his pain is her joy, his blood on her powdered face wiped off by that white-gloved hand.

One more photograph in the English papers: 'Singing Star's Husband In Fascist Attack'. Alone with her coffee, in a Berlin café, Emilia sees it. She hates his anger, his pain and his spilled blood. Emilia Jeffries, his rejected love, still loves him in spite of this. If Ivy had known, she would have laughed.

Forty-One

Don't forget me, my young friend. I am waiting for you. Still here, while you unravel the past. It was not all pure and sweet. Believe me. It never is. Put your young brain to the task. Focus and penetrate. You, all of you, can learn from us. Don't sever the thread. I need you to find me. I am waiting for you.'

Austin Randolph, Tung Ping Chau, August 1967

Now fully bearded, his hair growing long, his new gold-rimmed glasses slipping slightly down his nose, Stephen was dressed in a new but crumpled linen shirt and thin, rough-woven trousers in indistinct shades of straw. He was sitting in his recently perfected lotus position, in the sun, on the white wooden chest in Dys's window. He looked at his brown toes, the symbol of the journey that he had made that summer. His skin had turned nut brown, like the seedpods of a greenhouse plant brought on by the heat of the sun; now he too was ripening, coming to fruition.

Dys had come back after the party at The Toadstool: she didn't say where she had been or who she had been with and Stephen didn't ask. He had learnt, with some difficulty, not to encroach on her private space. She had gone away many times before, always suddenly and without explanation, but mostly, these days, they had been together – practising yoga, swimming in the sea, lying naked in the sun on the roof of Gresham Villas; but always their preference was to return to their bed in Dys's whitewashed room, the centre of their lives. They saw more of Mark, Rosalie, Mick and the others; there were late night debates and sitar ragas in Paul's incense-perfumed room, extravagant gatherings at The Toadstool, and bonfire parties on the beach where the sweet smell of marijuana mingled with the ozone as they watched the sea from sunset to the new dawn. They were like members of a mystic nomadic tribe moving through a landscape of their own making, with Stephen now one of their number.

Dys came into the room, always lightly, like a ballerina, and threw her arms around him.

'You're like a guru sitting there lost in your own meditation. What were you thinking?'

132

'About you, I guess. I was thinking how little I know about you and yet I seem to know all about you and to have always known you.'

'You know all there is to know,' she whispered as she pushed her fingers through his hair. 'I'm here, my long-haired man. You see me, feel me, talk to me. What else is there to know?'

'Oh, I know that's true but I have so many old habits. I can't help wanting to know about the past, your past. It is just how I am I suppose. I'm a historian at heart, still a historian I fear, even though you don't approve. I want to know where you come from and things like that.'

'It doesn't mean anything,' she repeated. 'Honestly, it doesn't matter.'

She sat down behind him on the chest, her legs enfolded round his torso as she slowly massaged his neck. 'The past doesn't exist for me, my love. I died and was reborn – you won't know me any better by knowing my past. That's all labels, no more. You know: "Here's the lovely Dys, eighteen, loves horse-riding, reading and meeting people. Her hobbies are stamp collecting and big game hunting." You can't sum people up like that. I don't care what you were like when you were twelve – I want you now. It's always sad, damaged people who are obsessed with the past – they are victims of it. It used to make you sad too: I could see it. Why should we dig it all up? Who cares? So, my love, don't try to trap me under one of your definitions.'

'But what if...'

'Oh no you don't!' she laughed, kissing him to silence.

So they went to the beach and behaved like lovers do, walking along the water's edge; they deliberately sought out romantic locations, settings eroticised by myth. His life, at that moment, was concentrated within the sensations of wet sand under his feet and the warmth of Dys's hand in his. The sea lulled them and silenced their words and, once more, their world was telescoped until it was an abstract – a joyful haze of blue.

When they got back to the house, Dys scooped up an envelope from the doormat.

'It's for you,' she said. 'See you later.'

She had gone before he opened it.

'Dear Mr Dearsley,
This might be helpful for your book.'

The typewritten note had no address or signature, but enclosed was a cheaply printed notice advertising a lecture series to be held in a church hall in Hove. One entry had been circled in ink – it was a lecture that night. 'Those Were The Days – A Talk on Musical Comedy. Guest Speaker Miss Ivy Cooper.'

Forty-Two

'That's right, my friend. Dig out the dirt. It is where I swam; where I wallowed. Dig it all out. Expose it to the sun and when all the filth cracks, remember me.'

Austin Randolph, Tung Ping Chau, August 1967

The afternoon light shed an elegiac glow over the town, warning of autumn. It cast its nostalgic spell over Stephen as he made his way to St Pius Church Hall on the sleepiest side of town, tucked away behind the shops in a tiny road that you would only go down if you wanted to visit the hall. Stephen suspected that not many people would feel that particular urge.

He had walked down busy streets full of afternoon shoppers and had come across the odd band of young hippies – now it seemed like they were members of his own secret society. Today, though, they seemed frail and vulnerable as the edge went off the summer sun – he hoped that they would survive the first frost. In the heat of the afternoon, winter was still a remote threat, but the seasonal clock had moved on and Stephen felt an involuntary shudder. It could have been the light, the temperature, or a feeling of guilt. He hadn't told Dys about the letter and she hadn't asked about it.

In the dingy church hall, rows of wooden chairs had been prepared for the lecture, but only the front two rows were occupied – and, even then, not all the places were taken. The high-ceilinged Edwardian building was no longer a respectable meeting place for St Pius's pious congregation. The church, one of many surplus-to-requirement Church of England buildings, was long demolished. The land had been sold to the council to build flats for the elderly and the hall was now used for various ill-attended community projects aimed at occupying the minds of local impoverished pensioners. Crumbling plaster and descending damp patches broke up the monotony of the dirty magnolia walls.

At one end there was a stage with faded blue velvet curtains forming a backdrop to the afternoon's main attraction. An elderly man, in a grey tweed suit, was standing stage left with a portable gramophone on a table. He was tremblingly manipulating the stylus onto a vinyl record while, centre stage, isolated on a shabby leather chair, sat, Stephen assumed, Ivy Cooper; once a glamorous singing star, now a plump elderly woman with thin, hennaed hair and a fleshy rouged face enlivened by an inaccurately applied smudge of scarlet on the lips. Her beauty had faded in a similar way to St Pius Church Hall Stephen thought, unkindly. Both had survived beyond their glory days to become crumbling symbols of their own obsolescence.

While Stephen surveyed the scene, the gramophone produced a faint recording of Ivy singing 'The Desert Song' from a musical show now mostly forgotten. Stephen guessed it was one of her own performances by the way she sat smiling at the ceiling, as if she had escaped from this world where the audience sang along, drowning her out, in quivering voices. Stephen, unsure of why he was there, sat at the back and watched.

The music finished, there was a clatter of applause, the old man lifted the needle, dropped it back onto the vinyl, swore, retrieved it a second time and walked carefully back to a seat at the side of the stage. Ivy waited for him to settle, with an instinct born of a lifetime's experience, then rose to her feet. She wore a tight floral dress, mostly orange chrysanthemums on a red background, that had been designed for a younger and shapelier Ivy Cooper but now just emphasised the rolls of fat that were trying to escape such cruel confinement. Lighting a cigarette and inhaling it, she maintained a theatrical pause before allowing her girlish, unnaturally high-pitched voice to project around the hall. As she spoke, her bright red mouth was set in a perpetually sweet smile – a technique acquired by all young soubrettes in the Thirties.

'For our last record, I thought I would save my favourite.' She made a simpering giggle, hoping for a murmur of excitement that never happened.

'I have the fondest of memories for the show I did with Mr Ivor Novello many years ago now. He was such an amusing man and so generous too. He could be so romantic and he was always quick to praise any little quality that his co-stars might possess. I found him quite delightful to work with and, whenever I hear this song, I am reminded of dear Ivor and the smell of the theatre in those days – when people truly appreciated style and romance.'

There was a ripple of agreement from the audience who, somewhat surprisingly, all appeared to have memories, accurate or not, of more glamorous days.

'Unfortunately, we never did record this lovely duet together but, if you're ready Mr Snewin, here is an equally dear friend, Mr Al Bowly, in Ivor's role. We recorded this not long before Al was tragically killed during the London Blitz, such a long time ago now.'

Throwing a thespian look at the nervous Mr Snewin she sat down, and instantly, as if the chair had magic powers, her girlishness vanished. The music's youthful romanticism had survived but it was made all the more poignant by the elderly recording and the ancient gramophone player. Ivy slumped in her chair puffing on her cigarette – she was an old woman again.

'It was nice, wasn't it?' was the much repeated comment as the old ladies made their way out, but enjoyment did not show on their faces.

'The music was lovely,' they all agreed.

They had each come back from a happier time – back to their aches and pains and the memories of their losses. Their woolly hats and tweed coats warned Stephen that not everyone had been celebrating a Summer of Love. He was also aware that they edged away from him; a chasm had opened between the generations and, as they inched past him, some of them whispered their disapproval of his appearance. 'Disgusting…' a gentle old lady said too loudly, once she was out in the street. 'Long hair like that and nothing on his feet but those sandals… They don't know how to behave, young people these days. He shouldn't have been allowed in.'

Ivy waited for them to leave before making her own way down the hall. She was not firm on her feet and it was some time before she reached Stephen.

'Miss Cooper?'

'Yes, dear?' came a deep voice, unrecognisable after the high soprano of her stage persona, and with an accent matured in thespian extravagance.

'My name's Stephen Dearsley. I wonder if you remember someone called Austin Randolph?'

'Jesus be praised!' she exclaimed with a coarse laugh. 'Talk about grave-digging! And why should a young man like you be asking me questions like that?'

When he told her the reason she guffawed in disbelief.

'And what the hell has he done to warrant a book, I should like to know? Apart from marrying me that is! He disappeared with the bath water years ago, darling. If you want to know all about him, ask away, I could tell you loads.'

'Could we go somewhere to discuss it?'

He was trying to sound earnest and interested, but he could imagine Mark's disapproving voice scoffing at his persistence with the past. He was giving way to bourgeois values, helping to perpetuate a past that should be giving way to the Age of Aquarius. He had tried to stop caring about Austin Randolph and the odd, incoherent story that he was constructing. Ivy Cooper had been sent to tempt him back, but his curiosity was now mingled with guilt. In this desolate place, in the battle for Stephen's mind, Austin Randolph reasserted his power.

'If you let me get my money for this little bit of business, you can take me home,' she said. 'Have you got a car?'

'No, I don't drive.'

'Well, we'll have to take the bus then – I have a little flat not far away, so we can go there if you want. I'm quite full of curiosity to find out what the old bugger's been up to!'

Back on the trail, Stephen used Austin's money to buy two single bus fares, one with an old age pensioner's pass, and also a small bottle of whisky from Ivy's local off licence.

'Usual brand, madam?' said the shop assistant, a middle-aged man with a bored expression, passing her the cheapest bottle. When Stephen paid, the man rolled his eyes wearily.

Forty-Three

'I think a drink is called for, don't you, dear?' Ivy said as soon as they came into her small sitting room. Stephen's first impression was that the tiny apartment stank – an unpleasant combination of damp and urine. The unattractive and ill-matching furniture reflected the taste of a mean landlord rather than an incompetent homemaker. A job lot from a junk shop, the upholstery barely hygienic, everything about twenty years old, Stephen thought, and the 1940s was not a good decade for interior design in his opinion. It was either trying too hard to be Fascist, with its brutalised art deco, or it got lost trying just as hard not to look monumental.

Age had withered everything here, including the tenant. Ivy had done very little to add her personality to the place beyond littering it with her detritus – empty bottles, plates with the fossilised remains of meals, improbably large greying undergarments in piles on the floor and, in multitudes, framed black and white theatrical photographs from the 1920s and 30s hanging on the wall or standing on every flat space. Stephen assumed that Ivy did not realize the value of the pewter art deco frames. Many of the photographs had the elaborate signatures of long forgotten variety artists and provincial matinee idols.

One face reoccurred in a number of the pictures – a platinum blonde woman in full stage make-up. In one, she presented her coyly dimpled smile through a misty gauze to the camera. In another she was laughing with a frozen pose of stagey artificiality. In each she represented the eternally worldly woman, a man's woman: an idealised barmaid, milkmaid, tart – man's real best friend, no matter what dog-lovers claim. Draped either in white fox fur, shimmering chiffon, or body clinging satin, she was unmistakably Ivy Cooper.

'I was a bit of alright then, wasn't I? That was a lovely dress. Pink lace, handmade, from Belgium. Oh well! The Lord giveth and the Lord taketh away – the mean old sod.'

They sat down in two old armchairs with their tumblers of whisky and Stephen offered her a cigarette.

'Thanks, love, I'm dying for one. They're the only pleasures an old bird like me's got left – fags and booze. Though I can still appreciate a good-looking young man like you, even though they don't come my way very much any more. But don't worry, darling, I only look these days, Heaven help me!'

Stephen was holding the whisky to his nose to lessen the room's odour of decay. As he sat back in the chair, his body began to itch and he tried to ignore the probable cause.

'I thought you might be one of those solicitors at first. You know, the ones who come from nowhere to tell you you've inherited a fortune from a relation you didn't know you had. Not that you look much like a solicitor with your dandy looks and your lovely long hair! And I don't suppose there'll be any money from Austin – that was a bad penny if ever there was one.'

'That's what I want to find out.'

'What? If he had any money?'

'No, I meant him being a bad penny as you call him.'

'So you want all the sordid details? It's a dirty job digging around in the past, dear. You dig up some pretty rotten things – and you might put your hand on something really nasty like my old man Austin.'

She took another drink and settled into her chair, pulling at the skirt that had stretched tight over her thighs. Involuntarily, Stephen noticed the large knotted garters of grimy elastic that held up her stockings.

'Why did you marry him?' he asked, averting his gaze to his whisky.

'It's a long story, dear, but the main reason was that he was lovely looking. Another thing was that he had a way with him. His eyes stripped the clothes off your back the moment you walked into the room. He knew what women wanted, you know, in the bedroom, and he let you know that the moment he met you. I was successful, pretty attractive as you can see, and I could have had anyone I wanted – and that's mostly what I did. I had all of them, dear, don't you worry. But Austin, he was a beast, a devil really – but God, was he a lovely man!'

She laughed coarsely at the memory. There was no doubt about her thoughts as she gulped her drink.

'I loved him, dear. It's as simple as that. I made a bloody fool of myself and then he left me – the bastard.'

'Did he leave you for Emilia Jeffries?'

'So you know about her, do you?'

'Yes, we've met.'

'Jesus God! You're serious about all this aren't you? Emilia Jeffries! Posh little Miss Jeffries. Yes, he left me for her. She was a pretty little thing, I'll admit that. She doted on him, little fool that she was. She never stopped chasing him even after I warned her about him. Told her what he was like, about his little habits, if you know what I mean. But she would hear none of it – all she could see were the stars. Her ears were full of heavenly choirs but he was made of earthier stuff, I can tell you. Actually, when he was gone, I missed him. We saw eye to eye, you see. We knew that this is a rum old world and that there aren't any pots of gold at the end of any rainbows. I don't think Emilia ever saw that.'

'She told me that they became lovers when he was still living at Frampton and that they split up in London. She didn't tell me about you though.' Stephen could feel the story was spinning out of control again.

'I bet she didn't! I bet she didn't tell you one half of the truth either. Cunning little vixen! They split up all right, but that wasn't the end of it. Not by a long chalk. Yes, they were lovers in the good old days. The days of yore. When they could both afford to be all lardy-da. But Austin, the dirty little bugger, messed things up, didn't he? Got chucked out of the stately pile for getting one of the maids up the duff and ended up with nothing. I wouldn't be surprized if he even 'ad a bit of 'ow's yer father with his mother, the dirty cow! But then, he'd poke it anywhere he could, the dirty bugger. Emilia and he fell out but he carried on falling. All the way. That's where I came in. Enter a showgirl.'

'What do you mean?'

'Well, it was quite straightforward. I was doing very nicely thank you. I was doing a musical in the West End; I forget which one, probably something by Ivor Novello, that old poof. I was on top of the world, topped up with champagne and looking for fun. I walked right into him. Down and out, dirty and ragged, not much more than a kid with nowhere to go, but he was still something. He had what it takes. You could say that I saw his potential and couldn't resist it.'

'So what happened?'

'Come on, love! I bedded him – after scrubbing him up a bit first of course. And then I wedded him. We spent loads of money, partied a lot, drank a lot, and then little Miss Perfect came back on the scene and he buggered off. There you have it. Big-hearted Ivy lost her boy.'

She took another swig of whisky, gulping it noisily.

'Where did they go?'

'Oh, I don't know. Abroad somewhere, I heard. I never found out – I didn't much care, to be honest. There were plenty more fish in the sea so I wasn't going to waste my time with the ones that got away. No, Austin and Emilia went off into the sunset and I got on with my life. And a funny old life it's been too.'

She patted him on the knee, using him as a support to lever herself up.

'I'll get us a couple of drinks and then I'll show you Austin Randolph.'

From the recesses of a drawer, she produced a black covered photograph album. Stephen moved his chair closer to hers as she flipped through the pages that documented her life as Mrs Austin Randolph. Typical of their day, the photographs were mostly of groups at special occasions. One showed Austin and Ivy pulling jokey faces to camera, he playing the he-man and she the vamp. Others had them in evening finery with friends at some evening dinner table, or in swimsuits lounging in the sun, cocktails in hand. They could have been stills from a film – Ivy and Austin were the perfect glamorous couple, daringly modern in the high fashion of the day and confidently extrovert in front of the camera. There was no denying his charismatic appeal – he was the tall dark man of Hollywood legend. No longer the young aristocrat of Mrs Irving's picture: with marriage to Ivy he had become a star.

'What do you know about the British Union of Fascists?' he asked, getting to the point, he hoped, at last.

'Oh, so you know about the Blackshirts too. I told him he was a silly bugger getting involved but he wouldn't listen – he enjoyed the excitement, the idiot.'

'Why did he join? Was he involved in politics?'

'No, it was just a bit of a game, like I told you. He said they were going to get the communists but I don't think he really cared who it was. He was after a fight, that's what turned him on you know.

142

They liked him for being posh and, of course, he could cut a dash. He was always good at that.'

'I thought they were against the Jews.'

'Oh I don't think so, dear. No more than a lot of people were in those days. I knew a lot of nice Jew boys before the war; there were always a lot of them in the entertainment business. I nearly married one once – God he was handsome too. I was a fool not to, and I can tell you there was nothing wrong with him. Austin thought he was being smart saying bad things about the Jews but I don't think he meant it, not really. I don't think he really cared one way or the other about anyone apart from himself.'

The more familiar he became through the pages of Ivy's album, the less Stephen understood Austin Randolph and the less he liked him. By now he knew the face well, but the man was receding further and further from his understanding. He declined a third whisky and persuaded Ivy to lend him the album.

'So you'll put pictures of me into your book. That's a good boy! The world should not forget old Ivy Cooper. I tell you, luvvie, on a good day I was up there with the best of them.'

Surreptitiously, with an uncertain sense of its symbolism, Stephen slipped a ten-pound note, Austin Randolph's money, onto the sideboard and left Ivy to finish the bottle. He walked home feeling disturbed, challenged and depressed. He had got so near to giving up the project and then this happened. He had been drawn to Ivy against his will and now he had found out that Emilia had lied to him. He called her from the phone box on the corner of his road; it took a long time for her to answer.

'I'm sorry, Stephen, but this is a bad time. I'm desperately packing and I'm off to France tomorrow for four weeks' holiday. It's the perk of being a school ma'am. Call me when I get back.'

Charming, as always, she managed to cut him off before he could even mention Ivy's name, but he knew her well enough to recognise the anxiety in her voice.

Forty-Four

Stephen, from an unusually early age, had felt that he was part of a historical chain. The links added up to his beloved, sometimes mystical, sometimes woolly concept of Western Civilisation. An inheritance that he felt was handed down to him personally by Michelangelo, Shakespeare and Beethoven – something that he had tried to honour above all things. However, he was humbled by it, inspired by its legacy and increasingly aware of his own ignorance of it. He believed that those three geniuses themselves were worthy of a lifetime's dedication and study. He could never know enough, read enough, experience enough; but it was the water he swam in, whether he liked it or not. Sometimes he basked in its warm depth; sometimes he was tossed against the rocks.

This cultural chain also kept him from falling into the chaos that he had often glimpsed fearfully in his worst depressions: a world where there were no lessons in the stones of ancient architecture, no messages in books, and no spiritual link with his saints – Michelangelo, Beethoven and Shakespeare. Without them, there was freefall and the terrors of the void, but with them too those terrors were never far from the surface. Until now he had always been careful to stay away from such a dangerous cliff-edge by keeping the past ever present in his daily life. Those three living dead men, plus the many more that he had discovered for himself in the pages of library books, comforted him and partially explained a confusing and alienating world to him.

Now, when he was trying to discover a life, he had to hide these thoughts from his friends and even from Dys, for it was something, he believed, that they would never share with him. Georges Villard had said that the world had been a long time dying – he had meant that his cultural world was ending and that a new age was dawning. People spoke of the Age of Aquarius; some even believed that it was dawning around them now in 1967.

Maybe Villard would have been more in sympathy with Dys and Mark, who refused to give any importance to Ancient Greeks, Romantic Poets or the Old Masters from the Italian Renaissance, finding them simply irrelevant to their lives and their hopes. They wanted to be free of history and the restrictions it imposed on them. They made sentimental exceptions for a select band of personal heroes like Marx, Buddha and Vincent van Gogh, as well as some liberal-minded novelists like DH Lawrence and Thomas Mann: modern minds, all of them, born into the wrong era and who, they were sure, would have joined them if they had been alive today. They wanted to start again, to create something entirely new, but Stephen suspected that their confidence was based on ignorance and that he would never be able to go the whole way with them.

Although no one was trying to stop him writing, and they all respected the power of words, he was hurt and insecure about their disapproval over his hankering for the past. Maybe he was not as secure in his love for his inheritance as he believed. Silence and tolerance descended whenever his book came up in conversation, eroding his energy in pursuing it and partly converting him to the idea of giving it up. When he was with Dys, he felt the joy of living for its own sake without putting himself continually into context. She was telling him simply to embrace the moment, and that maybe Austin Randolph and his love-damaged circle were relics from some old superstition that he had to outgrow.

Yet, with the smell of Ivy's flat still in his nostrils and Emilia's panic-stricken tone alerting him to secrets that he had not yet unravelled, he could not dismiss it all from his mind or ignore his need to finish the book. They too had had their moments of joy, more than he had ever had, and now their anguished voices were invading his happiness, warning him about his own life, eating away at his growing desire for spontaneity.

'What will you do when you grow old?' he asked when they were all gathered in Paul's room.

'I don't want to,' said Mark. 'I want to die feeling like I do now.'

'Won't that last until you're old?'

'I'd rather not risk it.'

Joints were passed round and Paul created the appropriate ambience with his sitar. As the drug soothed Stephen's gloom, he looked at his friends. He felt as close to them as anyone that he had known: it was the first time that he had been part of a group and he was grateful to all of them for putting up with his odd ways. Sitting next to him, their legs touching, Dys was silent and tranquil. He could feel the warmth of the blood circulating through her body

145

and yet he feared that she and all the others were really still strangers to him.

'Don't let it get you down,' said José in a gentle, concerned tone. 'We're all in it together.'

'I'm a long way behind you all,' said Stephen. 'I would like to get there. I really would, but something keeps anchoring me down.'

'Just stick with it, friend,' the Puerto Rican whispered, his gravelly voice floating on his breath. 'That's all you've got to do.'

'That's what's so difficult. For you it seems so easy, like in the song, but I don't think it is.'

'Just relax and it will come, man,' José said, passing him the joint. 'You can do it.'

'Of course you can,' said Dys, laughing knowingly. 'All you need is love.'

They all laughed – each fanning the others' hysteria and fuelling the narcotic's effect, until they collapsed back onto their cushions exhausted, with aching lungs and watering eyes. All of them except Paul of course, who continued to play a long sensuous line of melody, continually prolonging itself, avoiding its cadence, promising another existence beyond the mundane, and maybe beyond Stephen's imagination. Stephen carried on laughing, tears filling his eyes, his stomach contorting in spasm. He laughed but he knew that it was not funny. He was fighting himself over this and he felt very unsure of the outcome.

Forty-Five

'I thought you were dead,' said Dys when Stephen woke up the following afternoon. She was sitting next to him on the bed, bringing him back to consciousness, smoothly massaging his arm with trembling hands. Smelling of the sea, still wet from her swim, she was wearing a towel tucked tightly under her armpits, her hair up in combs, with traces of seaweed in her tangled curls. 'You were so depressed last night. I thought I was losing you.'

'I'm fine,' he replied, smiling at her and giving way to the now determined pressure of her fingers. She worked her way to his abdomen, further relaxing muscles soothed by long sleep.

'Do I cage you in?' she whispered in high seriousness. 'Sometimes I feel I do.'

'I quite like the cage,' he said, his words scarcely articulated on his breath as she smoothed the skin over his pubic bone.

'But sometimes you don't like it. I felt that last night. I felt that we were moving away from each other.' She pushed harder with each sentence, brutally gentle, her voice catching the hint of a sob. 'I thought that I was denying you your freedom, and this morning, while you were asleep, it was worse. I went down to the sea. I wanted to share it with you and I knew that I couldn't. I thought you'd gone, that I had driven you out and that we would never do this again. I was thinking about you and remembered that time when I groped you on the stairs. I was so mean to you in those days, I could feel your embarrassment but I just didn't care. I wanted to break through to you. You seemed so invincible, so untouchable. I needed to break through your defences. I suppose I still feel that even though now you've nothing I can't touch – nothing concealed. And yet still something keeps us apart, doesn't it? Last night I thought you might even hate me.'

Momentarily, she released him from her touch, sitting back on his thighs, taking all of him into her stare.

'I was confused,' he answered. 'I felt lost between two worlds.'

She went back to work – his muscles had tightened but her fingers were undoing the damage.

'You mean your book, don't you? I'm stopping you getting on with it; I'm stopping you being yourself. I want my freedom but I deny you yours – well, I want that to change. I've been thinking about it all day. I want to help you – even if it's only sharpening your pencils. I want you to tell me all about it even if it does mean talking about a load of creepy old people. Even if you bore the crap out of me!'

Now was not the time for talking – the massage had taken its course: he was gasping, unable to speak, but moved by her offer. Letting her towel drop, she sat astride him, taking him with her beyond conversation, beyond words even. Later, lying back with her beside him, he tried to let her into his solitude. Allowing her into his so studiously private mental life after she had given herself to him physically was the most challenging leap he had made yet.

Georges Villard, Austin Randolph, Emilia Jeffries and even Ivy Cooper – they were all furtive secrets that had never been mentioned in their life as a couple. He had always recognised them as forbidden fruits in Dys's present-tense universe. Breaking through that taboo enabled him to tell her not just about the book but, for the first time, to stumble towards telling her what it really felt like to be him. Lying naked on the bed, they celebrated the loss of his cerebral virginity. Now he really did have nowhere to hide.

Forty-Six

Mick, the pony-tailed elder statesman of their group had heard it from someone who knew someone at the Town Council. The Toadstool was on the bailiff's list and the squatters would have to go. A note telling them to leave was received a few days later and, in the spirit of peaceful resistance, Mick persuaded the others that it would be pointless trying to stay. In fact it would be counter-productive, even reactionary to do so. It was difficult for some of them to accept at first but Mick asserted his unofficial role as leader and it was decided, after a gradual show of hands to hold a large farewell party to which, of course, the bailiffs would be invited

'It would all be just too materialistic making a fuss about possessing the house – even if possession is nine tenths of the law,' Mick argued. 'We should prove that possessions mean nothing to us. If we can't live here – we'll live somewhere else so, instead of resisting, we should leave willingly – even joyfully.'

'That's fantastic!' Rosalie enthused. She had only just moved in with Mick after a very long period of what she herself described as hero-worship. She had created a mystically inspired love nest for them in his bedroom with plenty of psychedelic shades of hanging silk, Indian beadwork, copper incense holders and Buddhist statuary; she described it as Tibetan Brothel Chic and had been very upset by thoughts of its imminent destruction.

'There are plenty of empty houses,' said Mick. 'We'll just find another one. A house is no more important than an old coat. When it's worn out, you get a different one. No big deal.'

The initial depression lifted as the members of the house prepared for a farewell gathering. News went out on the underground network that there was to be a 'happening' at The Toadstool; Mick was vindicated and the eviction had been turned into a celebration. The partially successful vegetable patch at the back of the house was harvested for Rosalie to make the vegetarian buffet. She was disappointed that all her recipes turned into identical-looking mixtures, dull green in colour and sticky in texture, but there was an enormous quantity and no one would have to go hungry. José, demonstrating the loss he was to the American army, came back from a night raid with several boxes of

149

fireworks liberated from a local factory. Mick dragooned a number of the others into an all-night decorating job on the outside of the house. Remarkably, on the day of the party and the day before the bailiffs were due, the crumbling exterior plaster was covered in bright primary colours applied in haphazard stripes, spots and zigzags – Hove's first public psychedelic experience. The neighbours were outraged but passers-by were amused and a small crowd gathered in the street drawn to a notice that had been posted in the small front garden. 'Farewell Party at The Toadstool. Everyone welcome tonight. We love you all.'

All the regulars, except the marijuana dealer, arrived during the course of the evening but the invitation was not taken up by the local community who preferred to stay behind net curtains watching and waiting for what they assumed would be the inevitable riot.

Tranquillity and anticlimax was the mood inside as no more than twenty friends sat in a circle on the floor picking at Rosalie's cuisine and listening to the improvised music. Jo and Viv, wearing identical buff-coloured kaftans and wilted daisy chains around their necks began the entertainment, playing on their matching acoustic guitars – they were a musical duo now. The Id had broken up when the bass guitarist hitched to India on a pilgrimage of self-discovery. Always playing the bass line and standing at the back of the line-up had depressed him, Rosalie suggested with a giggle. The lead guitarist had left soon after.

'Well he was the spare prick at the wedding,' José pronounced, winking knowingly towards the remaining musicians. Without their band, Jo and Viv had discovered that they preferred playing together, just the two of them, performing their mutual love songs, singing in dreamy high-pitched voices and strumming together in close harmony. Stephen had still not plucked up enough courage to ask if they were male or female and who was which. Later they were joined by some of the others: Dys delicately pinged finger cymbals sitting in the lotus position, José slowly and earnestly shook a jam jar filled with dried lentils, Rosalie nervously tried out Paul's tabla and Paul himself led from the sitar tracing an unbroken line which the others struggled to compliment. Homemade candles, joss sticks, cigarettes and joints filled the room with smoke and

150

perfume. Stephen watched Dys but listened to Mark who was arguing with Mick about the need for militant action.

'We're just lying down waiting to be trodden on,' he was saying. 'This is fine. I support you on this but, as a group, we're too passive. Too self-indulgent. Christ! There's a war going on, in Vietnam but also here, there's a class war, man, and what are we doing to stop it? What can we do?'

'We can have events like this,' said Mick morosely. 'We can show that there is another way. Don't underestimate the power of social non-cooperation. We're frightening people by showing them that their much-loved social order is about to be thrown out by a new generation who don't want any of it. We're going to inherit the Earth, man. These world rulers are old men, all of them. One day they are going to die and their rules and prejudices are going to die with them. That's what we're preparing for. We are building the alternative way and the old people are frightened. So they should be.'

'But we're not building enough,' Mark protested. 'We need to bring more people in with us. We can't just wait for some ideal time in the future – people are dying in Vietnam. They've been dying in wars, nuclear explosions, in capitalist-inspired famines, in prisons and death camps since before we were born. If we're not against it we're supporting it. We have to bring people to us. We have to persuade people like Stephen here that it's no good just sitting around discussing the tragic history of mankind – I tell you, man, if we don't change it, it will change us.'

'What do you want me to do?' said Stephen.

Mark's answer was lost as the music staggered to a standstill. Paul had been gradually turning paler as the improvisation progressed; his playing had grown wilder and increasingly discordant; gradually the other players had abandoned their instruments unable to keep up with him. Paul continued strumming his sitar, pounding it violently and shaking it as if he couldn't get enough volume from it. Then it became too much for him and he threw it down, holding his head in obvious agony. He looked desperately at the others with terror on his face as blood squirted from his mouth and nostrils and he lost control of his body in a frenzied spasm. Wriggling, limbs flailing wildly, he was calling for help, but only inhuman guttural sounds expressed his desperation;

with eyes bulging, he fell to the floor then his body slumped, limp and immobile. Mark too went deathly pale, ran over to him and cushioned him in his arms, sobbing and rocking him like a baby. No one moved, they were frozen in shock. Everyone knew that Paul was dead.

An ambulance followed by a police car arrived noisily in the street, giving the neighbours what they had been expecting and, without admitting it, what they had been hoping for. It would always end like this: hippies and their drugs and their other unspeakable habits, it was bound to end in tragedy. No one was surprised; it was what all the papers had predicted; it was what they had all said would happen. For all their expressions of horror there was relief along the street when the squat ended violently. It would be several months before the coroner confirmed that Paul had died of a brain haemorrhage but no one believed that he had died from natural causes. Paul, the gentle musician, had died the death of a degenerate. Something like that was bound to happen in a 'hippie house'.

Forty-Seven

Paul was given a decent Christian burial – inappropriate for a devout Buddhist but reassuring for the parents who insisted on it. He was praised by the local vicar as a dutiful son and as a bright hope for the future, tragically cut short in his prime. The ceremony, from Cranmer's sixteenth-century prayer book, and the burial, in a picturesque country churchyard, were in a small village in County Durham. None of his friends were invited, not even Mark who had locked himself into their bedroom hiding away in his grief. None of them even knew that Paul had been born in the North East – he had never talked about his past. The sitar and a small cardboard box of clothes had been collected by Paul's grandly cold parents who packed them into the back of their ostentatiously large red car, ignoring the shocked faces of their son's friends.

They would not accept Mark's special relationship with their boy either, or his right to mourn him. There was a hint of accusation when they found that there was so little to collect – their Paul had died years ago and they had never understood his wish for a possession-free journey to Nirvana. The sitar would sit in melancholy state in Paul's childhood bedroom along with the football posters and model aeroplanes from uncomplicated schoolboy days. When they had gone, José produced the fireworks that had never been used on the fatal night. Paul's real funeral was held on the beach, his life celebrated with rockets exploding over the sea and silver starbursts in the midnight sky. Only then did Mark decide that he could join in with the ceremony and allow his tears to flow in public.

The death changed things: The Toadstool had ended and the squatters dispersed. Mick and Rosalie moved to a rented flat paid for by Rosalie's work as a waitress. Jo and Viv gradually fell out of love with each other but were spotted by a record company scout and groomed for stardom, recording their love songs whilst repressing their mutual disdain. Gradually they became famous and were claimed as their own by Brighton's growing homosexual underworld, and they would always turn out for parties and talk fondly of their 'hippie days' to the musical press. Later Jo came out as a woman to everybody's confusion.

José moved into Gresham Villas, sharing Paul's old room with Mark who was frightened of living alone. Everyone kept an eye on Mark who became increasingly introverted. The rent had to come from Mark's university grant when Paul's parents cancelled their payment after finding out that, unwittingly, they had been paying the rent on the whole house for years, paying for everyone except Stephen who now agreed to take on the financial responsibility. It was a good use of Austin Randolph's cheque. Money was then forgotten and Gresham Villas settled down to a new routine.

Dys cried for twelve hours after Paul died; she wrapped herself tightly in a sheet and threw herself around the brass bed in near convulsions. Stephen couldn't calm her. He sat in silence watching her agony, looking out for her safety. She had controlled her fits by the time Paul's parents arrived but she was a spectral presence at the fireworks night. She clung sexlessly to Stephen in bed, stayed close to him whenever they were out and resisted any form of communication. If Stephen tried to talk to her, her eyes would fill with tears and she would crumple into his arms. For two weeks she clung to him – never letting him leave her – and then, one morning, he woke up to find that she had gone.

He was used to her disappearances; they were part of her personality, her fear of being tied down or having to explain herself. This time felt different however. She had been ill, depressed and frightened by Paul's death and Stephen was worried. No one had seen her and even the all-knowing Rosalie looked concerned. Gradually his anxiety turned to a cold feeling of repressed panic when he ran out of places to look. He was already grieving her loss as he repeatedly tried to convince himself that she was going to return at any moment.

He walked along the promenade, trying to stay calm, looking for her among the meandering holidaymakers; he visited all the places that they had been to, invoking memories of their time together, upsetting himself all the more and increasing his sense of fear. Fear for her and fear for himself – it was as if she had been amputated from his body, he could feel her phantom presence but the wound, he thought, would never congeal. Tired, dejected and emotionally turbulent, he returned to the house convinced that she had left him. Unable to face their bedroom when he found that it was still

154

empty, he went, for the first time in weeks, back to his own room in the attic.

There she was; sitting surrounded by his papers, photographs of Austin Randolph, letters supplied by Emilia Jeffries, Ivy Cooper's albums, newspaper cuttings and his own notebooks. She jumped impetuously into his arms when he came in – they hugged with an intensity that bordered on suffocation. They were both in tears when they loosened their grip.

'I've been through it all. Do you mind? I did tell you that I said I wanted to help you.'

'I'm amazed,' he admitted, unashamedly showing his happiness. 'I thought I had lost you. I never thought you'd come up here.'

'To your dusty old bachelor's pad, you mean? Well, if I have to love you, crusty old academic as you are, I guess I'm going to have to understand all this, aren't I?'

She never mentioned Paul again. Instead she gave herself up to sifting through papers and journals, helping him chronicle the sketchy history of Austin Randolph and his circle.

'They led Hollywood lives,' she said when she had read Austin and Emilia's correspondence. 'I'm sure that they were in love and everything but it all sounds so artificial in their letters. So dusty, so conventional somehow. It makes them sound like children play-acting. Using grown-up words for love but not thinking about what it really means. I wouldn't want people reading my letters years afterwards – I think you have to say what you mean now and get on with it. Why did they keep everything like this? So that some hippie boy could sit around reading their thoughts. I would hate that – I'd hate to be remembered as the person who hoarded a few smelly bits of yellowy paper. What they had is gone – that's all. Anyway, I don't really care about being remembered.'

'That sounds very harsh,' said Stephen.

'Does it? I'm sorry. I don't mean to but I agree with Mark. We wallow around in all our yesterdays and there's no point. It doesn't make you happy does it?'

He felt she was starting to attack him again so he changed the subject. 'Poor Mark. You know I never realized they were lovers.'

'Yes, poor Mark. He has to get over his past now. My poor innocent Stephen, you didn't know? I do love you for your innocence. Never lose it, promise me that.'

They went back to work on the papers. Among them there was an unopened letter from Philip Irving. He had written to say that his mother had found some documents that she wanted to give to Stephen. The letter had been lying in his room for weeks and Dys took this as proof that she was ruining his work.

'You love all this, I know that, you love all these old documents, relics and everything,' she said. 'Just because I can't see the point doesn't mean that I can't help you. You must carry on with it because it's what you want to do. It's who you are and what you're good at.'

They agreed that he should go back to Frampton House and that she would go too.

Forty-Eight

They are German enough – by adoption, by choice, partly by blood and mostly by convenience. Austin and Emilia hug motionlessly in the Schiller Park in Berlin for a very long time in that winter of 1936. On a cold Prussian day they are frozen in time like a statue by Rodin, standing there oblivious to everything else in their black winter coats, their breath rising like smoke over their heads. They ignore everyone in the frost-crisp park, even the soldiers marching in procession, boots harsh on the grit. They have escaped; they are liberated and together again. The English rose and her Hollywood man have found their freedom in a militarised state. They are lovers touring Berlin, taking in the sights but lost in each other – General von Öchen's grandchildren, these loving cousins are German enough.

Marching men, all equal, part of a whole, all committed to one cause, one country, the Fatherland, his maternal grandfather's land. No more begging, no more favours, no longer the servant's boy, the rent boy, the gigolo, Austin Randolph can be a hero at last.

Forty-Nine

'Tie it all up. Hurry, my scribe. Expose it all. See how they twitch when I call. They cling to my boots as I march away. Write it all down, the pain and the tears, their bitter souvenirs.'
Austin Randolph, Tung Ping Chau, August 1967

Equipped with new rucksacks, bought with Austin's money, they travelled to Huntingdonshire Dys's way – by hitching. At remarkable speed, due to Dys's canny proficiency in the art of picking up lifts, they completed the journey in a day with the help of two articulated lorries, a very uncomfortable two-seater sports car and an old van full of secondhand television sets. On each occasion Stephen had stayed out of sight while Dys stood, pleadingly and beguilingly, by the roadside. Chivalrous drivers were consistently disappointed when Stephen appeared with their rucksacks but Dys entertained them with a thick Eastern European accent telling them preposterous stories about how they were cousins from Yugoslavia trying to trace their ancestors who had left Belgrade for England three hundred years ago.

It was late afternoon when they walked down the lane to Frampton House. With no rock festival attracting the crowds, the village was getting on with its own life. An old woman with swollen legs trudged past with her basket full of greengroceries, a man in a dirty grey suit and flat cap greeted them from his sturdy black bicycle, a plump woman in a flowery overall retrieved her washing from the line in a cottage garden full of gladioli and lavender bushes while her collie dog ran after them barking until they reached the gates of the big house. Dys pushed her arm between the straps of Stephen's rucksack and hugged him as they kicked up dust from the sun-baked tarmac.

'Do you think we should retire to the country?' she said. 'I would do all your washing and ironing and you could do the vegetable plot.'

'I don't see you as the washerwoman sort,' Stephen replied dozily happy in the heat of the day. He was thinking about all the changes in his life since that solitary journey of only months before.

158

'I see you as more of a goose girl. Geese would love you. You could keep them all under control and they'd follow you everywhere.'

'Yes, I could do that,' she said, but her joyfulness had turned doleful. 'Did you know that they pair for life? When one partner dies, the other goes into mourning. They even get lines under their eyes.'

The collie unearthed a rabbit and chased after it across a field as they opened the gate and carried on up the long drive. Dys tightened her grip; Stephen could feel her shudder when the rabbit's death cry struck its desolate note.

'I won't have to say anything, will I?' She had begun to sound frightened again. 'I'm only here to be with you. I don't care about talking to them; I would rather not get involved. That *is* alright isn't it?'

'Of course,' he replied, squeezing her waist and glad that, this time, he was no longer alone.

'The weather's made your hair grow,' said Philip, after the awkwardly formal introduction of Dys. They were not going to be friends. Dys shrank into her private space and Philip focused on Stephen. 'It suits you longer – very modern – and the beard is very fetching too.'

This time there were no drinks downstairs; Philip took them straight up to Mrs Irving's room.

'Mother has been sorting out some papers and things for you. You've come just in time, she's not been so well since your last visit and she sleeps a lot of the time. Don't stay with her too long, will you? She gets very tired.'

He poked his head round the door before showing them in. 'Stephen Dearsley is here to see you, Mother. Are you decent?' His boisterous, nursemaid tone turned to a whisper as he ushered them through. 'Come down for a drink when you've finished,' he added ominously. 'There'll be things that you will want to ask.'

The darkened room had not changed since his last visit but Mrs Irving had grown very frail. She was propped up in bed wearing a black lace bed jacket with her white hair hanging loose around her shoulders. She waved her bony ring-covered hand in greeting, beckoning Stephen to sit on the bed. Dys smiled shyly and took a chair in the shadows.

'So you've got yourself a pretty girl!' the old lady laughed with that high fluty voice that sounded as if it had come from another century. Stephen could hear the hint of German now that he knew more about her. 'She's done you good, you don't look nearly so solemn and serious. You've done a good job, my dear.'

The bed was strewn with papers and Mrs Irving's hands hovered over them as if she was wondering where to begin. She had spent the time since Stephen's visit sorting through boxes of documents that Philip had carried up from the cellars for her. She had found Austin's birth certificate and his adoption papers when he took the name of his new father and became Austin Randolph Irving. There were some letters from Emilia and Mrs Jeffries written to thank Mrs Irving for various summer holidays at Frampton. Emilia's childish hand listed the main attractions – riding with Austin, swimming with Austin, playing hide and seek with Austin and having picnics with the whole family.

Most interesting of all were the photographs. Yellow with age, often torn or bent round the edges, they documented Austin's childhood and early manhood. Certainly he was handsome, with a dark swarthy complexion, large, heavily-lidded eyes and the easy photographic laugh so often found in pictures of wartime heroes or the romantic idols from vintage American films. Also, unmistakably, there was that wild expression that had been described by the people who had known him. Unlike the others in the group photographs, he loved the camera and radiated confidence in front of it.

Blond-haired Emilia, still in her teens, had a soft shy beauty as she stood coyly next to her sturdy Teutonic mother. Mrs Irving, more beautiful and assured than her sister, wore dark satins and silks and, bizarrely, in all the photographs, while the others looked into the lens, she was always staring intently at Austin. Mr Irving, showing signs of the premature senility that would make these pictures the last records of an uneventful post-war life, hid behind the masculine trappings of a country gentleman – thick grey beard, tweeds and knobbly walking stick.

Philip Irving was there too, but here he was not the bulky presence of the man waiting for them downstairs. Slight, with nervous squinting eyes and a small thin smile, he was limply effeminate next to his virile brother. In one picture, the two of them were caught after a swim in their waterlogged woollen swimming trunks – Austin's proud pubescence contrasting comically with Philip's childish frame. As they stood together, probably at the pond in Frampton Park, Austin grinned towards the camera, holding out a frog for inspection while Philip, with quiet tenderness, gazed at his brother with a look and an intensity inherited from his mother.

'You will make good use of them, I know,' Mrs Irving said as she put them all into a box. She took Stephen's hand in both of hers and squeezed hard.

'I could have sent them to you, I know. You know that too, I'm sure. You must know that I didn't ask you here just to give you these. I'm an old and very impatient woman – much too old for my own liking. And I am still an old fool for Austin. Whatever he's done, I don't want to die without knowing what has happened to him. Can you understand that? Ever since you came here I've been wondering: why a book? All I can think is that he must have got into trouble and I just can't leave it alone. It's terrible sitting up here all these years not knowing what happened to your child. You know that he was my son and my joy. I don't want to die like this, so please, you must help me. I truly believe that you will.'

She renewed her grip on his hand to show that there would be no refusing her. Stephen knew that there was not much to say but he tried to comfort her with reassuring generalities. He had hardly begun when she cut across him, her arms gesticulating wildly.

'Emilia took him back to Germany. There! I've told you!' She interrupted him with this information, not wanting to hear anything but facts. Her eyes had the large moist blue pupils of old age, giving her a romantic look made desperate by her yearning.

'They went to my parents' house in Berlin, but later, in 1945 as you know, Berlin was not the place to be. Everywhere was bombed. Emilia had gone by then but my parents and Austin disappeared. Under the rubble or so I used to think. But you tell me different. You say he is in Hong Kong. Well, I want you to go there. To see him and to find out what has happened to him. I want you to tell me, do you hear? Before it is too late. It all depends on you. On you going to Hong Kong.'

161

'I shall go there,' Stephen said, quietly putting his other hand on hers. 'He has invited me. I shall definitely go and I will tell you what I find. I promise.'

Margaret Irving lay back on her pillows with a tired smile of relief and Stephen let her hands rest on the bedspread. Involuntarily he patted them, noticing the vulnerable raised veins dark with the blood that was still pumping through her frail body. He had grown so used to Dys's young translucent flesh that the sight made him shudder, prophetically disturbed by the contrast.

'It was all because I loved him, you see. That should be forgiven, don't you agree? It was not such a sin, was it?'

She carried on muttering as she fell asleep. Stephen turned round to find Dys – she was sitting quietly, paler than the old lady and with tears glistening on her face.

Fifty

'Poor old tart!' Philip said, offering them glasses of water – Stephen and Dys had turned down his homemade gin and tonic. While he had been getting the drinks, they sat silently in the living room looking out over the parkland at the rows of lime trees with their yellowing leaves. There was something cruel about the season change, nature flaunting its power, warning them about things unspoken. Harsh cries from the resident crows carried over the lawn, now an unmown field, celebrating Frampton House's desolation and anticipating its return to the wild.

'She's worried about him for all these years and now she'll never know the truth.' Philip pronounced pontifically from his armchair after an enthusiastic mouthful of gin.

'What do you mean?' Stephen asked, putting his hand on Dys's knee.

'She's on her way out, I'm afraid, as you can probably tell. It's strange that you can hate someone all your life and when they reach their dotage, there's nothing left to hate. I even admire her in a way – indomitable spirit and all that.'

'Is she really that ill?' said Dys.

'Oh yes. The doctor says that her heart will pack in any day now – in fact she should be dead already. That's why I wrote to you – she's talked of nothing else except you and your blessed book ever since you left. She's taken quite a shine to you, poor old love.'

He was talking to Stephen but his eyes darted lizard-like towards Dys every few moments, as if he was trying to work out why she was there. Dys's presence, her intensity as much as her femininity, inhibited him in his reminiscences. Intuitively, she asked if she could go for a walk in the grounds.

'Of course, my dear. You'll be quite alone, no marauding boy scouts around this time of the year. The hostel isn't doing that well actually – there's been no one here for weeks.'

Letting her out through the French windows, Philip waited, watching her walk away towards the trees before saying anything. 'Emilia didn't tell you that we were married then?' he said suddenly as if the very process of saying it gave him pain. 'I suppose she thought it wasn't relevant.'

'No, she didn't,' Stephen responded with feigned cool, but he was stung by the surprise, the shock and by Emilia's skill in selecting which truths he should learn and how little she had really trusted him. That same old capacity to surprise seemed very near to trickery, telling him that he was naïve to believe any of them. Unprofessionally, he was also hurt. He had thought that Emilia had tried to be his friend.

'Maybe it wasn't relevant. Well, we did. We tied the knot and made everyone very happy, I don't think! But we did the deed and little good it did any of us.' Philip had slumped back into his well-worn armchair during these revelations, reinforcing his new rush of truthfulness with another swig of gin.

'It was when she came back from Germany at the beginning of the war. She was interned with her mother and my mother-dear — they did that to all the Germans, during the war — especially with Austin's history. She got very depressed — I would have too, being locked up with her mother! God how that woman talked! I suppose I was pretty down too. I'd gone into the Air Force — didn't get on too well with regimental life, if you know what I mean. Well, I guess when we knew how things were going, we propped each other up, Emilia and me.

'It was as if we wanted to try living the life we were meant to live, the life we would have had if we had not been who we were and if Austin had never been born. In other words, it was a sham. Pitiful really. Maybe we had just given up on love. We went to Germany as soon as the war was over too. Did Emilia tell you that? I suppose we were both hoping to find Austin again — unchanged, the man he had been before. We found no trace, of course, but our grandparents were dead. We saw the remains of their home. They and the family house were wiped out — I expect one of my old Air Force chums did that. So, that was when we fell back on the original plan, Emilia and I — we were always meant to be married after all. Mother and Aunt Julietta had always planned it that way until Austin messed up their little scheme, of course. Mother so hated the idea of Emilia marrying Austin. It was quite pathological.'

Another refill of gin unlocked his discretion even more and the conversation took on the tone of a confession.

'We both missed him so much, you see. I suppose I had always loved him — he was my brother, of course, but he was more than that. Nothing happened, don't get me wrong, but if he had wanted it, I would have done it. No question about that. He was the undoing of me really.'

Philip sat lumpenly fingering the rim of his glass, watching his own circle-making with exaggerated interest and gulping back his emotion.

'What did you mean by Austin's history?' Stephen asked when Irving had regained some control.

'So Emilia didn't tell you that either? How very discrete! Oh, Austin liked a bit of excitement, as you know. He messed around, even Emilia failed to keep him on his leash, and the family had ousted him after he got some poor cow pregnant. They got rid of the kid and Emilia went back to Mama. I'm surprised she didn't tell you all this. You know, I am sure, that he fell into bad company. He would have found it all very exciting, I think. London life with Emilia gone had its compensations. He knew he could charm the ladies and loosen their tight little fingers from their purses so he made a living, got to know people, mixed in posh circles, that sort of thing. That's how he fell in with the Mosley lot. The Blackshirts – the British fascists. I thought you would have found out about all this.'

'I think everyone has been trying to hide it from me,' said Stephen, wryly accepting his own incompetence. 'But I did know about the Blackshirts.'

'Well, it was very much the thing for some. We were all a bit anti-semitic in those days, I think. Well, round here there weren't any Jews – nobody whose family hadn't been here for centuries – solidly Anglo-Saxon, us lot. Everyone apart from Mother, of course. She is Prussian to the core! So you could dislike the Jews without offending anyone. You could be anti-anything if you liked around here – as long as you were loyal to Frampton and the idea of good old England! In London it was different, of course. Austin loved all the excitement – he could go hunting again, that's how he saw it, and he loved that. Of course he did. Oddly enough, he wasn't against the Jews or anyone else really – he just liked the danger. I remember that he was beside himself; he was so exhilarated after the East End punch-ups. It may sound perverted, but, I have to admit to you that it was that spark in his eye that I loved too, the killer instinct in him. We all loved that, if we were

165

honest. I know I did. We were all mad about Austin, ridiculous isn't it? Then he got all muddled up with that drunken old soak, Ivy Cooper; some washed up stripper or something, I forget what she did, but something in the entertainment business. Emilia, of course, came to the rescue. She could forgive him anything. She did it over and over again.'

'I met Ivy Cooper,' Stephen said, trying to gain some credibility. 'She lives in Brighton now.'

'I know. I sent you the information on her. I assumed that Emilia wouldn't want you to know any of the salacious bits. I guess Ivy filled you in though! God knows what the world will think of us if you ever publish. It's typical of Austin that he wants to drag us all into this again. I suppose he wants his revenge.'

'What for?'

'Oh, you know. Rage against his bastardy. Against Mother's obsession, the family's betrayal. I suppose even what you could call my unhealthy devotion. He wants to take us all with him I'm sure. That's what I think. Well, I've got used to the idea now; I won't blame you if you tell the whole story – whatever that may be. In fact, I would quite like everyone to know the truth. Mother will have no objections either – she'll be well out of it by then.'

Another round of gin sent the conversation plummeting into maudlin incoherence and it was not long before Stephen took the opportunity to go. He went to the French windows and said his thanks as he stepped outside. Philip was now too drunk and too upset to notice or care.

Walking towards the waiting lime trees with the rucksacks and the metal box of photographs, Stephen watched the crows circling in the evening sky – the chill of autumn deepened his depression. He had lied to Irving and said that they were booked into the local inn. He was following his instinct to leave, to get away and to avoid too much emotional involvement with Austin's desolate witnesses. Also, he wanted to protect Dys from the oppressive mood of the house. She was where he knew she would be – sitting on a tree trunk by the pond. No longer the golden pool of high summer, it was dark and damp and buzzing with desperate insects instinctively acknowledging their winter extinction. Sitting down silently, he hugged her. It was obvious that she had been crying.

'It was so awful,' she said without looking up. 'It was all so long ago but they are still tormented by it. What makes people love like that? It's not what we call love, is it? It does no good – it only stops them living. That's not what love is supposed to be. I couldn't bear that.'

She started to sob, pressing her face into his chest, needing his body, his young body, not his words for comfort. He too drew consolation from her body; she was so fresh and warm, too beautiful to wrinkle and decay. She spoke to him of eternity – the eternity of the moment.

Fifty-One

They pitched their tent out of sight of the house, slept huddled in each other's arms and awoke cold, shivering and dew-soaked to a sunny September morning.

'I don't believe I can be so cold and so happy at the same time,' Dys said, kissing Stephen's icy lips.

They bathed breathlessly in the pond, laughing at such a series of body shocks and repeatedly hugging each other joyously in an attempt to gather even the smallest hints of each other's body warmth. Laughing, they dried each other tenderly but hurriedly with their shirts before breakfasting on the season's first crop of blackberries. Still shivering and naked, they lay on the grassy bank, clinging together, warming each other with each other, laughing uncontrollably at their own foolishness and looking up at the sky as a small aeroplane weaved thin white patterns in the blue, its metallic body sparkling like a daytime star.

'We wouldn't need a revolution if everyone found the world's natural rhythm,' Stephen said, watching a small shiny beetle crawl single-mindedly over his bare chest. 'You never see neurotic beetles – it's all just food, survival and sex to them and there's not much wrong with that.'

'Shall we do it then?' sighed Dys. 'Let's find a ditch somewhere near here and just live like beetles, or maybe like creatures that eat blackberries or even blackberry pie. Yes pie and custard – I'm not sure about beetle food.'

'Quite,' said Stephen his laugh disappearing as he looked through the trees. 'Or maybe we should just go.' He had seen an ambulance speed its way up to Frampton House.

'It'll be the old lady, I know,' Dys whispered as she dressed in a hurry.

They crossed the country in a series of short car journeys, almost on the run from those memories of the Irving household. They were not alone that season, young Britain was on the move and they met fellow travellers at almost every dropping-off point. At times they joined long queues of hitchers even on remote country roads, spending hours in convivial ditch-side conversations about cross-country adventures. It was the end of the hippie summer and

168

young people were returning from journeys across Britain, Europe and beyond. They met hitchhikers from all over the world – some on their way back to other continents, some coming home and some neither arriving nor leaving, just journeying for the joy of it.

A commercial traveller selling plastic kitchen utensils across southern England told them how much he envied them their freedom and how, one day, he would pack this in and hitch to Tibet and beyond. Dropping them off at a garage, he continued his journey to the hundreds of small shops that would either buy his wares or not, but who would probably never about know his fantasies.

'I'm sure that they could use washing-up brushes in Tibet,' Dys said as they watched him drive off.

'I'm beginning to think that we're half-way to Tibet ourselves,' said Stephen. 'We're miles off route for Brighton.'

'Yes but well on our way to Salisbury,' Dys responded slyly. 'I want you to meet my friends.'

After another night in a ditch, they got a lift in a lorry all the way to Salisbury. From its high cockpit, they had a wonderful view of the open road, sitting next to the driver, grinning at each other, exhilarated by the primeval attraction of the countryside still luxuriating in its own burgeoning autumnal abundance. Hampshire was bringing in its harvest from the golden dry fields along their way and the driver, converted by their enthusiasm, became their guide, pointing out the perfect Gothic spire of Salisbury Cathedral as it came into view behind miles of open fields.

Stephen felt a surge of emotion and imagined that this is what it must have looked like centuries ago as travellers made their way cross-country to the ancient city. He wondered if even the most impressionable of those long-dead adventurers could match the excitement he felt right there, sitting in that cockpit next to his girl in that vehicle packed with washing machines and tumble-dryers for very modern Hampshire households. As usual, everywhere he went he studied the layers of history revealed in his surroundings. Now these observations mingled with a thrilling sense of new adventures in the making.

The lorry left them on the outskirts of the city but Dys knew the way and, without a pause, she insisted on almost pulling him onwards in her excitement. They made their way through narrow streets, drawn on by Dys who was now constantly competing with the sights that clamoured for Stephen's attention. The architecture, for him, described Salisbury's history; the Middle Ages met the eighteenth century and moved on into the nineteenth in buildings jostling together, almost shouting their stories at him and tempting him with their tales of continuity.

History would never leave him, he knew that as he tried to absorb the essence of this archetypal English market town. Salisbury would have been the ideal environment for the unreconstructed, bookish Stephen, but now he had to hide his reluctance as Dys, ignoring the architecture, sped him past shops smelling of leather and freshly-ground coffee, past the cathedral itself standing in its lawn-covered square, glorifying reason as much as God. He felt a guilty sense of well-being in the solid permanency of civilisation and wanted to confess it and to linger in the cathedral's Gothic cloisters as the cathedral bells chimed the hour, but Dys was still rushing on ahead and soon, much too soon for him, they had left the city centre behind far them.

'We're here!' she shouted excitedly when they turned into the driveway of a blackened Victorian mansion. A hand-painted sign read: Wessex House. It looked like a residential home for the elderly.

Fifty-Two

The door was unlocked and they went in without signalling their arrival. Far from being a rest home for the elderly, Wessex House was empty. The wide entrance hall with white walls and a black and white marble floor was clean, with a strong smell of what Stephen assumed was disinfectant – it was totally unfurnished. They went through a large newly-painted white door into another large empty room; this was also painted white and had a floor of highly polished wooden floorboards. White was obviously important here. When they closed the door there was total silence.

'They must have gone,' said Stephen.

Dys didn't answer. She went through another door that had been jammed open.

'They can't hear us, that's all,' she whispered.

She walked, almost tiptoeing, to a pair of large oak doors at the other end of this inner room and pressed her ear to them. Looking at Stephen, she grinned and put a finger to her mouth.

'We must be very quiet. They're in here. Come in and do what I do.'

They entered and found themselves in almost total darkness. When their eyes adjusted they could see another long, wood-panelled space that must have been a dining room but now, like the other rooms, was completely bare. Its wooden floor was painted black, as was the glass in the large casement windows. The only light came from a small group of no more than five or six small red candles and, by these flames, Stephen could make out the figures of nine people sitting in a circle on the floor. His eyes were now accustomed to this new environment and he could see that they wore simple white cotton shifts over their ordinary clothes. Barefooted, they were sitting cross-legged with closed eyes and hands uniformly placed on their knees. They were intoning in a low murmur – the sound never increasing or decreasing in a unison that sounded as if it had been practised many times before.

Dys sat down at a distance from them and Stephen did the same, but soon regretted taking a cross-legged position when he realised that they were to be there for a very long time. Dys began to hum gently in time with the others; he tried to follow her but felt ridiculous and embarrassed even in the darkness, so he kept the sound to an inaudible breath, feeling like an intruder. Gradually, though, he became attuned to the collective voice and his stiffness softened as the sound began a long diminuendo towards silence. Time was suspended; nobody moved, he too became lost in the moment before movement returned, bodies flexed and came to life. Sporadically and silently they got to their feet, these monk-like men and women, and individually they left the room quietly and solemnly without looking at each other. Dys got up when the others had gone and led Stephen by the hand out through the doors to a room that dazzled him with its brightness.

The outer room was, yet again, painted white but this time furnished with dozens of large colourful cushions with geometric patterns in pillar-box red, purple, orange and green. When his eyes got used to the contrast, Stephen saw a tall long-haired, bearded man coming towards them. Wearing jeans, a checked open neck shirt and brown working boots He was the blond, rugged and gently smiling Jesus of Victorian paintings.

'I'm sorry that you missed it all,' he said, obviously recognising Dys. 'It was very powerful today.'

'I've brought a friend,' said Dys. 'Stephen, this is Andrew.'

'Welcome,' said Andrew. 'Spend us much time with us as you want.'

As the solemnity of their meditation wore off, the members of the group, now in their everyday clothes, denim jeans, brown and white checked cotton shirts and brown working boots, just like Andrew's, filtered back into the white room as if they had all come from different directions. Everyone was obviously happy to see Dys again; they hugged and kissed her before they all settled on the cushions, passing round mugs of iced tea. Dys, beaming with pride and affection, introduced them all to Stephen. Later she told him more about their previous lives before they had been drawn together by Andrew's muscular charisma.

They may have retreated from the world but Stephen thought that they still personified this brave new age that he was only just beginning to understand. Anna, a dark, big-boned woman with long brown hair tied in a ponytail was in her mid-twenties and had been a teacher until she met Andrew. When she joined the group she brought her friend Julia, a nurse, a ruddy-faced extrovert with hair of tight golden curls cut in a short boyish style. Monica, a small almond-faced woman with long straight, oriental hair was also in her twenties; she had worked in a clothes boutique in Carnaby Street, London's newly fashionable centre, and had come to Wessex House with her boyfriend, Will, who had given up his job as a car mechanic. He had grown his black hair and his beard long and had given up everything from his former life except his taste for oily machines. His work had indelibly stained his thick brown fingers with a black graininess, identifying him as a practical man in aesthetic company.

Beautiful golden-skinned Allie had worked as a trainee hair-dresser and receptionist as a money-earner to pay for the English part of her world tour. She was Australian, with a qualification from an agricultural college in Queensland, but she had abandoned her travel plans and had joined Wessex House with her boyfriend Dave, who had worked in the London parks growing plants for municipal flowerbeds. Besides a shared taste in horticulture, they were both black belts in one of the more obscure Japanese martial arts and, consequently, their bodies were bulgingly muscular and toned to peak condition. Dave, thick bearded like all the other males, had introduced his friend Carl to the others.

Once a carpenter's apprentice in Burnley, Carl had always dreamed of making beautiful things but he had dropped out of regular work to come south, drawn by the much-publicised activities of 'Swinging London'. He was slighter than the others, with delicate features and cornflower blue eyes and a rudely sensuous mouth that often got him into unintended situations. His straight blond hair was tied back with an elastic band and his matching beard hung down to his chest in sparkling golden wisps. Carl's looks had found him temporary fulfilment taking advantage of London's many opportunities for promiscuity and decadence but things had turned sour long before Dave found him broke and homeless in the park, sleeping rough by one of his ornamental displays of scarlet geraniums and salvias.

The final member of the group was tall, slightly muscled Lawrence who was an electrical engineer who had worked in a recording studio. Now a cropped-haired man in his late twenties, he had worked on an album that Andrew had recorded at the height of his fame as a rock musician. Andrew it seemed had been a star. With its psychedelic message and hauntingly strange production effects, the record had sold in millions and become one of the most influential albums of the times. Its unexpected success had introduced Andrew to the life of a rock star that earned him a great deal of money, which in turn, led to his retreat from the world.

Andrew had written songs about an imagined perfect community, freed from the pressures of money, class and sexual elitism. He had recorded them: his folk-singer's voice and simply strummed acoustic guitar mixed with multiple layers of psychedelic sound effects and a gentle battery of African drums. His utopian dream had sparked a reaction in the record buying public; his album sold so well that he earned more than he would ever need in dream-fulfilment money. Like St Francis of Assisi, his Sunday school hero, he wanted to give everything away so that he could live a life without materialistic distractions. All his money, along with much smaller amounts, token and democratising investments from the others' savings, had been put into buying The Wessex Centre and establishing the commune, a latter-day but very secular Franciscan order. Everyone was to give their expertise as well as their money, there were to be no personal possessions, no hierarchies and, it was hoped, no taboos.

'No one believes that we can do it,' said Andrew, taking Stephen out into the gardens while Dys caught up on the news with her friends.

'We plan to be totally self-sufficient. We have all the skills needed to create our own community and to let it grow. In the short term we have had to use our own money – money earned in the straight world, I know, but we started in the straight world so it's only fair to use its resources to help us leave it. I know what all the cynics think and I don't care. We are earning our freedom and it's hard work.'

There were several acres of gardens at the back of the house. A substantial part had been cultivated into methodical plots for vegetables, fruit and flowers; there were soft fruit cages, orchards of precisely pruned fruit trees and two long greenhouses heated by a noisy electricity generator that also fed the house. Behind them, in a number of outbuildings, were workshops filled with sophisticated tools and equipment for achieving the commune's desired self-sufficiency. The rest of the land was left for recreation – lawns, terraces and shrubberies had been restored and replanted and a high brick wall enclosed the whole property.

Inside, it was only the entrance hall and the first inner rooms that were unused – an eccentric camouflage to discourage unimaginative intruders. Apart from the rooms that Stephen had already seen, there was a small refectory where the community ate round a single trestle table. Again, as with the other rooms, it was painted white with minimal functional furniture. Everyone slept in a dormitory, a large high-ceilinged room that looked more like a gymnasium, with a wooden floor, tall windows and nothing except a pile of rush mattresses stacked neatly at one end. Andrew explained that these simple beds could be placed on the floor to suit every possible sleeping arrangement.

'We don't believe in monogamy,' he said, smiling knowingly at Stephen. 'We are one family here and we share everything.'

Next door was the bathroom, completely tiled in white and uncompromisingly communal with its large bathing pool, suitable for a football team, sunk into the middle of the floor. Unenclosed showers lined the walls and slatted wooden benches provided the only seating but, to Stephen's relief, the lavatories, in an enjoining room, were enclosed and private. He was not at all sure about these arrangements but he made no comment, even though he was beginning to dread the challenges ahead for someone of his fastidiously introverted nature.

Upstairs, there were a number of single rooms with small tables, chairs and mattresses for individuals who needed temporary escape from the group. At one end of the top floor was a large room, similar in size to the prayer room but which was sound-proofed in white cladding and filled with expensive-looking hi-fi equipment, a white concert grand piano and a glass-encased recording studio. Andrew's music was now to be recorded for its own sake and tapes were to be given away to anyone who wanted them.

'You are very welcome to stay with us for as long as you want.' Andrew repeated. 'If you have any special skills it would be good to know about them. There may be things that you can do for us.'

'I'm afraid, I am not very useful, I'm only a writer,' said Stephen. 'I don't know what I could offer.'

175

'You can meditate with us, I'm sure, and you can share yourself with us. Bring some of yourself into our midst. We would be grateful for that. In return you can use one of our rooms for your writing.'

Stephen felt reassured by Andrew's uncompromising warmth and tried to move away from his own inner doubts about this new idyllic-seeming community.

Dys ran between them and put her arms around their waists, hugging them both excitedly as they walked.

'I've wanted you to come here for so long,' she said.

Fifty-Three

'We're like a monastery, I suppose,' said Dave, the plants man, in his gentle rural Lancastrian accent. 'Only I like to think we're a bit more open to suggestion. We do pray in our own way too, though; it binds us together, I think.'

'People think we just take drugs all the time,' said Anna, the teacher, taking in the others with an inclusive schoolroom smile. 'We've all taken the Acid Test, of course, but we want to move beyond that. I know what people think but we're finding our own way, if we can only be left in peace.'

'People want us to fail,' said Andrew. 'Everyone wants definitions so that they can work out what's right and wrong, where they sit in the hierarchy and how things are meant to be; it's really all very unimaginative. If anyone tries to do it a different way, it's a threat. They kill your ideas with ridicule – that's the English way at least. We're saying: No thank you very much. We'd like to go our own way and we will if you leave us alone.'

They were eating supper on the second day – marrows stuffed with lentils, potatoes mashed with garlic, and broad beans. When it was over, the washing up and clearing away happened imperceptibly, everyone doing their duty with often-practised fluency in the shining steel kitchens next to the refectory.

Stephen had talked to them all by now, one by one, all day. He had survived his initial fears and was quickly forming what seemed to him like an attachment to these kind and gentle folk. Yet again, invitations to stay were renewed and, as the sun came down on the first day, the outside world already seemed very far away.

Dys had talked him through the routine, loving being his guide and excited that he was joining in. He had undressed discretely and slipped under the blankets on their joined mattresses, and she snuggled up to him there in the dormitory darkness. He got used to the sounds of unidentified couplings and the involuntary sounds of deep sleep as Dys explored his body with her hands. He was excited to share these moments in proximity to other people's eroticism and its sense of shared communal intimacy. As the days passed, he became relaxed and familiar with their monastic routine. The communal bathing was awkward at first, he felt very naked and hoped that his full body blush didn't show too much, but very soon he had become quite uninhibited.

On his second nude descent into the water, with Dys's hand massaging his buttocks, he felt that he had bonded at last with his naked companions. It was, he thought, the most liberating experience of his life. With those early moments of uncertainty behind him, the others no longer seemed naked; rather they were revealed, more complete as individuals and newly opened up to him. He grew familiar, even fond of their bodies, both male and female; they had never been individualised by their uniform shirts, jeans and boots, but now each of them took on his or her own unique appearance. From this point onwards he always thought of them without clothes as their naked selves, their real selves, with human bodies, all different but also not so different from his own. He surprised himself by finding each of their bodies physically attractive.

No longer self-conscious about nudity, he began to lose his other inhibitions too. He even joined in chanting the mantras in the prayer room, quickly mastering the simple repetitions, letting his voice link him transcendentally to the others as he joined the rhythm of the community.

That night, needing to disengage for a while, he lay on his mattress in the dark letting his mind drift, carelessly enjoying his gradual loss of focus. So many new thoughts and experiences had come his way in these days that he felt suddenly scrambled and desperate for some moments to untangle himself before he reverted to his usual state of tension. Some of the group had gone to bed early, others were sitting up talking in the next room.

He was floating between sleep and wakefulness when, hours later, quietly, as if not wanting to disturb him, Dys slid her mattress next to his. He could feel her breath on his body as she knelt over him; he was not ready to return to her but her hands caressed him until he could resist her no longer and now, unembarrassed by the lack of privacy, he gave in to her delicate inducements. Later, exhausted and spent, he could feel her gaze in the darkness as she lay next to him and he lingeringly and with happy tranquillity slipped into sleep.

In the morning, he was alone. Dys and the others had risen before him. Draped in his towel, he made his way to the bathroom and found everyone in the water, Dys in the middle.

'Come in,' she said. 'We've been waiting for you.'

He climbed in and sat down beside her.

'I stayed upstairs last night. I hope you didn't mind – I just couldn't sleep.'

Stephen said nothing but a glow of embarrassment spread through his body and his eyes passed over the smiling faces of his new friends.

It was the same the next night, only this time he was excited by the thought of the unidentified lover. He wasn't sure whether it was Dys or not until it was too late to care. Only then did he hear her reassuring voice in his ear. On the following night, he passed his hands over her skin only to find voluptuous handfuls of flesh where he had expected Dys's tiny form.

'It's alright, we're all friends,' whispered Anna, still the teacher, as she rolled on top of him. 'Dys is quite happy about this. Don't worry – if you like this, then it's good.'

After a week he knew that he had slept with all the women in the house, sometimes knowing who they were and sometimes not. Sometimes too, Dys would join them on his mattress, and the other woman would leave or not, depending on invisible signals between them.

One night, a new partner joined him and he was already in the early stages of arousal before he recognised a distinctly masculine touch on his skin.

'It's alright,' whispered slightly muscled, blond-haired Carl. 'We all love each other here. Don't hold out on us man.'

Like so many experiences in this place, the first time was always the most difficult, but Stephen was now beyond resistance and Carl taught him some exciting and unexpected sensations. As the days and nights passed, Stephen was more than enjoying the unpredictability of each new erotic encounter from, in the end, what he took to be every member of the community. In the darkness anything was permitted and nothing was beyond exploration. It was a very secular laying on of hands. In the daylight, there was an intimacy now between them all that added a pleasurable dimension to those morning baths where eyes met and lingered indulgently.

'I really like you. You know that, don't you?' said Dys one day when they were on their own in the garden. 'I wanted to share you with my friends. I love them too, you see.'

'I thought I was betraying you at first,' he replied sheepishly, 'but it isn't like that, is it?'

'No. Not at all,' she said, kissing his mouth and running off, leaving him to smile – only slightly saddened by her disappearing form.

Later, at supper, Andrew patted him on the back and massaged his shoulders affectionately. Stephen recognised his touch from one of the previous nights and welcomed his warmth.

'Dys tells me that you're ready for the Acid Test – do you want to try it?'

'I suppose I do,' Stephen answered – fear mingling with his excitement.

'It can be a great experience but it's not the whole thing,' Andrew said severely. 'Sometimes it's good but sometimes it's bad. Whatever happens, my friend, it will be memorable – I can promise you that for sure.'

Fifty-Four

And it was.

In the white padded room, listening to Andrew's psychedelic music projected through speakers hidden in the walls, the group shared Stephen's first acid trip. All in a circle, with Dys facing him, sitting on the floor with soft fruit and homemade cordials between them, Stephen took his pill, ritualistically like a novice in a temple at the beginning of his own personal journey.

At first, it was just a relaxed evening-in listening to music with friends. Maybe this would not live up to his expectations; maybe he was too resistant to letting his mind roam freely, or maybe he was just not imaginative enough. He was expecting failure when it all changed.

In a rush of mental energy he saw himself crouching in terror in a darkened corner. Dressed only in a loincloth he was staring back at himself looking at himself looking at the man in the loincloth who was looking at him – it was a long and perpetual stare and he was terrified. No one could calm him, not even Dys with her sweet words and proffered plums. Only he could see its significance – he was looking at the truth. He had always been that terrified boy – nothing would ever change. His friends surrounded him, calming him, helping him, stroking his head. They were all there – Dys and Andrew and Anna, Carl and the others, a multi-limbed massaging body caressing him at first but then entangling him into a suffocating knot, gripping him so that he struggled for breath as he heard his bones snap within him.

He was back in Brighton, there was Rosalie and Mark, their flesh transparent, their entrails alive with naked and hungry newborn rats. They were crying out for his help while more embryonic rodents climbed out of their mouths. Emilia Jeffries was pouring his tea from a bone china teapot and stirring his metal mug with a knife, making sharp-edged ear-piercing sounds while Georges Villard looked on, his face a death mask of smooth and smiling alabaster. There was Philip Irving, a young man again, hiding in the shadows, furtively yearning, pleading and desperate for a hungry climax which he reached with a bitter gurgling groan. Then long-dead Paul with blood pouring from his nose screamed out to him, telling him to follow as he strummed frantically at his sitar, lacerating his fingertips in his frenzy. Most frightening of all, Austin Randolph was laughing at him – a handsome mocking Satan kicking him repeatedly with knee-high boots; kicking the small naked boy in the corner; never stopping not even when his face had turned to pulp – filling his vision with liquid red as those naked rats swam through his eyes.

Then it changed again.

Stephen stopped screaming and his desperate friends let go of him and returned to their places. Now he was smiling happily, he had gone somewhere new. They were much relieved when they saw this changed expression. Wherever he had gone it looked good.

And it was.

Fifty-Five

In their regulation checked shirts, jeans and working boots, Stephen and Dys entered the life of the community; weeding in the vegetable patch, sweeping the paths, watering plants in the greenhouses and polishing the acres of floorboards; anything, especially as far as Stephen was concerned, that required minimal skills. At night in the refectory they banqueted on the produce of their labours, drinking their own wine and playing music together with everyone singing folk-inspired anthems, accompanied by guitars, African djembe drums, flute and harp.

For a period every day, Stephen went up to the small writing room and tried to progress with his book. Everything that he could need was there, a table and chair, white of course, a view from the window which, in reality, was as much as a distraction as it was an inspiration, stacks of paper and an invention new to him, a fearsome electric typewriter, shining like a racing car, challenging him, daring him even, to write. Carl patiently explained how it worked and equally patiently disentangled the paper, ribbon and anything else that Stephen managed to mangle up in it.

'Just call me if you need me, I'll be in the next room,' Carl told him, squeezing his arm reassuringly and running his fingers down Stephen's spine. Sometimes, Stephen took up the implied invitation and spent some time with Carl in private before getting back to his work.

Mostly, he just sat there thinking, gazing out of the window, sometimes guiltily enjoying his solitude but at other times celebrating the total lack of privacy that he found with these people who were teaching him what felt like a new mastery of his mind and body. The community had given him that and much more. He had, or at least he thought he had, passed the Acid Test. It had not been a miracle cure but it had brought together, in one intense moment of incoherent but intense self-revelation, many of the experiences and desires that had changed his life that summer. It had calmed the turmoil that had been a constant ache deep inside him since his childhood and, in an odd non-specific way, it had focused his thoughts even if he would have struggled to say what they were. He could not explain it fully and, knowingly, no one asked him about it. He had seen himself, liked himself enough maybe for the first time to view the future with optimism, and, so it seemed, now he was learning how to live with himself without that voice of doubt constantly resounding inside him.

'You should stay – the monastic life suits you,' Dys whispered to him one night, as they lay nestled together on their mattress. 'You would be happy here.'

'Maybe. One day perhaps. For now I'm still discovering the big world out there. Our world. What about you? Could you stay here permanently?' he asked, already noticing how she had excluded herself from the idea.

'I don't like to think anything is permanent,' she answered, with a touch of bleakness in her voice. He could not see her face but, with a shudder of sudden unhappiness, he knew that it was time for them to leave.

The next morning they said goodbye to everyone at the house; handshakes were held with lingering melancholy pleasure, hugs enfolded them with affection. Even though Stephen had only been there for a short time, they had become intimate friends – physically and emotionally bonded. He had gone there as Dys's friend but he was leaving in his own right, a novitiate in their enclosed order; he would take that with him, he thought, wherever he went.

'We have formed a circle of love,' said Anna, giving him their parting present, a knotted and beaded ankle bracelet plaited with lengths of hair from each member of the community.

'You can keep it on no matter what you wear and, even if you conceal it under your clothes, we will still know that you are carrying us with you.'

She knelt down and fixed it round his left ankle, kissing him on the shin in benediction.

Dys watched, quietly standing at a distance with her arm squeezing Andrew's waist. Her face, Stephen kept noticing, looked different, something new was giving her that radiant expression, something that he could not decipher. She was watching him, maternally, her face like a Renaissance painting, he thought – the Virgin adoring her Christ Child, the Mona Lisa, or a saint transfigured. He was lit up by her passive joy, receiving it as a gift, but he still retained that sense of sadness too that had coloured his thoughts since the night before.

'We love you, Stephen man,' said Andrew, hugging him with an affectionate bear-like grip and lifting him off his feet. 'Come back anytime.'

'Yes, don't forget us,' Carl added with a lingering smile.

Stephen and Dys were beyond words as they walked back into the city. For Stephen, those medieval street scenes were now seen through a watery haze and he held onto Dys's hand with a firmness born of fear. They walked into the graceful Gothic of Salisbury Cathedral that he had wanted to visit on their arrival. Now it was no longer an issue between them, Dys remained lost in her deepest silence as they sat in the nave looking up through the long avenue of pillars to the great east window. The September sun filled this, the lightest of cathedrals, with a burnished autumnal refulgence that lit their faces as they sat next to each other, body pressed to body, for a very long time, in what seemed like an unbreakable silence.

Stephen was at one with the many troubled souls that had found solace in these quietly elegant arcades. Since medieval times, people had come here to celebrate national and personal triumphs and to mourn public or private sorrows. Concentrated emotion lingered in the stones, adding to his mysteriously growing tranquillity. Once more, as he would always do now, he let the past into his present. He had neglected it for too long. Knowing this, he put his arm around Dys, whose emerald eyes were watering too as she gazed up the aisle.

'It's not just a vicar thing here, is it?' she said quietly. 'It feels really spiritual – not just Christian.'

'Yes,' he answered. 'It was built to let in the light, to bring wonder and peace. And it does that still.'

'Wonder, peace and love,' Dys added with gentle emphasis. 'It speaks of love as well.'

'Yes.' He smiled.

They sat there in silence. Something unsaid was known to both of them but needed to be spoken here in what they both, for different reasons, felt was a sacred place. Eventually she put her hand on his thigh, turning to him with that Leonardo smile but with tears in her eyes.

185

'We have known love,' she said. 'You know that, don't you?'

'Yes. I do,' he said, sadly smiling too.

'That's why I'm not coming back with you. I want to go now while we are both full of joy. Both full of love. Do you understand that?'

'I knew that you were going to say it, if that's what you mean.'

Abandoning cathedral decorum, they embraced passionately, joyfully – happy suicidists drowning, clinging to their last moment of intimacy.

'Where will you go?' he said when they disengaged.

'Don't ask,' she said, sniffing and laughing simultaneously. 'Somewhere new, that's all. Now you can write your book, live your life and things like that.'

She kissed him hurriedly on the cheek and then, as so often before, she had gone.

He didn't move. This time he would not look for her. He stayed in his pew, outwardly calm but internally offering up his wounds for healing. Seven hundred years of dimly understood benedictions descended on him, giving him strength without numbing his pain. It was physically present in his muscles, in his stomach, in his lungs and in the cold shudder that ran down the sinews of his limbs, to be comforted.but not stilled by that anklet above his left foot. He was good at controlling pain, he always had been – he felt that he had been preparing for this moment all his life.

'Excuse me, sir,' said a black-gowned verger. 'Are you staying for the service?'

'No thanks,' he answered with a voice on the verge of breaking. 'I've got a train to catch.'

Fifty-Six

Austin and Emilia walk through shadowy streets on a summer night, in love, in Berlin, in 1938. A night at the opera, Beethoven's Fidelio, the triumph of love over oppression; German opera in Nazi Berlin, German idealism in Nazi Berlin. She, perfectly poised, hand on his arm, white silk dress adorned with gardenias, sings Beethoven quietly, his hymn to liberty, her hymn to hope. Magnificent, resplendent, unbendingly proud in his military uniform, Austin guides her through those shadowy streets. On guard, excited, aware of the danger, he is the General's grandson, the dashing young officer, Emilia's love and now Germany's son.

Gunshots: she hears them after her body had jumped. 'It's probably thunder,' he says, trying to hasten their pace, but she sees the man. He dies slumped in the street in a circle of blood. There is so much blood in a dying man. She rushes to help, kneels to hear his gasps, to see the bayonet wounds and the pumping blood.

'He's dead...'

'A communist, probably......but, anyway, he's a Jew......a communist Jew. Come away Emilia, you will do no good here.'

Blood soaks her feet through her open-toed silver shoes; her white silk dress is bespattered in gore. Embarrassed – but for what? – he tries to take her away. She screams in animal pain. Not just for the Jew dead at her feet; she screams for her love dying there in that street.

Fifty-Seven

Stephen went back to the Reference Library, determined to get on with his work on the Randolph book. He was still numbed by the loss of Dys, but that numbness brought its own tranquillity enhanced and strengthened by his Salisbury awakening. Now a longhaired, bearded and sun-browned student type, he was not recognised by the assistant librarian when he asked her about the periodicals that had been requested months before.

'We've kept them for another gentleman but I'm not sure if he still wants them,' she said but, when she realised her mistake, she blushed and grinned awkwardly.

'Oh, I'm sorry, I didn't recognise you with your beard and your...'

Stumbling over her embarrassment, she didn't finish the sentence. Bending down behind the counter, she produced ten thick volumes of local newspapers covering the Frampton area in the 1930s.

'You'll have to read them here, I'm afraid,' she said. 'They're not allowed out but we can keep them for as long as you need, as long as no one else wants them, of course...'

She was wittering nervously as she carried the first of them to his usual desk, proud to prove that she remembered him.

'Just leave it here when you've finished. Let me know how long you will need it and when you want the next volume. Oh,' she added with forced lightness, 'it's good to see you back. We thought you'd left us!'

So there he was – back in his usual seat, the summer past, Dys gone but everything else where it used to be. All the same well-remembered smells – dust, old paper, furniture polish, body odour and that smell of stale face flannels that he had always associated with old men. Far from depressing him, it was comforting, bolstering him up in his yet-to-be-acknowledged bereavement. The bad-tempered old man, in his usual tweed jacket reeking of old tobacco, showed just the same lack of charm as he had done through Stephen's most lonely times. His irritable glare sent the assistant librarian on her way; there was no welcome back from the sullen denizens of his old world. It didn't matter. Here, in the former centre of his experience, nothing had changed. He was pleased about that. Part of him had always belonged here, he had returned to reclaim it and to measure how far he had moved on.

By researching Austin Randolph's life, he had hoped to write a social history of the English landed classes before the war, with Austin, its central character, as both its archetype and its exception. Now that he had learnt more about the German connection, he doubted that he was writing the right book. He was still a long way from the truth but, whatever it was, it had begun in the fading pastoral of those early Frampton years. The book that he had found so difficult to write within the high walls of the Wessex Centre now became an important distraction from his still pain-cushioned grief. He would now bring the book to its conclusion.

Turning through ten years of local newspapers, he saw the many reports of flower shows, village fêtes, Rose Queen Parades, Christmas pantomimes, livened up by the occasional accidental death or farming tragedy. The years moved on and the journalism kept time – each year there were slightly different pieces on the same annual events. Sometimes the same proud gardener would win the dahlia prize two years running; Stephen would look for signs of change, of ageing or even for a different facial expression, but a pattern had been set and everyone in the Frampton and District Journal knew how to behave in front of the camera, always smile as you look into the lens.

Even Mr Irving senior, in spite of his wasting disease – even he could muster that local newspaper grin. Every year he was there at the agricultural show, giving the cup to the breeder of the best heifer, the star prize. Benignly patrician, he beamed with photographic sincerity as he shook hands with each year's winner. His reassuring words were lost but their impact was reflected each year in the dutifully respectful peasant smile of each recipient. He disappeared from the 1938 show and his obituary followed a month later. In 1939, the cup was presented by the vicar – apparently, even though it was not mentioned, Mrs Irving's German nationality ruled her out in such troubled times.

There was no mention either of the internment camp where she had been sent with her sister and niece. It was very different in the early Thirties. The Irving ladies were often photographed at charitable events, elegantly dressed, aloof in their chic superiority –

perfect images of English life. Austin Randolph-Irving, as they still called him, only appeared after he had left Frampton to become Mr Ivy Cooper – the paper had chosen the most glamorous photograph of the pair to illustrate a short article about their marriage. Stephen moved on through several more agricultural shows until he spotted Austin Randolph's second entry:

Frampton Man Arrested after East End Incident
Mr Austin Randolph-Irving, the son of the Frampton Irving family, was arrested this week accused of incitement to riot and causing an affray. As a member of Sir Oswald Mosley's British Union of Fascists, it is alleged that he led an attack on various Jewish-owned properties in London's East End resulting in substantial damage to several premises and, in the ensuing rioting, it is also alleged that he caused actual bodily harm to a number of people who were defending the properties. He was due to appear before the local magistrates' court today.

There were a number of other stories in the following weeks – the court case, the mitigating circumstances, the substantial fine and the supportive wife. Then the story was replaced by local news including Julietta Jeffries' exhibition – 'Frampton in Oils' – which was being held at the local library. The photograph showed Mrs Jeffries with her sister Margaret Irving at the opening – they were standing in front of the romanticised picture of Frampton House that Emilia now kept in her spare room. It was 1938 and everyone was laughing – presumably at the photographer's long forgotten joke – it was the perfect image of civilised English life and the Irvings' final appearance in the local newspaper.

Stephen packed up, leaving the volume closed on the desk. He would return again tomorrow and again after that but, today, he had crossed a frontier, he had remained objective, business-like even, in a world still haunted by Dys; now a neutral environment without her. He went out into the street, to the darkening evening sky and a mist of rain. Without the sun's insistence on exposure, bodies everywhere were concealed under raincoats, huddled under umbrellas, removed from public scrutiny. Welcoming the opportunity, Stephen wore his long overcoat like a bandage, collar

190

turned up, face hidden from view – protecting himself while, underneath, he hoped, he began to heal.

Fifty-Eight

At Gresham Villas, like bedsits everywhere, absences were smoothed over rapidly, gaps were filled and life continued to its slightly altered rhythm. Rosalie had moved into Dys's room, filling it with handmade flowers, and pink and green hand-painted pine furniture. The walls were covered with oriental shawls, chains of tiny hessian-covered mirrors and wind chimes hung in the window, while the lighting came from several wrought iron candle lanterns.

She never mentioned Mick but she had arrived at the house with a badly bruised face and a suitcase. Mick never visited. Mark and José had turned Paul's old room into their own space, filled with printing equipment for their new venture – a weekly pamphlet, The Happening, that mixed politics written from an anarchist perspective with local and international news and advice on alternative life-styles.

'If we can change our own space, then ultimately we can change the world. Purify your own patch, that's what we are about. The world is just a lot of backyards so if we can only convince everyone to keep them in order then…eureka! The Happening can do that here.'

Mark was now truly inspired. 'That's where you can really help, Stephen. You have an eye for detail – all your history stuff gives you that, I concede it, alright? I'd really like it if you could write for us, but first of all,' he added with a mischievous twinkle, 'you have to tell me what has happened to you to turn you into this beautiful young man!'

Stephen blushed beneath his tan but was happy to accept Mark's physical acknowledgement, just as he was excited to have his love of history accepted by one of his few good friends.

So Stephen helped – both as a writer, on the lighter, mostly non-political subjects, and as a street-corner distributor of the finished paper. From his regular position, not far from the Reference Library, by the Hindu Gothic archway entrance to the Pavilion Gardens, he braved disapproval in the rain and enjoyed furtive moments of subversive camaraderie with street-wise hippies and would-be fellow travellers. He went on marches to London, Manchester and in Brighton itself, handing out leaflets on the way, and, stirred by the spirit of solidarity, he too intoned 'Ho Ho Ho Chi Minh', the highly charged syllables of the North Vietnamese president's name, a chant now sung around the world in protest about the war in Vietnam.

Never quite sure of his stance, he joined hundreds of others, a confluence of the radically political with the growing numbers of pacifist hippies, many wearing pieces of military uniforms – not khaki battle gear but colourful toy soldier jackets – seaside bandstand soldiers looking for fun. They were a ragamuffin army, marching with the excitement of being a part of something that really was going to change the world. Rumours spread that a revolution was happening. In Washington DC, The Pentagon, so they said, had been levitated by the mystic chants of anti-war demonstrations. It would be a revolution by the miraculous exorcism of the spirit of war. It would be easy, as Stephen's lapel badge read: Make Love Not War.

In Brighton, they had a number of successes – exposing local politicians, promoting political meetings and demonstrations, campaigning against the Vietnam war and the nuclear arms race. Paul's Room, as it was always called, lost its tranquillity and became a nerve-centre for Brighton's underground culture. Often it was full of volunteers making banners, collecting copies of The Happening, arguing politics, typing up stories on an old typewriter or running off copies on the Roneo machine that José had requisitioned from an unknown location. Paul's gurus were replaced by new icons – dominating one wall was a poster of the revered Leon Trotsky, welcomed by Mark as an honorary contemporary, while on another, over a table with a regularly replaced vase of flowers, hung a small framed image of the recently executed, Che Guevara. José had added his own tribute, painted directly onto the wall in red letters: 'Venceremos!'

Up in the attic, Stephen settled back into the smoking room ambience of his old abode with its seedy junk shop Victoriana. He could have changed it, making a public comment about himself, but he decided not to bother. His only concession was the skilful addition of a few framed pictures: an erotic expressionist poster of a languorous naked couple with a taste for red velvet, a set of early photographs of a naked man running and, most prominently, Aubrey Beardsley's illustration for the elegy to his dead brother by the languidly mourning and suggestively bare-torsoed Roman poet Catullus – 'Ave atque vale, Hail and Farewell'.

There was excitement enough around him. His room needed to be a quiet space, maybe a melancholy place but somewhere to hide when the revolution got too hot. It was also somewhere to work, to write the articles that now flowed with satisfying fluidity. He knew his subject: Brighton, its eighteenth and nineteenth-century legacy, his own sense of its sanctity, expressed in its meeting of the urban with the primevally maritime. He wrote about the errors in demolishing what some called the slums but he saw as historic buildings, holding the spirit of citizens past and the promise of community in the future. He had met Mark on his own ground; he had even unleashed his own inner anarchist, a delicate avenging angel perhaps, but one that was at war aesthetically, emotionally and unforgivingly with the repressive culture that had reared him.

'You miss her, don't you?' Rosalie said one day when they sat drinking china tea on his bed. Languorous in her uniquely fleshy way, she lay on the bed as if she had been one of those Expressionist models.

'I'm sorry,' he answered automatically. 'Is it that obvious?'

'No. You're doing a great job.'

'Yes, I do miss her but I'm also partly relieved that it's all over. She was a mystery to me you know. I knew her totally and yet I didn't really know her at all. It was always going to end, I knew that; I was always frightened of facing the moment. I suppose that's how we look at death.'

'Sometimes it can be beautiful, you know. If you're really prepared,' said Rosalie, penetrating his reserve. 'I think we should enjoy endings. You know, look boldly down the barrel of the gun.'

'I did. Now it seems like my time with her was an initiation ceremony, its purpose was all in the initiating – there could be nothing beyond it. We couldn't go any further, maybe I always knew that; she was frightened of what we might have seen, or, I suppose, what we might have become. So we reached a moment, the moment and then it had to end.'

'She wanted to live at the same pitch all the time,' Rosalie added, sympathetically filling his pause. 'She hated coming down – leaving the excitement. She will always be moving on – that's her way. I just hope that things stay exciting for her.'

'I never even really knew her name,' Stephen mumbled – close to tears but now able to hold onto the emotion, extend it and even to enjoy it, to feed on it without letting it reach its climax. 'Dys is not a real name is it?'

'She didn't want anyone to know,' Rosalie laughed. 'Poor thing! I saw an official-looking letter she received once. It had her name on it – she was very upset when she saw that I had read it. Gladys – that was her name. Can you imagine! Gladys Atkins. No wonder she wanted to keep it secret!'

Names meant very little in themselves, he knew that, but he was still upset. Gladys Atkins was a different person, unknown to him – maybe she was someone else again now, always changing with every new experience, every new relationship It had been challenging living up to her philosophy – always existing just for the moment. No one could do it, he thought, not all the time, not even Dys but especially not him. Everyone should have somewhere to keep their slippers and their cocoa mugs. Rosalie needed that too. She gave him one of her Russian cigarettes – black papers with vermilion filters – and they acknowledged the inevitable with glances stolen through the smoke.

For that moment, at least, and on the other occasions that followed, they could give each other comfort and a kind of love. When Mark joined them, they silently recognised a mutual bond: all three of them stood on the outside now, partnerless, unconventional in their desires and united by an almost certainly ill-conceived sense of optimism. They were friends like never before and, here in Rosalie's room, they could say or do whatever they wanted and so they did. Sadly though, as they opened up for each other, they recognised that each of them was still pursued by ghosts.

It had been snowing; the sharp cold light froze out the colours from the town, turning the white Regency stucco buildings yellow like rotting teeth. Stephen walked down the streets, on his way to the library, feeling that he was in an old black-and-white film. Rosalie and Mark had brought him more than solace, they had made him feel adult; he, like them, was a survivor washed up on a foreign shore, homesick for a remembered paradise where people behaved differently and loved differently. Happy though he was to have made these friends, he was a survivor like them nonetheless.

He stuffed his hands into his overcoat pockets and waded through the slush. The world might end in another Ice Age. It would kill off all life before thawing and leaving a new purer world, maybe one that he would understand. If he could only hibernate until then, he thought, he would awake, like Noah, cleansed and renewed. Only it would never be like that, every day had its little deaths and renewals. Whenever he was sure of anything, something else would knock him off balance again.

'Excuse me, sir,' said a man, who with his companion had produced identity cards complete with unsmiling photographs. 'We're police officers. If you'd just like to step this way, it won't take very long, we'd just like to make a quick search, if that is alright with you, sir.'

'There's nothing to worry about,' said his companion, embarrassed but firm. 'It's purely routine. We're looking for illegal substances and we're making random searches.'

Before he could register his anger, they had fingered his coat and trouser pockets, the insides of his shoes and socks, giving each other the eye when they saw his concealed anklet, looking through crumpled papers, smoothing out bus tickets, chewing gum wrappers, taking the cigarette from their packet, dismantling his lighter and checking his wallet. Then they frisked his body with intimate efficiency, under his arms, between his legs, lightly brushing his crotch and patting his torso in an embarrassed bear hug.

'Sorry to have troubled you, sir,' said one of them with just a hint of a sneer. 'Enjoy the rest of your evening.' They left him shivering in the snow, an angry young man in black and white. The snow now heavy on his black overcoat, he was the brooding hero of a French art house film.

'I don't need your permission to enjoy myself,' he called out, more to himself than to them, enveloping himself in a cloud as his hot breath met the frozen air. He turned up his collar and lit a cigarette.

Back in his room, feeling violated and defiant, he remembered the packet of cannabis bought at the station months before. He had put it away in a drawer, saving it for Dys. It had been his first act of illegality, a rite of passage. Opening it, he found a small ball of silver paper and, inside, a handful of autumn leaves. He sat down in his winged-back chair, his eyes stinging with grief, before the humour of it all struck him and, by the time he had sat back, there was a smile on his face and there was also laughter, deep and explosive, inside.

He had been so naïve, such a victim, but he could still remember the excitement of breaking the law for that first time and that in itself was worth every penny. It had taught him whose side he was on. He was with Dys, with her refusal to conform, and he was with Mark and Rosalie and Andrew and the others: they were not for the law as it stood, they wanted it changed even if they did not always know why or what for. He was with them in spirit, now more than ever. It was only when the doorbell stopped ringing that he heard it. When it rang again, he ran down the stairs and, opening the door, saw a man walking away, monochrome in the blizzard.

'Did you want something?' he called, the snow settling in his mouth.

'I was looking for Mr Dearsley. Is he in?'

'That's me,' he replied, recognising Stanley Finch.

Fifty-Nine

'It will be easier next time.' The Colonel was reassuring, sensitive, caring.

It was easier the next time and the time after that. There, in occupied France, in the summer of '43, the blood on the whitewashed walls, the dead men, Frenchmen, executed for resisting, helping the Jews, being in the wrong place.

Austin Randolph, Kapitän Randolph, rising up through the ranks, gave the order to shoot and they fell, resisting no more, save one, wriggling where he lay, awaiting the young officer's pistol, duly delivered.

Easy.

Sixty

'I thought you'd forgotten me, my friend. I haven't forgotten you. I'm still waiting, still wondering what you have found. Don't give up now, you're nearly there and only you can end this.'

Austin Randolph, Tung Ping Chau, December 1967

'How did you find me?' Stephen asked, looking at Stanley Finch who was sitting breathlessly, unbelievably even, in his winged-back chair.

'You left your address, if you remember, sir. I'm afraid that I wasn't very helpful when you came to see me that day. I didn't want any trouble, you see.'

Stephen sat fidgeting on the edge of the bed, still getting used to the idea that Finch had actually sought him out. He studied the old man from an objective distance, while a surge of energy rushed through his body telling him not to let this interview slip into incoherence like the other ones. It was obvious that Finch had been through a bad time. His clothes were old and threadbare, the materials faded, his black suit had a green sheen to it, his white shirt cuffs had had the frays snipped off and his immaculately polished shoes were coming apart at the stitching; but in spite of that, he had retained his natural elegance and the calm dignity that Stephen remembered from the university canteen. He was still winded from the journey upstairs, but Stephen had no skill at small talk so it was left to the old butler to break the silence with breathless and facile pleasantries while Stephen leapt up nervously to make coffee.

'This weather eats right through you, sir, doesn't it,' said Finch, trying to be civil.

'I didn't think I would see you again,' Stephen said, ignoring the platitude as he manipulated the electric kettle and his cafetière hyper-kinetically. After all the vacillation with the Randolph project, he was genuinely excited to see the old butler at his door and now he was going to persist until he got some real information.

'I went back to the university but you had gone and no one knew where you lived.'

199

'Yes, I think I've behaved rather foolishly,' said Finch, recovering his breath and warming his hands on the coffee mug.

'Very good coffee, if you don't mind me saying, sir. It's unusual for people to get it right in this country, I find.' Stephen smiled but didn't take up the brewing topic. 'Anyway, I'm sorry if I caused you problems, Mr Dearsley. I packed in my job after you found me there in that awful canteen. I was frightened, you see. I wanted to avoid any unpleasantness, like I said. You have to understand that it was quite a shock hearing about Mr Randolph again after all this time. I wanted to hide away from it all I suppose. Anyway, I've been thinking about it and fate seems to have led me back to you.'

'What do you mean?'

'Well, I've landed a little job at the station, here in Brighton. I'm waiting at table in the small restaurant there. I suppose you would call it the railway buffet but that isn't strictly accurate. I thought if we were going to come to Brighton then I could hardly hide away from you, sir. We were bound to bump into each other eventually.'

'You said, "if we were going to come to Brighton", Mr Finch. So you have not come alone.' Remembering his earlier incompetence, Stephen was determined not to let anything slip. He was beginning to enjoy himself, even though he was coming across as uncharacteristically rude.

'Oh, yes. That would be Mrs Finch and me, sir. She's been very patient about all this. Very patient. I told her about it all, of course, and she said that I should come and see you.'

'Well thank you. I have been rather stuck without your help. I saw Mr Irving after you told me his address and I've met Emilia Jeffries and Ivy Cooper. The trouble is no one is really telling me the whole story.'

'Well, sir, I expect those ladies and the gentleman in question are worried about the truth just the same as I was but, judging by Mr Randolph's letter, it seems that he wants it all to come out, so I suppose I should tell you what I know. I hope you will understand why I wanted to be discreet. And then maybe, sir, you will understand why the other parties have shown a little reluctance.'

'I suppose you're referring to Germany?' asked Stephen, wanting to wade through the excuses and get to the point.

'Yes, that's it, sir. People don't take kindly to what they don't understand and I have had to look after Mrs Finch and myself.

200

Well, I'm not going to avoid the truth any more, we decided that it might be better that way.'

'I know that Mr Randolph went to Germany with Emilia Jeffries after his marriage broke up,' said Stephen, persevering with the increasingly talkative old man who was sitting upright in the chair with his mug balanced on his knee.

'Yes, sir. I suppose you know that I went with them too. It would have been in 1937, I think. It was a strange business and it was very sad when things didn't work out for them. He was very fond of her, you know, and it hurt him when she came back to England. Of course, when you look back at it, she was lucky to have got out when she did.'

'But you stayed?'

'Yes, sir.'

'But why? It must have been dangerous for you as an Englishman in Germany in those days and it sounds as if Austin Randolph can't have been an easy boss.'

'Mr Randolph certainly had a violent side to his character, I wouldn't deny it, sir. He was a very instinctive person, if you know what I mean, but it was not my place to tell him how to live his life. I felt that I owed him a certain degree of, er, of toleration. It takes more than a bit of pain to upset an old soldier, you must understand that. You see, I was messed up a bit in the war. The Great War, I mean. Like most of us who went through it, I grew up there. It gave me a certain tolerance of other people's foibles and it gave me this as a memento.'

He pointed to the scar that ran its crooked course down the left side of his face from left eye to the corner of his mouth.

'Not very pretty, is it, sir?' he said.

'I always thought Austin Randolph gave you that.'

'Oh, no, sir. It was a souvenir from the trenches. I was pretty badly shot up and was invalided back home.'

Once more Stephen's assumptions had been wrong. This simple correction shattered a number of Stephen's other theories too. Whenever he discovered something new, he felt that he was going backwards again – back to the beginning.

'Then I found that life could be even tougher,' Finch continued, now in full flow, 'when you try to make a living in your own country. I had no trade and no money so, you could say, that I slipped downhill a bit. I had a few medals and that earned me a bob or two from ex-officers and the like – I think they felt guilty seeing you on the streets down on your luck. My training as a gentleman's gentleman had got me nowhere now that I had this disfigurement. That was when I met Mr Randolph. We were comrades; I suppose you'd say. He was just a young fellow, of course but he was going through bad times too. We frequented the same places – the parks, the Salvation Army hostels. I had been doing it for years so I could show him the ropes.

'He managed to do a bit of business with the ladies, if you know what I mean, but he would always remember his old friend – he was a good sort, believe me, even if he had a reckless spirit. We'd share the odd bottle of cider on the proceeds, as it were; his immoral earnings, some might say. Well, he was a gentleman, I suppose. You can't hide that can you? When he landed on his feet with Miss Cooper, he took me with him. I worked as his valet but, underneath it all, we were always friends. I never took advantage of the relationship and I never tried to rise above my station but I like to think that I helped him. As I say, sir, we were comrades, you see. So that's why we could go into battle together, when the time came.'

'So you knew him when he joined the British Union of Fascists?' said Stephen. The old man took out a packet of untipped cigarettes and offered him one. Stephen accepted it and produced his lighter while Finch considered the question.

'That's a nice lighter, sir. Gunmetal isn't it? Petrol.'

'Yes, it is, Mr Finch, but what about the British Union of Fascists?'

'Well, that was something else really. He was a young blood, I suppose. He liked the excitement you see. He got in with a bad lot, I know, but I don't think he really meant it. I don't think he had any dislike of Jewish people or anyone else for that matter. He could have joined any group of young lads – it was just the same in the army. If you put a lot of excitable young men together, sometimes things get out of hand.'

'But he was arrested for criminal damage.'

'He was part of a group. He wasn't really political in that sense. You know, sir, a lot of the gentry in those days shared those views. They're not a lot better even, now, sir, if you see what I mean. The upper classes don't really understand the real world, do they, sir? A lot of them are not – if you will excuse me saying so – they're often not very clever, and Mr Randolph was not what you would call an intellectual. He only thought about these things later.'

'Well, it must have helped him get on in Germany,' Stephen said with a tone of malignant irony that even surprised himself. He could feel his anger rising and he was not about to share Finch's tolerance. 'That's what happened I assume. He went to Germany as a British Fascist and scored a bulls-eye.'

'Well, I suppose you could say that. Yes, sir. But his family was half-German as was Miss Jeffries', you must remember. When we were all at her grandparents' house in Berlin, it didn't seem that wrong being there. But I expect that you find that difficult to understand. Mr and Mrs Von Öchen, the general and his wife, were very nice people, you see. They were never fascists or Nazis or anything as far as I could tell. They were just like anyone else really, very hospitable and kind. In fact, I think they disapproved of Mr Randolph's involvement as much as Miss Jeffries did but I suppose by then it was all much too late.'

Sixty-One

They sat in the attic room until nightfall, swapping Stephen's French cigarettes with Finch's untipped Virginians while the story unravelled. Austin Randolph, the romantic lead, the handsome rogue, the bon viveur, was replaced by the naïf, then the unthinking but noble savage, and then the fool – the wealthy over-indulged son turned roué, down-and-out, prostitute, gigolo and, in an ever descending spiral, the anti-Semite and traitor. Was he any of these things, Stephen wondered. The man who was so easily loved and who had left such a poignant trail of sadness in his wake, was maybe less remarkable that he had thought. He had simply and quite unheroically walked into a trap in a moment of petulance. Mrs Irving's illegitimate son, with some help from his adoptive grandparents, became Randolph von Öchen, an officer in the German army. A year later, he was at war.

'Miss Jeffries had gone by then, of course. She wanted him to come back with her but he'd sensed adventure: that was always his problem, as you probably know by now. It was like a child's game for him. Nothing would dissuade him. I stayed for as long as it was safe then they arranged for me to escape into France.'

'And was that the last you saw of him?'

'No.'

Stanley Finch offered Stephen another cigarette and hid for a moment behind a welcome moment of smokers' camaraderie.

'When things started going wrong, the old General von Öchen smuggled him out too. The same route, into Paris then into hiding – he had to avoid the Germans as well as the British now, if you understand me, sir. We met up again in southern France. He was then more like the man I had first met; we were both in the same boat, really – stateless without a penny to our names but still comrades, you see, sir. Always that. We had both been to war, we had both suffered. It strengthened our brotherly bond and, somehow, in spite of all that he had been through, he had kept his innocence; well I like to think it was that or something like it. We had both messed up, of course, and he was in some ways broken, slightly haunted I believe, but he was still excited by that old sense of adventure, maybe more so than before. He loved being on the run, I think but he would not have minded being caught, he might even have welcomed it.'

'Do you know what he did in Germany?' Stephen was beginning to suspect yet another whitewash.

'Not really. He was always a brave man and, if I'm allowed to say so, I don't think he would have done anything terrible, if you know what I mean. Anyway, things didn't turn out well for him. I think things went wrong with the old General too. He wasn't an admirer of Hitler; I think he tried to object to things and it wasn't liked. Then questions were asked but only Mr Randolph got out.'

'How did you get out of France?'

'There was a network of brave men; we were taken care of by a group of Frenchmen, partisans, I think you would call them. There was a man known as Maynard; that was a code name, I believe. He found ways of helping us – he was helping hundreds of people at that time, not Germans of course, but British, communists, Jews of course, and other partisans. At first he didn't know about Mr Randolph's involvement but, when he did, he let it go. Mr Randolph could be very charming sir, if you understand what I mean. He got us to Gibraltar. I went back to Britain but Mr Randolph would not have been very welcome here so he went out East. That's all I can tell you, sir – I didn't know even if he was still alive until you startled me that day in London.'

'It's an extraordinary story, Mr Finch.' Stephen had grown used to lies and half-truths but he was drawn to believe Finch's improbable tale.

'Yes, sir. I know it's extraordinary.' Stanley Finch looked pale and tired when he had finished. 'I suppose people will think that he was a fool, a ne'er do well, or even a monster and that I was a fool and a traitor too to follow him. I suppose they would be right, I was wrong to go to an enemy country, stupid in fact and lucky not to have been punished for it, but there was something about him, Mr Dearsley. He could make life seem exciting, worthwhile somehow. You wanted to see the world his way, sir, because often reality can be pretty bleak.'

'This Maynard, do you know much about him?'

'He was a great man, sir, a hero really. I don't know much more than that. He had been a writer, I think. He'd lost his wife – to the Germans. He'd given up his books, he said, until he'd got nothing

205

better to do. He hated Fascism, obviously, but he was against all forms of bigotry – I think he found something worth saving in Mr Randolph, in spite of it all. I think he was a wise man, sir. They talked a lot. Mr Randolph seemed moved by him, humbled even.'

'You say that Maynard was a code name. Did you ever know his real name?'

'Oh, I don't really remember. Georges, I think. Yes, it was Georges.'

'Georges Villard!' Stephen said, suddenly realising what had been happening.

'Yes, sir. That's it. I believe it was Georges Villard, or something very similar. How did you know that?'

'A voice from the grave,' said Stephen.

Sixty-Two

Gallic humour was not Stephen's speciality; often Villard's wit had confused him, leaving him feeling relentlessly Anglo-Saxon, doltish even, but he had never been so confused by the old man than he was now. As he sat in his room after Stanley Finch had left, he tried to remember the details of his conversations with the old Frenchman. It might have been intended as a helping hand or as a trick or, even, as he began to suspect, just a joke. The letter from Austin Randolph had been a coded message; maybe the book was to be a piece of posthumous vanity publishing, an immodest act of self-vindication from a dying man. Maybe it was all mockery or, maybe, there really was something about Austin Randolph that Villard wanted to see in print.

Whatever the truth, the chain of lies had completed its circuit; Georges Villard, the reluctant war hero, was the latest in his cast of characters to deceive him; he no longer knew what or who to believe. No one had been wholly honest with him; he had misunderstood most of the people involved in the story, misjudged them, trusted them when he should have been more suspicious, been suspicious when he should have been more trusting. He despaired of ever finding the complete truth. It seemed that Villard had predicted this and that there was a wry humour in his legacy. Maybe he was telling him, in a cruelly tangential way, that his idea of being a biographer was wrong, misconceived, and much too literal. He was laughing at him, kindly, he assumed, but all along he had told him not to trust simplistic notions of truth and falsehood.

Maybe Mark had been right all along. It was no longer relevant; this story populated with disappointed, unfulfilled people and its magnetic, destructive hero, the old-fashioned man of action, an admired archetype from a discredited culture, who now turned out to be at best a fool and, at worst, a war criminal. Maybe it was better to bury the past and reconstruct the present. Stephen had written down everything that he knew so he decided to go through it all again, one last time, and to decide whether he should or even could continue. If necessary he would tell Austin Randolph that he didn't want to carry on and that this unpublished material should remain unpublished.

He précised his notes, creating a long document full of contradictions and assumptions based on the evidence of Randolph's chosen interviewees. He sat up all night and most of the next day, writing, trying to make sense of the confusion. Randolph's witnesses had all been his victims: Emilia, Philip, Finch, and even Margaret Irving; all had been drawn to his flame and damaged by their love. Maybe they were better served with silence. As for Germany, Georges Villard had judged Randolph innocent, according to Stanley Finch at least. It was possible that he was merely doing his duty. He had been a soldier, obeyed orders, and survived in a brutal regime. He was guilty, no doubt, of disloyalty to King and Country, but that, to Stephen was no crime.

If there was more to tell, if there had been a crime committed, or, more likely, several crimes, then Stephen couldn't avoid it, he would have to go on whether he wanted to or not; he had become involved with that most awkward of burdens, moral responsibility. He would have to travel to Germany, access military records, find new witnesses and become a criminal investigator. If necessary, he decided, he would have to do this, but it was not what he had wanted when he set out on his literary adventure. This was too much like investigative journalism, or being a private detective even, an absurd idea and beyond his skills, but maybe no more unlikely than all the other changes that he had undergone since meeting Georges Villard. He had to stop himself from being buffeted around; he had to decide what to do. So he wrote to Hong Kong, including a copy of the précis and telling Austin Randolph that he would only continue with the book if they met face to face first.

José had told him not to bother. 'It's all over, man,' he had said when he read the document. 'Help us to make a difference now. These people, they're laughing at you. You don't need them, they're history. We must remember the people they killed and make the future a better one but let's not perpetuate these fallen heroes or their decadent world.'

'How do you know that there's any more to tell?' asked Rosalie. 'You could just be wasting your time. I agree with José. It looks like they're fooling you.'

'But what if Randolph was a war criminal?' Stephen objected. 'Is it that far-fetched? If he was then I have a responsibility to find out the truth.'

'He was a bourgeois reactionary,' said Mark. 'Forget about him, my friend. History is littered with men like him. He was getting his kicks any way he could. So ok, he was this big romantic lover man, donkey dick hero. So what? That's all Hollywood, man. He was part of the myth, the big lie. This century has had enough charismatic heroes, machismo self-seekers. He's a paper icon, that's all. Ignore him and forget his kind. If you want to punish him, tell the authorities, give them something better to do than keeping us down. Don't turn into a policeman yourself, man, it's a job for pigs.'

Stephen took a taxi to the cemetery; he wanted to see George Villard's grave but he was unsure whether he was going there merely to pay his respects or whether he had something to bury before he could move on. He had been dealing with things dying, the old order so hated by his friends; he could see their point and he wanted to join them, to share their plans, their ideals, to wipe away the past but still he couldn't let go.

Frost-hardened snow covered the scene, and the bright winter sunshine was reflected in the crystals encrusted on the monuments as they stood in rows, hundreds of them standing in the stiff white-coated grass. It didn't suit his mood. No longer a place of decay, it had become a place of hope; each grave sparkled, competing in brightness with its neighbour, representing a life that had once shone with just such a light. Those murdered victims of the Third Reich in their millions shone there in front of him. They must never be forgotten just as they shouldn't be seen as dead things, horrific statistics only. He stood and stared, his depression lifted, he was dazzled, in love with humanity once more, connected to its perpetually repeated hopes and sorrows. 'All you need is love,' he thought – it had been Villard's funeral song on that early summer's day and its message spoke just as strongly to him now as he stood in front of the tombstone in deepest winter.

'Here lie the mortal remains of Georges Dominique Villard. 1869-1967. Historian.'

Whatever his motives had been in involving Stephen in the Randolph book, Georges Villard had opened him up to those hopes and sorrows. He had pointed him outwards, away from his own little griefs, towards the world and its consequences, but he had also respected Stephen's sense of history and acknowledged his place in the great chain of human knowledge; he had teased him about his own generation, insisting that he should join it. This had led him to Dys and thus to his great unveiling but it had also led him towards Austin Randolph, the wild-eyed boy from Mrs Irving's photographs, and then to the others, the witnesses: sad and vulnerable they might be but they were also points of light. It would be too difficult to disengage, to separate past from present, the living from the dead – Villard probably knew that too.

Sixty-Three

'It's free,' Stephen said when the woman got out her purse to pay for The Happening.

'Oh, that's good,' she said breezily.

Stephen was in his usual position by the Reference Library, muffled against the wind, clinging onto the pamphlets with mittened hands. At first they didn't recognise each other.

'You're the writer, aren't you?' said the assistant librarian. 'We haven't seen you for a long time.'

'No. Yes, I'm sorry about that. The book's going through some problems at the moment and I've got involved in this. Spreading the message, you know. So I haven't been back for some time.'

'Well, that's sad – I mean the book, not these leaflets,' she said, blushing behind her scarlet scarf. 'I hope you can sort it all out.'

'Maybe,' he said. 'But this is important too.' He didn't sound convincing; he was disappointed that he hadn't heard from Austin Randolph, even though he was pleased with the essay he had written on the history of peaceful protest in England since the seventeenth century. He had become one of the main writers on The Happening, contributing a new piece each week and enjoying that feeling of regularly putting words on paper. Active as he was, he was still the silent one at meetings, a dutiful but sceptical foot soldier in Brighton's nascent anarchist movement.

'Well. I'm leaving the Library too,' she carried on, cheering up the conversation and trying to bring his eyes back into focus. 'I'm getting married.'

'Congratulations,' he said, in a voice that sounded like it was coming from someone else. He knew that it sounded trite, clipped, and insincere but the word had tumbled out unplanned. He was surprised too, maybe slightly disappointed, but whatever it was, he couldn't avoid one last look at those breasts, still proudly upstanding under her winter coat.

'Thanks. It's really exciting. My boyfriend's a photographer. He takes stuff for the music papers and he's just got a job in New York. He wants me to go too. I'm very excited but, of course, I'll miss you all, my regulars I mean, at the Library.'

211

Spontaneously, maybe to make up for his crass response, or to show that he wasn't like the others, not just one of the regulars, he kissed her on the cheek and took her hand affectionately.

'Well, good luck,' he said forcefully. 'I'm really pleased, genuinely.'

She blushed, squeezed his hand and rushed off, flustered.

It was a time for leave-taking. A few days later, Mark and José called a meeting, or rather, they asked Stephen and Rosalie to come into Paul's Room.

'We have something important to announce,' Mark said, portentously sitting back-to-front on a chair, hugging it slightly. 'Exciting things are happening here in Brighton but they are happening everywhere else too. It's time to move on. José and I are leaving, this seems the right time. And Rosalie, you know the ropes here, you can take over The Happening, can't you, while we spread the web further afield?'

Rosalie hugged them and kissed them before she stopped crying and soon they were all locked in one large inter-connected bear hug.

'I'm going to miss you guys, I really am,' Mark said, with eyes shining behind his glasses. 'Keep writing, won't you Stephen. You were always going to be a writer, you know, even though I didn't see it at first. You see the world with your feet firmly on the ground. We need people like you, believe me."

Always the sensible one, Stephen thought. He was disappointed that he still carried that tag. They squeezed hands, let the grip linger, and their eyes met in a moment of recognition. Maybe they had never given their friendship much of a chance, he thought. Mark was going to live with some friends, studying politics at the University of the Sorbonne in Paris; they were pacifist anarchists, he said, setting up their own student newspaper, they wanted Mark to be its fulltime editor.

José had decided it was a good time for him to go too; he wanted to take his chances back in the United States. He would, he said, burn his draft papers, like so many others had been doing, on the steps of the Pentagon itself.

'And then, who knows?' he said. 'I won't be fighting the Vietnamese that's for sure, but there are other wars to be won. I may just go down to South America, man. There's work to be done in Bolivia, Columbia and Brazil. Freedom there will mean freedom everywhere one day. Who knows, maybe I join with the Vietnamese.'

'We're on the same side, man,' said Mark, as the game of hugging continued 'but I'll never agree with you. Can't you see? We can do it peacefully. It's already happening – look what's going on in San Francisco, in Amsterdam and even here in Britain. Everywhere, people agree with us. We can't go on in the old ways; they didn't work. But we can stay pure, we can refuse to fight, refuse to cooperate, prepare for our turn; it's evolution, man, you know, things improve. Stick with us and we might just make a better future '

'You're a dreamer, amigo – but, hey, what's wrong with that? I'm older than you, older than all of you and I'm not so sure but I promise you this: if you make your beautiful revolution – if you win, I'll be there for you, OK?'

The London train was due to leave in five minutes. The three of them waited: Stephen on the platform, numbed by the end of an era, while Mark and José leant out of the window. Rosalie had already gone, she was preparing her first edition of The Happening. After so much talk, so many days and nights, weeks and months of inspired arguments, of political analysis, of cannabis and caffeine-charged debates, of slogans shouted on the streets, and of simple camaraderie, they were now embarrassed by those last minutes. The conversation was muted, with talk of train times and signals. Stephen distrusted moments of farewell, it was too easy to make rash promises and he could feel them rising inside him.

'I hope it works out for you both,' he said vaguely, already retreating.

'It will,' said Mark. 'You'll see.'

'Yes, my friends,' said José. 'When we meet again, we will all be living in a beautiful world. Just you believe it.'

'You could always come over to Paris,' said Mark, suddenly passionate as the train began to move. 'We will need all the help we can get and I would love you to come too. I'll miss you, you know.'

'Maybe,' said Stephen, but there was already too much noise and his words disappeared unheard.

'Venceremos!' they cried back to him, waving as the train rolled out of the station.

'Venceremos,' he muttered under his breath. 'I wonder.' An involuntary shudder shook him as he thought of Catullus: 'For eternity, brother, hail and farewell!'

Sixty-Four

'What are you waiting for my young friend? Come to me now and tell me my life. Spell it out. Spit it out. Nothing keeps you. Nothing holds you. Come to me now and put it to rest.'

Austin Randolph, Tung Ping Chau, March 1968

With Mark and José gone, Rosalie took over the editorial committee as well as becoming editor while Stephen carried on writing for The Happening. No longer lovers, even if they had ever seen themselves like that, they had slipped seamlessly back to a friendship now uninhibited and deepened by shared carnal knowledge. Gradually, as the other members of the group had moved away, Rosalie and Stephen became the main figures in their activist group. His articles had grown more political, evangelical even; he was less embarrassed at sounding naive as he caught up on his self-inflicted anarchist reading list.

He could now see where his preoccupation with history fitted in and how he had become a balance to his more wildly book-burning colleagues. Rosalie recognised this and encouraged him to spend more of his time on his journalism. She had found both her vocation and her voice; she put away her tarot cards, stopped worrying about her weight and both she and The Happening grew louder; she became, on her own admission, fat, and the journal became a fully-fledged newspaper – sometimes even running to six pages. She was happy, her confidence blossomed, she flaunted her cleavage in colourful tent frocks and she doubled the paper's readership – she had become both political and effective.

'Where's your piece on shamanism?' she barked, when Stephen sauntered into Paul's Room. 'We've got to get the paper on the road, love!'

He hadn't written it that morning because he had received a letter from Hong Kong, and, when he explained why, she cried and the hugging began all over again, smothering him in welcoming flesh.

'I knew this would happen, I just knew it!' she said, not knowing whether to be pleased or angry. 'You know I saw it in your cards a long time ago and I guess we can't deny our fate, I'll always believe that. I suppose it's really quite exciting! Stephen Dearsley goes East.'

'I have to go,' Stephen said. 'I can't just leave it now, not without knowing what Randolph really did.'

'It's up to you – I think you'd be better used here, helping us make a future, hopefully one without people like him in it.'

'Well, I can help by writing about it.'

For once Stephen was in no doubt; he had accepted the offer by return of post and the journey was already planned.

'Dear Stephen Dearsley,
I agree to the meeting even though I am unhappy at the tone of your letter. As you have already produced such interesting work it would be a pity if you were to abandon things so soon. I have taken the liberty of enclosing tickets, travelling instructions and a small cheque to cover your expenses. I live on an island not far from Hong Kong. Please confirm your decision to come out here. I am sorry that you have lost interest in our project but if you decide not to write the book after your visit, I will not pester you again. Please confirm your plans as soon as possible as there is now a certain time imperative.
With best wishes,
Austin Randolph.'

'You make sure that you're safe,' Rosalie said when she had read it. 'You're putting yourself into a dangerous situation, you know that don't you?'

'Yes,' said Stephen, quite liking the idea.

'I still want that article before you go though,' she said with a laugh – even though they both knew that she was serious.

Sixty-Five

Georges Villard is not so old in that summer of '44, in a suburban town, not far from Paris, German Paris. He is seventy-five, betrayed, captured, tortured, defeated. He sits crumpled, bound in a chair with red blood bright on his venerable white beard.

His captor, feeling no more victorious than his prey, is the young German officer, the Kapitän with the hunted eyes. Swiftly, easily, Austin Randolph had beaten the truth from the old philosopher, the diligent seeker of truth.

Now it was simple.

'We know you are Maynard and we know all your friends. It is time for a deal, for an exchange of favours.'

And so it was done. Easy.

They met once again, in sunny Provence, the professor and the English gentleman, in the café known to them both. A quiet establishment, minding its own business, helping Maynard, letting people pass through, discretely managed by Monsieur Finch and his young French bride.

They sat at a table, civilised, two glasses of wine, red on the starched white cloth. A sign of nerves, the glass slips at his lip, red drops on the white, Austin's hand shakes.

'Our secret, Maynard, that's agreed?' Austin Randolph was running again; pursued, hounded, but, as always, by something within himself.

'Agreed. It will remain a secret – just between the two of us. It is arranged, you will disappear,' said Villard, chilled, compromised.

Their eyes met in fear.

Sixty-Six

'You look like those Parisian students in the papers,' Emilia Jeffries laughed when she saw Stephen. 'I always knew that there was a touch of the Dostoyevsky about you.' She welcomed him at her front door, flicking her fingers through his now shoulder-length hair as she showed him into the living room. The crisp white blouse, short black skirt and black stockings gave her a business-like look contradicted by her nervousness as she shifted old editions of the Sunday papers from the coffee table and repositioned the cushions on the sofa. Coffee was prepared and there was much clinking of china.

'So you're going ahead with the book?' she said when she finally settled into an armchair opposite him. There was a frosty edge to her voice that had not been there before.

'Yes, I think so,' he answered, holding his ground against her under-played aggression. 'It's been very difficult sifting through the facts – working out the truth.'

'You mean seeing through the lies.' She was ready for a confrontation.

'Well, yes. Everyone has been very protective to say the least. It hasn't made my job easier.'

'So how much do you know?'

'Much more than you wanted me to.'

Stephen scored his point. Emilia visibly weakened. She took a lingering sip of her coffee, placed the cup gently on the table and nodded. 'Yes. I lied to you. I didn't want any of this to come out. I suppose I underestimated you – Philip and I thought we could keep you off the trail but you got there anyway. To be honest, I didn't expect you to carry on with it. You seemed so young and, well, forgive me, naïve, and there are so many more interesting things going on for young people today. I thought we might be able to slip away back into obscurity.'

'I'm going to Hong Kong next week. I felt I should tell you.'

'Thank you.' As she looked at him, her coolness turned to tiredness, something her make-up was unable to hide. She sat silently, visibly older now, the colour draining from her face as Stephen told her about Stanley Finch's visit.

'I'd so hoped that the past had gone away,' she said wearily. 'We try to bury it alive but it keeps on coming back, clawing up through the slime. Aunt Margaret made me realise that. I saw her just before she died, you know. You'd been there just the day before. I always blamed her for brooding on the past but, when I saw her lying there, I realised that at least she had been honest. There was nothing else she loved, no one else – only her forbidden son, the focus of all her passion, the reason for her great sin. She would have preferred him dead I think. Knowing that he was alive gave her a furious strength – the strength to live too long. That was cruel. Seeing her like that was frightening. I was afraid that it might happen to me.

'You don't recover from people, you know. A part of me is still waiting for him to return. Oh yes, even after all this time. When I left him there in Berlin, I thought that eventually he would realise his mistake, stop playing at soldiers and then come home or, at least, write. I suppose I still think that even now but I know it's foolish. I've seen it in war widows whose husbands went missing in battle. As far as they are concerned, their husbands are missing, not dead, and even though they feel the pain of bereavement, they can't stop hoping – hoping hopelessly. I suppose I'm like that, even though I know he's alive. I say that I've always hoped that he would come back but that's not true. I've coped with his loss; I don't want him to renew his power over me. I want him to be a beautiful ghost and, yet, inside, yes I do still want him to return, young and unchanged. Yes. Even as he was in Berlin.'

'In spite of his politics?'

'I suppose so. Politics is too big a word for Austin, you know. Even if I couldn't forgive what he had done, I'd still welcome him back. Yes. That is the terrible force of love, isn't it?'

'Did you try to find him after the war?'

'Well, we went back, Philip and I. I hoped that by some miracle I would see him again. You know, just bump into him casually and make it all up. Of course it wasn't like that. The house was gone. In fact the whole street and all the streets near it had gone. No one knew what had happened to my grandparents but it was all too obvious. We really did think that Austin was dead too.'

'Is that when you decided to marry Philip Irving?'

'So you know about that? We were both looking for the same thing and we thought it would help. It was a foolish mistake of course, but there you are. I suppose that that is where I leave your book, my dear Mr Dearsley. I become Miss Jeffries again. Spinsterly teacher – but not quite as spinsterly as you might have thought!'

They laughed but her levity was superficial; her weariness returned, she leant forward and held his hand.

'I've been playing a lot of music lately – mostly Schubert, he knows all about these contradictions. Let me play you something before you go. My grandmother taught it to me, my German grandmother – it's very comforting. Do you mind? Humour me if you do.'

She went over to the baby grand piano that stood in the bay window. It was covered with a gypsy shawl and on it stood a large bowl of chrysanthemums – brown, gold and amber. She sat down and opened the lid, her eyes glistening in anticipation. She began playing, her delicate touch producing exquisitely ringing tones; the ambiguous major key harmonies spoke of happiness tinged with sadness, or melancholy shot through with joy – the ecstasy of loss. As she played, her complexion turned grey but her eyes shone. Even Stephen's untuned ear was moved, but he felt useless confronted by such sadness. Youth could contribute nothing to age – or so it seemed to him then. He sat silently watching and listening, feeling her pain. When it was over, he could say nothing. She sighed and smiled.

'I'm sorry,' she said with a catch in her throat. 'I've done it again, haven't I?'

Emilia's sadness haunted and challenged him as he walked to the station through suddenly empty streets. Could he expose her suffering in a book? What right did he have to judge? He felt humbled by her passion, as insubstantial in his inexperienced youth as his dark shadow projected in front of him. February drizzle glistened in the streetlight; he felt a long way away from that already legendary summer: the summer of 1967, his summer. The sound of running feet woke him from his brooding.

'Hippie bastard!' a voice shouted. Spinning round in frightened self-defence, he saw eight crop-haired youths running towards him. The pattern had repeated itself, every positive needed its negative;

the Summer of Love had bred its antichrist. Skinhead gangs, street vigilantes, dedicated to violence, knew their targets: longhaired hippies, students, middle class kids, virgins in the urban jungle. Stephen was perfect, the symbol of his age, naïve as Emilia said, defenceless and alone in a darkened street. So they ran, whooping with laughter, swastika-studded jackets, steel-capped boots – united in hatred, they had started the chase, and their shouts of abuse mocked his escape.

Stumbling in panic, he hit the ground, the boots surrounded him and his ears hummed. In the flash of a second, he saw it all: a bicycle chain, a knife and an antique carving fork – early Victorian, no, probably Georgian – then blackness filled his vision and only for a second he felt the pain. He cradled his head, snuggled into the concrete and allowed himself to be lulled by their kicks as they pounded him painlessly, their jeers now dimmed – he would not resist. His mouth filled with blood, a comforting feeling, and Emilia's music sung him to sleep, welcoming him, gently leading him away to a better place.

Sixty-Seven

He woke up in a hospital, not knowing where he was or how he had got there. It was somewhere near Richmond and Rosalie was there with a nurse, looking down at him, chins doubled in caring attention. Hospital smells, clinical calm, some tubes coming from under the sheets, and a soothing anaesthetic rush told him that he was alive. Then he remembered what had happened and his body's reflexes flinched painfully. He could see it all again. He was wounded, with broken ribs, bruises, lacerations; his face was swollen and numb.

'It's alright,' Rosalie told him. 'You'll be fine.'

'Yes,' said the nurse. 'The little buggers messed you around alright but you're mending well. We've strapped up your ribs and we've had an icebag on your scrotum, but don't worry, you're alright in that department. You'll just have to wee through a tube for a bit. We fixed it while you were asleep.'

'Well that's good to know,' Rosalie joked, in her best jollying voice.

'You'll have to be careful, though,' the nurse continued, eyeing up Rosalie's weight as Stephen grew tired of her attention. 'While I think of it, you can't use the missionary position with broken ribs, love. My advice is that you'd be best going on top but you'll have to take care, you know what I mean. Anyway we'll have you out of here in a couple of days, Stephen, so you just lie back and talk to your girlfriend here; she's been very worried about you, you know.'

'Well, thanks for that, nursie,' he said, smiling through swollen lips when the over-attentive nurse had finally gone.

'They found your phone number in your pocket,' Rosalie explained, stroking his hand. 'They rang up last night. I got a lift up here straight away.'

'Thanks,' he mumbled. 'You're the nearest I've got to family.'

'Yes, right,' she laughed, sifting her thoughts rapidly. 'Just call me Mum; I'll always be there for you, you know that – missionary position or not.'

'Maybe not now, eh?' he said, looking at his wrecked body limply laid out on the bed.

'Yeah, but you were very lucky. They could have killed you. Someone disturbed them and rang for an ambulance. The bastards ran off, fascist thugs.'

'I could have died for the cause then,' Stephen joked, 'and I'd never seen myself as the martyr type."

In spite of himself, he felt a certain glow at the thought that he had been picked out as a hippie and that he belonged somewhere.

'Saint Stephen! Maybe not, eh? They threw stones at him, though, so maybe you're our very own little saint.'

'I really didn't expect it,' Stephen said, feeling the need to talk about it. His body was shaking and his mouth went dry, but his tongue had loosened – his words were now unstoppable. 'It isn't what's meant to be going on. I thought things were going to be different. You know, the times they are a-changin' and all that. They were dressed like Nazis, those kids, can you believe that? No one ever learns. Great. Let's all be Nazis and kill each other! Just for the hell of it. Let's hate each other; you don't need a reason, you can do it for fun. Just like Austin Randolph did.'

'They were just stupid kids,' said Rosalie, trying to calm him down. 'They don't understand. They have to learn that they need a share in their own world, their own street, because that's where we live, that's where we can build something for ourselves and for each other. I guess that's why I believe in our paper, in local journalism, in working at street level. People think it's boring but it's the way to change things, to show people that they really can make a difference even if it takes a life-time to achieve it. Now you forget about last night, do you hear? When the swelling goes down you'll feel a lot better and then we'll get you back home.'

He mended slowly and painfully, his mind haunted by reoccurring images, waking nightmares and gloomy visions. Whenever he closed his eyes he was falling again, hitting the ground, and there were the boots and, ringing in his ears, the mocking laughter. He healed well enough after a week and returned home with Rosalie to his room but still, when he was alone, the images returned with thoughts, negative abstract thoughts, that kept dragging him down, puncturing his hopes. He was, Rosalie knew, depressed. As the pain subsided, the shock grew; shock that he had become an object of hatred, with tribal enemies: ignorant, unthinking Nazi descendants finding warped inspiration, something to attack in his 'Summer of Love'.

'Oh, when they were undressing you at the hospital, they found this. I'm sorry but I forgot about it,' Rosalie said one day, as she began rolling up his left trouser leg while he lay on his bed.

She had the ankle bracelet from Salisbury, undamaged in the fight, and now she put it back where it belonged, where his Utopian friends had put it to create a circle of love. Rosalie's touch and the return of a treasured object brought on his tears and his long recovery began.

Physically, he had recovered enough for his trip to Hong Kong – it had been postponed but not forgotten. He had no intention of missing this final confrontation with the man who had haunted him on the battlements of his subconscious. Psychologically, he was still not prepared. He was angry; angry with his attackers, of course, and with what they stood for, but he was angry with Austin Randolph as well. He held him responsible: one bully in a long line of bullies, a hero for some, just like those skinhead kids would be to their friends, but a reactionary, negative force, preventing progress. He was angry that an Austin Randolph existed in every generation.

Feeling numb, depressed and still more than a little stiff in his joints, he packed a small rucksack with a spare pair of jeans, a few shirts and a notebook. He said goodbye to Rosalie and then he crossed the world.

Sixty-Eight

'I am still here, my young friend. Hanging on, feverish in anticipation. I sense you near to me now. So very near. Make speed, come to me and I'll tell you everything.'

Austin Randolph, Tung Ping Chau, April 1968

He found little excitement on the long journey: his first flight on a plane was, he thought, like a slow-motion accident. All those hours in free fall and nothing he could do about it. First Europe then Asia spread out beneath him. It seemed like he was being pulled away from the world. It would not have surprised him if the plane never landed at all or, if it did, it could have settled on some distant planet far away in light years from his drab parochial existence.

He did land, eventually, in the modern airport that was all that he would see of Hong Kong. There was no time for recovery or exploration because a stern young Chinese man in a grey uniform met him at arrivals with a neatly printed card saying 'Mr Steevan Dareslee'.

'Welcome to Hong Kong, Mister Dareslee. You come with me for Mr Randolph.'

He was led to another part of the airport where a small chartered helicopter was waiting. This flight was less terrifying than the long haul one, was almost exciting, and it nearly broke through his torpor. He felt, as they were tossed around in the air turbulence, that in an emergency he could just jump out and land safely in the sea. He would decide what to do about the sharks if and when the situation arouse. He had been travelling now for three days, alone, lonely and feeling vulnerable, so when the helicopter began its descent in small circles towards a small gem-like island in the South China Sea – exotically green and mountainously rocky in the sparkling blue, a holiday paradise without the holiday-makers, more beautiful that he had imagined – he still could not throw off the stupor, the depression, his post hospital malaise. It was now made worse by the jet-lag.

A car met him at the small private airfield.

'Welcome to Tung Ping Chau,' the Chinese driver said in polite but barely understandable English. 'I take you Mr Randolph house.' They drove in air-conditioned luxury along a dusty and primitive road to more than a house – it was Austin Randolph's colonial palace, hidden behind trees. It was more than just a big house. Its white, porticoed splendour was matched by a manicured tropical park, set out with constantly-irrigated lawns cut into geometrical shapes and divided by rows of brick-red geraniums, golden marigolds and yellow chrysanthemums where the land sloped away towards shining white sand and the sparkling sea in the distance.

A Chinese butler answered the door. He bowed and led Stephen across the hall; white marble floors covered a vast area, sweeping through arches to further reception rooms, high-ceilinged and elegant with gilt furniture upholstered in gold and scarlet. Their footsteps echoed on the marble as they made their way up a staircase of gilded colonnades underneath a painted ceiling illustrated with scenes of elephants and semi-naked princes and princesses, sentimentalised natives, noble savages in a gaudy paradise. Without speaking, they walked down a long corridor to a pair of double doors. Opening them, the butler led Stephen into a darkened room, heavy shutters blocking out the afternoon light. He indicated a four-poster bed, draped with mosquito nets.

'Excuse me please,' came a voice from the shadows. An old Chinese woman came up to them. She was wearing a long shawl, draped over her head; her small face peeped out enthusiastically.

'You are a friend of Mr Randolph?'

'Yes. I've come from England.'

'Oh, a very long way,' laughed the woman. 'Long way from Tung Ping Chau! Well, Mr Randolph sleeps. You want to wait? He may talk or he may not. No one knows.'

She pointed towards the shadowy figure, recumbent behind the muslin, and then she went back to her chair and her knitting. Stephen stood at the end of the bed and looked at the man lying there asleep. Only in his fifties, Austin Randolph was an old man. Thin, white hair clung in wisps to the pale skeletal face. It was the face of a dying man. His mouth was slightly open and his regular but effortful breathing indicated that he was very near to his end. Age and cancer had corrupted the handsome face preserved in Mrs Irving's photographs, but the features were like familiar landmarks on an eroded landscape. There would be little further alteration now when life left his body altogether.

'Would you like to join the other gentleman while you wait?' the old woman called, with an unceremonious lack of concern. She walked over to the ceiling-high French windows and half opened one of the shutters.

'He is on the terrace. You will find it good there.'

She was referring to the smell of death, which lingered in Stephen's nostrils as he walked out onto the terrace with its dazzling view of the sun-speckled sea.

A thickset man in a white tropical suit was sitting in a wicker chair with his head in his hands. The woman brought up another chair and the man looked up.

'Hello there,' he said, jolting Stephen with the unexpected sight of a haggard and sleep-deprived Philip Irving, whose weight loss already gave him the look of a widow.

Sixty-Nine

'I should have told you I was coming, I suppose,' Philip Irving said without any of his old bluster. 'I wanted to see him alone. It was selfish of me, I know.'

'Have you spoken to him?' Stephen asked.

'Only a bit. He's dying. You know that?'

'Yes. What did he say?'

'I've only been here since the beginning of the week. He was a bit stronger then. He spoke of your book. He was rambling some of the time – he kept saying 'the secret's out, boys' over and over again. He's very keen to talk to you. He thinks of you all the time.'

'What has he been saying?'

'Nothing intelligible really. He said it had all been wasted. It was all a waste of time. He kept repeating that. The old woman told me that he ran a lot of companies in the East. Obviously, he has made a fortune. I've never seen anything like this place.'

They were served tea by the butler and they sat in silence, like undertakers waiting for their job to begin. Much later, the old woman hurried out to them.

'He is awake,' she called. 'You must come. He talks!'

Back inside the darkened room, they gathered around the deathbed. Philip indicated the chair next to the bed, nodding gently to Stephen to sit there while he remained standing. Austin's eyes were open and they moved enquiringly to identify his visitors. A dim smile flickered on his face when he recognised Philip, then he stretched out his enfeebled arm and pointed to Stephen.

'So there you are, my young friend, my scribe. It is you, isn't it? Come closer.' He was barely audible, so Stephen stood and tried to ignore the rotting smell as he bent over the old man. The face was a skull – the skin had a green cast as if he were already dead. His cracked lips quivered as he spoke, parting to reveal white, glue-like saliva that played around his crooked teeth. Even though he was already decomposing, his eyes retained the Randolph magnetism that everyone had remembered. Vividly brown and shining, they darted from face to face. They returned to Stephen. 'You're a bright kid,' he said, grinning. 'Old Villard said so. I've read your

228

letter. It will do nicely. You know as much as you need for the book. You will do a good job.'

'Why do you want it written? Forgive me if I don't understand.' Stephen was feeling more anger than sympathy. Austin Randolph struggled to sit up and the old woman propped some more pillows under him. A rush of energy flooded into his face; he was enjoying himself.

'It seemed important then,' he whispered, articulating slowly, giving his words an added emphasis with effortful precision.

'Why did Georges Villard lie to me?' Stephen said, with a coolness brought on by the deep hostility that had been growing in him all the way from England.

'Villard was the man who understood me,' Austin continued, with his voice finding a reserve of strength. 'He was a writer, an observer. I wanted him to tell people about my life – as a warning – or as a way of finding forgiveness.'

After a few gulps, he found his breath again and continued to talk in clusters of phrases interrupted by lapses when he looked as if he were already dead.

'I thought Georges could do something... Could ease my passage... He had other thoughts of course... typical of him. He would not write, he said... He was through with that... He told me that I should find my own peace... That was like him... but it was too easily said... I insisted. People always give me my own way! I buy people, Mr Dearsley... I told Villard I would pay him... handsomely... or if not, expose our little secret. He still refused.'

He smiled, as if he was reliving the argument with Villard. There was a long pause while he summoned up his strength again and while Stephen recoiled from whatever revelation he had about Villard. 'Then something changed... Georges said he'd found an innocent... a man without baggage, someone who had never taken sides... Someone who could act as a jury... for both of us. We were, as you might have suspected, each guilty in our own way. That man without baggage, my dear Mr Dearsley, I'm afraid, was you... It was not a trick; don't think that... It was a gift.'

'I don't think so,' Stephen said, cutting in aggressively. 'I've picked up a few pieces of baggage on the way and I won't be giving you your final starring role. I don't see the point. I don't care about any secret you had over Villard. You've had enough attention already. I came here to tell you that I would not write the book.'

Randolph let his head lie back on the pillows and laughed gently and feebly, letting gusts of air rush from his weakening lungs. 'You could have done that by letter, my friend. Why did you come all this way to say it? You couldn't resist the offer. That's the truth, isn't it?'

'I needed to see what a hero looks like.' Stephen's voice was dissected by emotion; he was angry, unable to forgive. 'We read about them, we've read too much about them, but we rarely see them, only the damage they do. I needed to see one, that's all. To see what drew people to you, to see why the world loves men like you.'

He heard Philip's audible shock but he didn't look round, he couldn't hold back now. It had become a battle and Austin Randolph, for one last time, was enjoying the fight.

'People need heroes, young man. If we didn't exist they would invent us... Sad isn't it?... I understand your anger, my friend... I know what I have been. It offends your pure little soul doesn't it?... But now it's of no importance... Once I wanted you to write my confession, my explanation... my apology, dare I say? Now I leave it to you. Time is running out and now I don't care – life's never that neat... remember that, Stephen.'

Then his eyes filled with tears and his body began to shake. Holding tight to Stephen's hand, suddenly convulsing, he tossed from side to side. His mouth opened in a hollow scream of pain like an echo from an empty cave. 'Help me,' he whimpered. 'Help me, for God's sake. Can't you see?... I'm afraid.'

Stephen, now crying himself, squeezed his hand and the old woman rushed over with morphine. Austin was staring at him, his eyes fixed in terror, then he looked away, up to the ceiling, and began his decline, the shaking gradually ebbing away with his remaining strength. An hour went by. Philip sat on a chair by the window, eyes shining but looking away to the sea with the faintest hint of a smile. The unwiped tears dried on Stephen's face but he didn't release the hand. He stood there, awkwardly bent over the body until a barely perceptible change occurred. There was a profound evacuation of air and then it was over – the movie had ended with a freeze-frame.

'It wasn't how I imagined it,' said Philip when they were back on the terrace. 'And you surprised me, I must say. I didn't expect that.'

'Neither did I.' Stephen was still numb with the shock of his own emotions.

'You are right, of course. He blighted our lives but I could never have told him that, I couldn't have been that brutal. Not that I blame you: he deserved it and I think he wanted it said. He needed you to say it. I think that's why he wanted you to come here and why he wanted that wretched book. He wanted purgation, I think. You gave it to him, old thing. You were very brave.'

Stephen couldn't look at him; he too felt purged. He had spoken for himself and for his friends – even, he hoped, for his own generation, even for future ones. These obsolete people would pass. He wanted the world to be free of his kind; he wanted to believe that but in the end, he had been forced to recognise Austin Randolph's humanity, to have ignored that would have been to have joined him.

'When he went,' Philip said, putting his hand on Stephen's arm and looking out to sea, 'when he had gone, something snapped between us. In the end, I felt free. I suppose the past has been with me for so long, I haven't really had time to think about the future. But, if this doesn't sound too callous, I feel good about it. Pleased that he's gone. I feel like those Christians who talk about being born again. Maybe, I've just won my freedom.' He was smiling now, then his smile turned into a gentle laugh as he looked back out to sea. 'You know, I think I'm going to enjoy it.'

Stephen was still shaking. He was trying to control the spasm that was sending shivers through his body; it gradually passed, leaving him cleansed by his tears and amazed at his own outburst.

'But what about you?' Philip asked, his smile reforming consolingly. 'What are you going to do? You have so much ahead of you my young friend.'

'I don't know,' Stephen said, surprised somehow that it was all over.

When they returned to the room, the body was already shrouded with a sheet. The old woman showed them out with the same cheerful smile that she had worn all day.

'I will see to him now,' she said with a strangely knowing laugh.

231

Seventy

Stephen remained in the East. A friendly young cannabis dealer in Hong Kong told him about a hippie colony on an island in the Andaman Sea. Tired out by his past and unsure of his future, he decided to go there; somewhere that he had never heard of and which was not even marked on his map. So he joined the colony, a group of welcoming Americans, Australians and fellow British. He enjoyed the lack of a shared history, his regained anonymity, the free love, freely given and freely taken, of both the sexual and the platonic kinds, and he learnt to play the guitar.

He let the sun heal his wounds as he lay on the sand, by the sea, in the heat of the day, sharing his body and talking about Utopia – often dreaming that he had found it. Then he learnt some new skills: woodwork, gardening and fishing with a spear. When this latest smell of death finally left his nostrils, he began to buy the English papers, delivered occasionally and often two months late. In them, he followed the news about student demonstrations erupting in America, Europe, Japan, all over the world, and he felt guilty, but, he admitted, only mildly so.

He thought of his friends. He imagined that he saw Mark in a photograph of the student protests in Paris when over six thousand students brought the city to a standstill. Rosalie would be pioneering in Brighton without him; he was sure that she would have been in London too when thousands more took to the streets and marched on the American Embassy in protest about the war in Vietnam. He wondered about José, assuming that he would have been with the Puerto Rican contingent in the Poor People's March that had turned into a riot in Memphis and then spread to Washington DC. When the stones were thrown, José would have been in the midst of it and Stephen should have been there too, he knew that now – maybe not in Memphis but somewhere in the world where he could have joined the others on the streets and added his voice to the throngs who wanted to change the world.

He hoped that Andrew's idealistic community had survived at Wessex House. He was tempted to go there but feared it had gone. One day, maybe, he would risk finding out. Then he thought of Dys. They were not so different after all. Sadly, he thought that he, like her, was just a traveller, absorbing his surroundings, taking what he wanted before moving on. Maybe he was, after all, as Georges Villard had said, a man without baggage. He hoped not.

He came back to Brighton on a hot high summer morning, some five years later, with a guitar on his back and a newly finished book in his bag. This book had nothing to do with Austin Randolph's unpublished material; he had abandoned his ambition to write historical biography for a work of fiction, an account of an imagined Utopia. The traveller returned with Polynesian brown skin, full black beard and waist-length hair. Sandal-shod, wearing his crumpled safari suit, a faded denim shirt and tiny purple sunglasses: his Pacific look.

He walked through the town, drawn back to it, feeling that he would never quite leave it, a modern Flying Dutchman, his ghost haunting the streets forever. He delighted in the harsh screeching welcome of the herring gulls and the English seaside air with its hint of vinegar and stale urine. He walked down to the sea, so European grey after the Tropics, and remembered those times, so recent and yet now so rapidly retreating, so nearly forgotten, when he had first come to life. He threw a stone, hopelessly, into the waves and climbed back over the shingle hills to the shining white stucco town above.

Lovingly, he trod the pavements around the Royal Pavilion, the Public Library and the Dolphin Fountain – he had, he thought, helped to smooth each paving stone. The breeze caught a string of bells placed in an open window; its sound took him back – his hair rustled round his shoulders, his body flexed, his heart leaped, but then the moment was gone. He was a pedestrian again just passing through. He fingered Dys's plaited hair bracelet still on his wrist, as treasured as the anklet, faded but still visible above his left foot. He had loved those people; from them, he thought, he had learnt how to love but, even so, he was still alone. He often thought of them, wondering if even a small part of their Utopias had materialised. All they needed, they thought, was love. It was never going to be as easy as that had sounded in those heady sunlit days when he was last here in this town.

He had grown nearer to Dys the further he travelled. He remembered her need to move on – once it had frightened him but now he felt it too. As he walked through the streets that they had once shared, he hoped, half-heartedly, that if he only looked hard enough, he might see her again. The past would never leave him, he knew that now, but it would no longer hold him here either.

He acknowledged his fate and went into a shop. He bought a stick of Brighton rock and, like the sightseer that he had always been, he crunched it contentedly enough and walked on.

About the Author

Colin Bell was born in a Franciscan convent in Surrey but grew up in Sussex – everything that he has done, he did for the first time in Brighton. After half a lifetime in Manchester working for Granada Television, he returned to Sussex and now lives in Lewes, the urban equivalent of BBC Radio Four.

At Granada, after working in every department from politics to light entertainment, he became a producer-director of arts documentaries and then Executive Producer, Music and Arts, making arts series for ITV and Channel Four. His television credits include Celebration, God Bless America, It Was Twenty Years Ago Today, My Generation and Menuhin's Children.

He has fond TV memories of writing scripts for Kenneth Williams, unwittingly asking Sir Lawrence Olivier to find him a transistor radio, being the regular voice of 'sneering authority' on the investigative journalism series World In Action and setting the music questions for University Challenge. He is also proud of having written three children's books (published by Novello's) to accompany the Early Reading series, Story World, and of working with most British rock bands from The Beatles to Oasis.

Following an urge that would never go away, he gave up television deciding that he had to try to become a full-time writer and thus fulfil his life's ambition. While working on his novel and a number of short stories he suffered a brain haemorrhage that was meant to kill him but failed. Described as the neurologist's 'miracle patient', he made a full recovery while discovering the virtual world of Second Life and a previously unexpected ability to write poetry. *Stephen Dearsley's Summer of Love* is his first novel.